Steaming Beneath the High Seas

By Lorretta Smith

Star Sapphire Press
Darby, Mt
2019

First edition
First printing 2019

Book design by Lorretta Smith Cover art by Lorretta Smith

Library of Congress Cataloging in Publication Data Smith, Lorretta 1972-
Steaming Beneath the High Seas: Star Sapphire Logs / Lorretta Smith -- 1st ed.

ISBN: 978-0-578-21720-8

Library of Congress Control Number: 2019901721 Star

Sapphire Printing / Star Sapphire Press
629 Bridge Lane
Darby, Mt 59829

Printed in the United States of America

Born and raised all over the Northwest, Lorretta makes her home in Darby, Montana where she lives with her two pugs, Lollah Loo and Corona Cerveza, and her Maine Coon Cat, Clyde. They live in the tiny house she built herself on the banks of the Bitterroot River. When she isn't writing, Lorretta enjoys camping, hiking, rafting and kayaking.

Lorretta is divorced with one child, twenty-year old son, Cory, who is the love of her life, partner in adventures and comic relief in life. She earned a Bachelor's degree from Eastern New Mexico University in Psychology and Sociology. Prior to her writing career, Lorretta worked as a social worker.

Photo by Renee Knowles

Dedication

To Grandma Carla and Granny
Smith
for always encouraging me to read,
partake in adventures and never

shirk science.

1

"Gangplank retracted, anchor released. Ready to exit Aconcagua Port!" Brannon announced. Engines hummed to life, preparing to propel the airship away from the largest dock in the western hemisphere.

"Once we clear the docking area, begin ascension." The throaty voice of the captain projected across the bow of the *Star Sapphire*.

Initiating his boot thrusters, a figure leapt aboard, tumbling across the deck, then rolled to his feet. With a cocky grin, he saluted his pursuers, ducking around the side of the pagoda, hiding behind several large fish bone baskets.

Just as she provided the order to ascend, the ship rocked slightly to the side. Kabe adjusted the stabilizers, compensating and leveling the airship "What was that?" Captain Alexandrea Canatolli asked.

"Don't know, Lexi. Maybe another ship's wake? We're fine now," the ship's navigator, Kabe, replied. "Beginning ascension."

Fabric lifted from the masts, filling with hot air. Scalding water siphoned from the ocean pumped through the converter, extracting the salt and water. Mixing with helium, heat quickly inflated the sails into a balloon, levitating the ship. Airships docked at port shrunk as the *Star Sapphire* rose into the sky.

"Once we reach two thousand feet, lay in a course for Mount Elbert Port," Lexi informed Kabe.

"The wind turbines are fully operational, Lexi. We can transfer to wind power once we reach cruising altitude," Tink, ship's mechanic broke in. Groans greeted her comment. "I'm fairly confident I fixed most of the problems allowing us to probably remain airborne," Tink valiantly failed to reassure

1

the crew.

Created by Tink, the design of the dual energy ship continued as a work in progress. Minor bugs reared their ugly heads, requiring emergency ocean landings on several occasions. Perfecting the marriage of wind and steam proved more complex than Tink originally thought.

After a few moments of silence, "Let's hold off engaging wind power until we leave sight of port. I don't want witnesses if we fall out of the sky. Again," Lexi decided amidst chuckles. The inflated balloon rose to cruising altitude. Steam powered turbines fired up, propelling the ship on the course laid out for Mount Elbert Port, one of the few docks constructed on solid ground.

Starting with a chain of earthquakes, lava spewed from the center of the earth, melting the North and South Poles. Continents flooded with ocean water. The melting occurred quickly, within a year's time, providing civilizations, governments, and countries little time to prepare. Most of the Earth's population perished. Only the tallest peaks rose above the water. Countries with naval fleets built seaports and living quarters for some of their citizens. Who lived and who died? Each country chose independently. Some picked scholars, scientists, doctors, and leaders. Others selected whoever possessed adequate resources to "purchase" continued existence. And the rest? Well, it boiled down to who provided for themselves. Noah Canatolli worked as an accountant for a trade company. He dreamed of sailing the seas. When the announcement came about impending doom, Noah and his best friend, Charles, built a sailboat. Noah designed it, while Charles manufactured the motor and propulsion system. Caroline, Noah's wife and Mary, Charles' wife, along with Charles' mother, Granny, planted a garden aboard the vessel. The engine utilized heated ocean water for propulsion. His design removed salt from the water. Steam fueled the motors, while heat inflated the balloon. Purified water fed the garden and became potable. Noah and Charles sailed with their families, prior to the continents drowning. Noah had one daughter, Alexandrea, and one son, Kabe. Charles brought his two daughters, Khara and Charlene, or Tink, nicknamed for her love of tinkering with everything.

2

After the ship traveled for several hours, Lexi sighed heavily, "Switch to wind power. We propelled a safe distance from port and no other ships appear in sight."

Lexi, Alexandrea Canatolli, Captain of the *Star Sapphire*, understood the importance of perfecting wind power, providing the ship with a valuable second energy source. It provided a boost, faster speeds above and beyond steam power, when the wind cooperated. Tink just needed to figure out how to harness it, calculate longevity, and safely transition between the two. She successfully harnessed the wind. How long it lasted and transitioning between the two? Nope.

The engines whirred while converting ocean water into hot steam. As the wind turbines took over, the engine noise ceased. Wind power felt like a bird floating on a breeze. No noise, no vibration, easy sailing. Until the wind stopped or changed direction. Then, the ship plummeted until the steam engines kicked in. Tink focused on calculating when the winds may change and starting the steam engines PRIOR to plummeting towards the sea. For some reason, the crew harbored an intense dislike of plummeting.

As the engines grew silent, Lexi hoped for two hours before the impending dive to the Pacific Ocean. Leaving the controls in her first mate's capable hands, she walked onto the deck. Before her, lay an endless blue sky, punctuated with white clouds here and there. Below, a darker blue ocean rose and fell with white capped waves barely visible from this height. She breathed in salty air. Her only memories consisted of life on the sea. She couldn't recall houses, meadows, buildings, parks or cities. Strolling the deck, she reached the stern. Aconcagua Port disappeared from the horizon. The highest point in South America, it served as a major port for trading resources. A few dots marked ships on the seascape. The *Star Sapphire* navigated towards Mount Elbert Port, the highest point in the continental United States. After the flood, it now served as the recognized capital. The *Star Sapphire* transported trade goods of fruits, vegetables and wood.

Lexi stood on the aft deck, gazing off towards the port they vacated. A scraping noise behind her, interrupted her thoughts. Turning around, ten fish bone baskets were stacked against the storage cabin. She approached them, trying to identify the sound. A boot appeared between the cargo. With a push of a lever on her right arm, a brass short sword extended eighteen inches out, hilt landing in her hand. One of Tink's inventions.

She stalked towards the tall basket, using the cargo to shield her approach. Squeezing in between the goods, she swung around the final obstacle, leveling her sword chest height to the stowaway.

Lexi thrust her blade up against his heart. "Who are you and what are you doing aboard my ship?"

Extending his hands, a man walked out from behind a barrel, a heart stopping smile blazed across his face, "My name is Jareth Montague." Looking sheepish, "I needed to leave port quickly and your ship happened to begin ascent at the most opportune time!"

Lexi lifted an eyebrow. "Why did you need to leave?" Shrugging, "Minor misunderstanding with a hot headed Argentine over a little card game. I don't hear steam engines running. How are we afloat?" Using his right pointer finger, Jareth attempted to push the sword off his chest. The sword, however, refused to budge.

"Wind power. Stowaways are not appreciated." Lexi informed him "Will someone be chasing you?"

Laughing, Jareth replied, "He didn't lose that bad! I'm sure he already forgot! Wind power? What a concept! It's so much quieter, peaceful." Nodding his approval, "I like it."

"So pleased to earn your endorsement," she replied, sarcasm covering her indecisiveness. No one stowed away on the *Star Sapphire* prior to this. Poking him in the chest with the sword tip, "Step out here, where I can see you better."

Complying, again he flashed a sexy, easy smile. Lexi recognized the arm guard on his right forearm held a sword and a rope with grappler hook, similar to hers. Several other attachments appeared unfamiliar. He wore black breeches and a navy silk billowy shirt displayed an ample amount of chest, including nicely formed muscles. A black leather coat fell to his knees. A brass monocular surrounded his left eye. Almost identical to Lexi's, it held lens for telescoping and microscoping. His black boots, adorned with brass buckles, reached his knees, sporting steam propulsion and springs for jumping. Six foot tall, a navy ribbon tied his black hair back.

"How can I assuage your concerns, Captain? Pay for my

4

passage, work it off, entertain you," with a devilish smile, his voice deepened, "in many different ways."

Using her sword, she led him to the bridge. "Start walkin' Romeo. We'll see what the crew thinks," Lexi remarked dryly. He sighed and moved in the direction she indicated. They climbed two flights of stairs, reaching the middle of the pagoda. Jareth hesitated before opening the door. Inside, Kabe, Brannon and Tink monitored the wind turbines, calculating and attempting to predict any changes. All three looked up as Jareth and Lexi entered.

"Crew, meet Jareth, the stowaway. Jareth, my crew," Lexi stated, wryly.

Bewildered, surprised and dumbfounded looks met the introductions. Tink stepped forward, as part owner of the ship. "What the hell do we do with him?"

"I must compliment you on your enhancements! What accouterments do you possess in your arm?" Jareth asked, eyeing the brass arm guard covered in gears, gadgets and levers.

Tink broke into a smile. "Thanks. I designed it myself. I built in a screwdriver, drill, metal cutters and a torch. Every tinker's necessities. What's in your arm? I recognize the torch, sword and grappling hook."

Lexi rolled her eyes while they compared hardware. Jareth looked chagrined. "Uh, well, this here's a lock pick and this is brass knuckles. As a child, I ended up locked in a closet for a long time and kinda freaked out. Now, I don't get locked up." He shrugged his shoulders, flashing the killer smile.

"Brass knuckles? In case you must fight your way out of a closet?" Brannon, first mate, commented, dryly.

Chuckling, "Something like that," he responded. Lexi rolled her eyes, again, heading below deck to notify the rest of the crew of the stowaway.

"So, where are we headed?" Jareth asked, casting a glance at the map laid out in front of Kabe.

"Mount Elbert Port. Our cargo includes a load of timber to deliver," Brannon answered.

Jareth appeared pleased. "Any stops planned along the way?"

"We'll drop anchor at Huascaran Port and several other

ports. We trade up and down the coast," Kabe explained.

"What brought you to Aconcagua Port?" Brannon asked.

"My employer hired me to retrieve an item from a collector. I booked passage there and back." Hesitating slightly, "After the poker game, it became imperative to move up my departure time. Some people are just sore losers." Jareth responded with a lopsided smile.

Lexi returned to the bridge. Noah and Granny wanted to meet him. "I'll apologize in advance for our Granny," Kabe commented as they exited. Jareth shot Lexi a quizzical look. She just nodded, leading the way below deck and into the hydroponic garden. Khara, Caroline, Granny and Noah worked in different areas. A multitude of crops grew under the transparent deck. Light shone through plastic windows and ceiling while a maze of pipes supplied purified water.

An incredible variety of fruits, vegetables, herbs and nuts flourished. "Impressive! I envy your set up here. I collect seeds. Are you interested in trading?" Jareth gushed. "I don't recognize…" Abruptly he stopped speaking. Khara walked around an apple tree. Wearing an emerald skirt with a black top, a green waist cincher scrunched her waist to impossible proportions. Her ample breasts gleamed milky white above her top. Copper tendrils curled whimsically, brushing her breasts, flowing to her hips. "Wow."

"Who's this?" Khara asked, carrying a basket loaded with assorted vegetables.

"Oh my. What a handsome stowaway! Are you a pirate? As a teenager, I dated a pirate for a few weeks." An elderly woman peeked out from a tree holding a sack filled with cherries.

"Where is a hurricane when you need one?" Noah groaned, shaking his bald head.

Caroline chuckled as she walked down a row loaded with corn. "Patience, dear."

Gallantly, Jareth bowed deeply. "I am overwhelmed by the beauty of the women on your ship, sir. And such a fine gar- den, as well. Your ship fulfills my wildest dreams!" Glancing at Lexi and Khara, "All of them."

Khara smirked, walked over to Lexi and kissed her, sliding her tongue along her bottom lip.

"I just died and went to heaven," Jareth murmured, awestruck.

"No teasing the boy, ladies," Granny walked up to Jareth and peered at him through spectacles. "Now, where did you come from?"

Finding his voice, reluctantly turning away from the two women, "Originally, Montana Territory. Today, Aconcagua Port. I won at poker and my opponent failed to rejoice in my luck. Your ship ascended just as I needed to leave."

"Lexi, a ship is sailing towards us on the horizon," Brannon announced through the ship's communication system.

Uncommon to encounter airships once out of port, Lexi raised an eyebrow. "Keep an eye on it. See if you can identify the ship. If it continues to gain on us, let me know," Lexi responded over the inter-ship communication device, a brass horn connected to a web of pipes. Directed towards Jareth, "Somebody chasing you?"

He laughed and shook his head. "No. Like I said, my winnings at poker dealt more with a loss of self respect rather than money. Chasing me costs more than the Argentine lost." Jareth flashed a smile melting a thousand icebergs, then, faded to pensive. "At port, multiple sailors reported pirates working this area. Is the balloon deep blue and white? Blending into the sky?"

Lexi glanced at Jareth warily, then clicked the toggle switch activating the horn. "Brannon, what color is the balloon?"

Several moments passed before a response came through the brass horn. "We can't make out the colors. Right now, we see the ship's outline and steam," Brannon responded, his voice, tinny as it traveled down the brass pipes.

Wrinkling her brow, Lexi shot a wary glance at Jareth, then ran up the stairs on deck, out to the stern with Jareth following. Turning a couple knobs, she selected a telescopic lens on her monocular.

Surveying the horizon, Lexi spied the vessel. The outline stood out against the sky, but the balloon blended in. She chose another lens, bringing the ship into clearer focus. It approached rapidly. Through this lens, the blue and white balloon stood out somewhat from the sky.

"It's the pirate ship! We need to run!" Jareth exclaimed.

Lexi turned her gaze to him. He too, surveyed the ship through a telescopic lens on his monocular.

"Brannon, did we receive any information on a pirate ship working this area?" Lexi questioned over her shoulder.

Hesitating, Brannon responded, "Not that we heard. What do you want to do?"

Lexi felt torn between protecting her vessel and aiding a possible escaping criminal. Eyeing the ship, she looked for signs of weapons. "Tink, fire up the steam engines but don't engage them yet. Continue under wind power, for now. Start up the water pump, too."

"Aye, Lexi."

Within moments, the noise of the steam engines growled from the belly of the ship. The vessel vibrated, signaling water moving through the pipes up to the deck. Lexi walked over to an enclosed box. She opened the lid and assembled numerous brass fittings.

Jareth watched her actions over her shoulder. "Is that a large gun or a small cannon?"

"It's a water cannon," Lexi responded as she connected the cannon to the base where a hose hooked up. Once secured, the cannon swiveled in any direction the operator wished. "Keep an eye out for any weapons mounted and readied for attack."

Nodding, Jareth walked back to the railing, and continued to scan the other ship. "They approach at a high rate of speed. The crew scurries across the deck," Jareth reported. "What is that… Holy Siren's song! It's a large bow and arrow!"

At his exclamation, Lexi looked up from the water cannon. Jareth's play by play proved correct. "Kabe, take the helm! Brannon, report to the stern!" Utilizing the screwdriver on her arm band, Lexi removed the brass horn from the deck intercom and strolled to the railing. When the ship reached about five hundred yards, Lexi placed the horn to her lips. "This is Captain Canatolli of the *Star Sapphire*. If you approach with honorable intentions, slow your approach!" As an aside, "Brannon, ready the cannon to defend against attack." The ship failed to slow.

Brannon clicked in a lens on his monocular allowing him to scope out the opposing deck. Using the peep sight, he zeroed in on the ship and watched for them to launch an arrow.

"Ready, Cap!"

As the ship gained, "Tink, engage the steam engines!" Lexi moved back behind Brannon, stowing away the horn.

The engines burped into action, jolting the *Star Sapphire* forward. The pirate ship fired an arrow. Tracking its path, Brannon retaliated, hitting the arrow, knocking it off trajectory, into the endless sky. A second and third arrow followed quickly. Brannon hit the second, sending it careening into the ocean. The third, he nicked the fletchings, causing it to graze the side of the violet balloon. The balloon squealed as hot air escaped. The airship lurched to the left.

"By the hair of a merman's chest! Take evasive maneuvers!" Lexi ordered. "Fire upon the pirate ship!" Opening another steel box, she removed a piece of fabric, along with a canister of adhesive. Initiating the steam propulsion system in her boots, Lexi leapt high into the air, landing near the tear. Quickly, she pulled the trigger on the canister, shooting adhesive along the edges of the rip and slapped fabric over the hole. Using her body weight, Lexi laid across the patch, assuring the adhesive bonded to both pieces. Heat from the balloon sank into her clothing. Biting her lip, she withstood the pain.

During her ministrations, the *Star Sapphire* fell about two hundred feet in a wobbly uneven path. After ensuring the patch held, Lexi propelled down to the deck.

"Evasive maneuvers!" Brannon relayed to Kabe, at the helm. "Firing on the rotting fish pirates!" Brannon aimed the water cannon at the keel of the ship, cutting a hole in the bottom, exposing the engine room. Mechanical parts fell to the ocean.

"Drop down two hundred feet, steam engines to full power, wind turbines full power!" Lexi commanded.

The *Star Sapphire* dropped drastically while gaining forward momentum. The pirate vessel grew smaller as the distance between the two increased exponentially. It disappeared on the horizon when suddenly, the wind turbines gave out.

Plummeting towards the water, Kabe righted the ship, compensating with the steam engines. A high pitched noise whistled. The added pressured caused a corner of the patch to give way.

"Brannon, take the helm. Kabe, locate the nearest island

or port to put down. Tink, let's examine the balloon and perform a temporary repair until we can dock to fix it. Tell Noah to report to the stern, to keep watch."

Once Tink reached the deck, she and Lexi propelled to the damaged spot on the balloon. Changing the lens in their monoculars to microscopic, they surveyed the temporary repair job. "The longer we keep our speed and altitude lower, the longer the patch holds."

"Yeah, that's fine and dandy until the pirates show up again." Lexi sighed, eying the spot through her heat seeking lens. Heat escaped one corner and leaked through minute areas surrounding the patch. They needed to drop anchor, repair the hole and give the spot time to cure before filling the balloon. "What do you think, Tink?"

Tink sighed, "If we land and spend twenty-four hours allowing the adhesive to fully bond once we fix it, it should be all right. But the longer we keep the balloon inflated and moving, the greater chance of complete failure of the patch." Tink diagnosed as she studied the patch through a heat lens and a microscopic lens in tangent.

"My prognosis, too. Damn." Lexi sighed. "I'll check if Kabe found a place to dock."

"Okay. I'll reinforce the small leaks."

Lexi kicked her boots, propelling to the stairs leading to the bridge. Jareth and Kabe compared maps. "Present me with options."

"Jareth's map shows a few islands we lack awareness of relatively nearby. The closest option possible," Kabe pointed to one spot. "Our position is about here. At our current speed, the islands lay about three hours away."

Studying the map, Lexi measured the distance of the islands from their immediate location and compared it to the mainland. The islands presented the best option for their impending predicament. "Are the islands inhabited? Any supplies?"

Hesitating, Jareth replied, "Few people know of the islands. I planted a number of different seeds, fruits and vegetables, trees. No one lived there the last time I stopped in." He paused, then continued. "I keep some supplies on the island for ship repairs, medical, the like."

10

"Do you think the pirates know about the locale?" Lexi questioned, glancing up at Jareth.

He laughed. "No. I," Jareth hesitated again, "conceal the islands. I've shared the location with only a couple friends. If you don't know about them, you won't find them."

"How do you conceal an island?" Brannon asked from the helm.

"Buoys made of mirrors refract light, sky and ocean strategically placed completely obscure the land mass. Manipulating the wind and ocean currents helps to steer ships clear," Jareth explained. "I guarantee our safety while Tink repairs the balloon."

Lexi raised an eyebrow, skeptical. "Jareth, can you direct Brannon and Kabe on how to reach the islands?"

Nodding, Jareth replied, "Of course."

Exiting the bridge, Lexi found her father, standing at the stern, searching the horizon with binoculars for the pirate ship. "Any sign?"

Noah shook his head. "No, I don't think they followed us. They probably stopped to repair their keel. What's our plan?" Sighing deeply, "Jareth knows of a place about three hours away where we can dock. He says he keeps the islands concealed and few people know of them." She explained the concealment process.

Stroking his neck, Noah considered the information. "Do you think it's a trap? Do you trust him?"

Lexi considered the possibility. "Jareth informed us the ship may be pirates prior to the attack. His warning allowed us to ready the water cannon. The island provides us a safe haven as opposed to trying to reach Huascaran Port."

"Could we make Huascaran Port?"

Lexi shrugged. "It's risky. We need twenty-four hours for the patch to cure before inflating the balloon. Leaks around the patch developed already. Tink is repairing the leaks. She advised we set down as soon as possible. Let's keep a watch going. If you take the first shift, those of us with heat seeking lens will maintain constant lookout through the night."

"Sounds like a plan."

Surveying the horizon, Lexi sighed, then returned to the bridge. "I'm going below to rest. The first watch tonight is

11

mine. Wake me before we enter the concealed area. You piqued my curiosity."

"Of course, Cap," Brannon remarked.

Jareth and Kabe stood hunched over, copying missing details from each other's maps. Both glanced up. "I assure your ship and crew's safety while on my islands," Jareth promised.

Raising an eyebrow, Lexi responded, "Forgive me for not trusting a man who stowed away upon my ship."

With a wry look, Jareth nodded. Lexi left the bridge and ascended to the sleeping quarters. she shared with Khara, resting above the bridge. She laid on the king size bed and instantly fell asleep.

2

"Lexi, we're almost to Jareth's islands. Brannon asked me to wake you," Khara's soft voice broke through the web of sleep entangling Lexi.

Groaning, Lexi rolled over and sat up, reaching for her boots. "No sign of the pirates?"

"Nothing I've heard. I think it's been easy sailing, given the ship's condition," Khara replied. "What's your take on the stowaway?"

"I don't know. We'll maintain an armed watch through the night. Speaking of which, I'm taking first watch," Lexi commented, dropping a gentle kiss on Khara's lips, stroking her burnt copper locks. "I better return to the bridge. I'm curious how one conceals an island."

Surprise crossed Khara's face. "Hmm, I think I'll accompany you. That sounds quite intriguing." Lexi smiled lopsidedly at her.

The last to arrive, Lexi and Khara descended the stairs. Everyone wanted to witness the spectacle. Jareth stood at the helm. He glanced over his shoulder as the two women entered the bridge. His eyes quickly noticed Khara's hand resting at Lexi's waist. A slow smile crept onto his lips.

"Just in time. I'll show you how to enter the concealed area." Jareth drew a lever back, releasing air from the balloons, dropping altitude. "Drop down to two hundred feet at this latitude and longitude. to reach the one hundred foot opening."

"Where are the buoys?" Kabe stood over the map, pencil in hand.

Jareth pointed to them. "If you look through a heat lens and UVA lens simultaneously, the buoys become obvious.

Two buoys rest on the ocean as well, creating a gateway, of sorts." Those with monoculars clicked in the appropriate lenses and surveyed the horizon. The buoys glowed against the sky and ocean. The heat signature differed slightly from the atmosphere and water. The UVA allowed them to obviously stand out rather than registering a slight change in ambient temperature.

Oohs and aahhs came from the assembled spectators. "Buoys surround the chain of islands on the water's surface and throughout the skies strategically placed resulting in hiding the islands behind what appears to be a glare upon the surface of the water. Without knowing where to find the gateway, ships sail by without seeing anything, other than the glare reflecting and bouncing off the buoys and ocean."

When Jareth finished his explanation, the *Star Sapphire* suddenly entered an area that appeared like an alternate reality. Four islands displayed a mosaic of colors: green, red, orange, yellow, brown and purple. The colors sprang from life, plant and animal. Birds of all sorts soared on wind currents, circling the islands, calling to one another.

The crew ran down the stairs, onto the deck, gazing over the railing at the sight below.

"Is this what the Earth looked like before the flood?" Khara questioned, turning to Noah.

Tears filled Noah's eyes as words escaped him. He merely nodded. Jareth circled the ship, landing on the water in line with the largest island, the second one. There, a dock made of wood and steel, extended out to the ocean. Lexi and Brannon retrieved ropes to tie down the ship as Jareth pulled up alongside. They kicked their boots to jump, quickly tying off. Once secured, Noah extended the gangplank. Jareth shut down the steam engines. The balloon slowly deflated. Lexi and Tink marked the tear, positioning the balloon to aid in repair. The rest of the crew gazed at the flourishing plant life. Chittering creatures unknown by most of the crew reached their ears.

"Is it... safe?" Khara questioned, hesitantly, standing at the gangplank, unsure whether or not to disembark.

Jareth walked up behind her, laughing. "Yes, it's safe. Along with plants and trees, I transfer animals and insects I've discovered from other places supporting life."

"Can I... Do you mind if..." Khara, at a loss for words,

unable to finish her request, gazed in wonder. "I've never seen so many varieties of plants and animals in one place."

Smiling, Jareth ducked his head. "I made it my mission to support all types of life. Plants and animals I discover, I transplant here and to the other islands. I keep track of what I place where and am constantly searching for other species. Would you like a tour?"

Eagerly, Khara nodded, as did most of the crew. "Tink, I'll help you with the sail. Let's finish it before the sun sets. We'll take the tour while the patch cures," Lexi offered. "The rest of you, feel free to take advantage of Jareth's hospitality."

"Catch up with the rest of the crew, if you like, Lexi. I prefer brass to plants," Tink smiled. "I'll maintain watch over the ship and sound the alarm if any issues arise."

The sun hung low on the horizon. Within an hour, darkness would creep over top of the light. Lexi scanned the skies. Birds and clouds dotted the upper atmosphere, but no ships. Nodding, "All right. Let me know when you tire and I'll take your place."

Lexi walked along the trail between the plants. She recognized tomatoes, onions and corn. A number of different trees adorned with apples, pears, plums and nectarines grew bearing small fruit, not quite ripe. Many different plants, Lexi failed to recognize. A smile crossed her lips. Khara found her vision of heaven here. Small animals scurried among the plants and trees while birds sang unfamiliar exotic songs. Sightings of birds occurred infrequently. Most of the world's population of animals perished with the flooding. Jareth created a Garden of Eden of sorts. Hearing voices and laughter in the distance, Lexi followed the sounds.

Khara knelt down, inspecting small plants bearing tiny red thin shaped growths. "Lexi! Peppers! Jareth possesses pepper plants! Did you see the vast assortment of flora? Many of them, I'm unable to recognize!"

"Quite a few of the varieties, I haven't seen since the floods," Caroline replied softly, tears filling her eyes, kneeling beside Khara.

"Feel free to take any seeds you want and I hope you plant your seeds I lack," Jareth offered generously. "I intend to keep as many species of plants and animals alive as possi-

15

ble and transplant them onto other islands and continents as I travel."

"I find your actions here very impressive and commendable," Noah remarked, as he smiled down at his wife.

"I assure you, we are safe here." After a moment, "I keep rowboats at the ends of the islands to access the next island in the chain. Feel free to explore all of them. I need to update my catalogue, plant new seeds I recently acquired and gather seeds for orders to deliver," Jareth announced.

"We finished the necessary repairs for the ship. Now, we must wait. This seems like a good place for a day of rest and relaxation," Lexi permitted, looking at the eager faces of her family.

"Can I assist you with anything?" Khara, gazed up at Jareth.

Jareth hesitated. "Why don't you pick out the plants you want. I maintain a detailed catalogue of all my flora and fauna. Once I finish updating, we can plant your seeds and gather the ones you desire." With a smile, he moved towards a trail, "Enjoy the islands."

Lexi woke to Tink cussing loudly. Walking to the railing, she peered over the side. Tink sat atop a round brass and glass orb floating in the water. She worked on her hydro-pod. Built to explore beneath the surface of the ocean, Tink spent any free time perfecting her invention.

Smiling down at Tink, "How goes it?"

Tink peered up at Lexi through her microscopic goggles. Her left arm glowed with a burning torch while her right held a piece of metal between a pair of pliers. "I figured a super secret port and twenty-four hours of down time provided the perfect opportunity to work on the hydro-pod. This land forsaken bolt doesn't want to seal," Tink grunted as she soldered metal around the offending article.

Lexi powered up her propulsion boots and floated to the pod. "How can I help?""

"Power up your torch. I think I need more heat."

Surveying the operation at hand, Tink attempted to seal the brass around a glass window, ensuring water wouldn't leak inside the hydro-pod. Lexi fired up the torch on her left hand, adding her flame to Tink's. The metal melted around the

16

bolt and along the seam where the tempered layers of glass met brass.

"All right! Now we must weld the rest of the windows and she'll be waterproof!"

The pod, made of brass, boasted six windows of tempered glass. Powered by steam from the heated ocean water, the pod protected the operator from the dangerous waters while allowing panoramic views below the surface. Outfitted with gears and levers, the hydro-pod operator piloted from inside, controlling the speed, depth and direction.

"Ha ha! We finished it!" Excitedly, Tink bounced up and danced around. "It's done!" Kicking her propulsion boots, she flew up and executed a back flip in the air. "Yah!" Sinking down next to Lexi, "Wanna accompany me on the maiden voyage?"

"What is that... contraption?" Jareth questioned, standing on the deck of the *Star Sapphire*. He gazed in wonder.

"It's my hydro-pod! I designed it to travel beneath the ocean, exploring sunken civilizations existing prior to the floods!" she exclaimed. "I think it's ready. We're taking it on its first excursion!" Tink grabbed the wheel on top and turned it clockwise, opening a hatch. She squeezed through the hole and dropped down. Popping her head up, "C'mon, Lexi! Let's go!"

Smiling, "I guess we're leaving. Brannon! We're taking the hydro-pod for a test drive." Lexi climbed down the hole and pulled the hatch closed. "How do I lock this thing?"

"Turn the wheel counter-clockwise, 'til it clicks." Click. Two seats sat in front of a row of levers, knobs, wheels, switches, buttons and gadgets. Lexi lowered herself into the chair furthest away from all the controls, while Tink fussed around. Studying the control panel, Lexi identified the depth indicator, compass, speedometer, and pressure relief valve. The levers? Completely clueless.

"Okay! I think we're ready," Tink sank into the pilot's chair and flipped a switch, illuminating the pod and the gadgets, buttons and switches. She pushed a green button and the steam engine growled to life. A purple button pressurized the pod. Pulling a lever towards her, the pod slowly descended. Water covered the windows as the pod sank. Tink pulled a

17

second lever and the pod propelled forward.

Lexi inhaled several shallow breaths and tried to relax, feeling a little claustrophobic as the pod submerged completely and moved underwater, further from shore and from the surface. Inside, the temperature rose slightly due to the hot ocean water. But no leaks appeared. Giggles escaped Tink. "It's working! Better than I imagined! Look at the fish! The plants! Everything appears so clear!"

Focusing on the scenes outside the windows, rather than her anxiety, Lexi gazed into the underwater world. "Wow. This is incredible! A whole other world exists under the ocean!" Awe evident in her voice. She watched a school of fish swim almost as one in front of the pod and dart off, disappearing into sea grass.

Tink moved a third lever to the left, turning the pod. She then, turned it to the right, with another giggle escaping, as the ship obeyed. The pod propelled about three hundred feet from the island, continually sinking lower into the ocean until the depth gauge indicated the pod reached twenty feet deep. Lexi vacillated between staring out the windows in awe and watching Tink operate.

The pod approached a pile of rocks. Tink brought the vessel to a halt. Lexi turned and looked at her. "This part will completely blow your mind!" Tink promised, grasping two levers. Two arms extended from the pod.

"What in Neptune's heaven?"

Tink responded giggling. Lexi began to worry about Tink's giggles. The two arms reached out to the rocks, picking them up and moving them around. She grasped a stone and retracted the arm back to the pod. Pushing a button on the control panel, Lexi heard metal clanging. Once the clanging stopped, Tink pressed the button again and a noise like air leaking filled the cockpit.

"What in Neptune's hell is that? Is there a leak?" Lexi squeaked.

Again, Tink giggled and flipped open a small door near her foot. She reached in and grasped the rock the arm retrieved, handing it to Lexi. It held the warmth of the ocean but felt dry. "Pretty cool, huh?" Tink responded, smiling like the pilot who caught a favorable wind.

Lexi broke into a huge grin, "This is by far your best

invention ever! Imagine all the exploring of old civilizations we can perform! All the maps we possess tell us where the continents used to exist. We'll become treasure hunters!"

Tink broke out in a fit of giggles, clapping in excitement, "I can hardly wait! This is going to be so much fun!"

After putting around underwater for a little while longer, Lexi sighed. "We better return to shore. Everyone may be worrying about us. I'm sure you need to take others for a ride."

Nodding, Tink manipulated the levers, turning the pod around and propelling towards shore. She experimented with changing the speed, ascending and descending on the return trip. Fits of giggles broke out of Tink frequently as the pod responded better than Tink dared to hope. Breaking the surface of the lagoon, Tink practiced with the controls on top of the water. The pod rocked back and forth, tipping as she worked on stabilization.

They pulled up to the dock and Lexi released the hatch, climbing out. She smiled as the assembled spectators sighed in relief at their arrival. "Tink's latest invention proves to be the most awe inspiring thing ever! It's amazing, the under water world! You must take a ride!"

Brannon raised his hand, "I call second!"

Lexi laughed, kicking her boots into propulsion, she jumped on deck of the *Star Sapphire*. "I'm going to check out the sails and ropes while we're in port."

"Hey, Jareth! Do you happen to have any firewood around to replenish our stock?" Tink asked, poking her head out of the pod.

"I'll trade you a whole island for a ride in your pod!" He offered.

Laughing, Tink replied, "No problem! As soon as we return, you're next!"

"Perfect! The third island grows a variety of pine trees. Feel free to scavenge whatever you find. If an unhealthy tree exists or if they grow too close together go ahead and cut one down," Jareth said.

Noah laid a hand on Kabe's shoulder. "Why don't we take the small skiff and see what we find in the way of firewood?" Kabe nodded, "Sounds fine to me. I'd rather stay above water."

Nodding in agreement, "I love the feel of solid earth under my feet." They moved aboard ship and readied a skiff for the short excursion.

Jareth observed the hydro-pod as they submerged and traveled away from the dock. Using the steam propulsion in his boots, he followed until they disappeared. He returned to find Lexi floating halfway up the main mast, examining ropes attached to sails. He activated the propulsion unit in his boots and joined her. "The design of the pod appears to be sheer genius! How did it operate at lower depths? Did the interior temperature rise from the ocean?" He questioned, floating next to Lexi.

Shaking her head, "She insulated the interior, protecting us from the heat. The temperature increased a little, but not uncomfortably."

"Did water leak inside?"

Again, shaking her head. "Nope. Air tight."

Cocking his head, "How about maneuverability?"

"There are levers, buttons, switches and all sorts of gadgets she uses to steer it in any direction she wishes. Tink adjusts the depth, stabilizes the pod against the currents, increases or decreases speed, turns to any bearing. Wait until you see the arms!" Lexi laughed, holding a rope in her hand, she slowly ascended, checking for defects.

"Arms?"

"She designed two arms she controls that extend out and grasp objects. Then, the arms place the objects in a pocket. From there, water drains out and you pick up the object from inside the pod. Under water. Tink is a certifiable genius!" Reaching the top of the mast, Lexi inspected the sails one by one, as she descended.

Jareth watched Lexi quietly, digesting the pod specifications. She discovered a small tear in the second sail. Pulling out a needle and thread, she deftly stitched the fabric.

"How does she provide oxygen to the pod?"

Shrugging, Lexi replied, "Tink created a motor that operates on steam. Her invention sends the heat in one direction for propulsion, and removes the salt and water, sending them in two separate directions. Some of the water breaks down into hydrogen and oxygen. The oxygen, she pumps into the air for breathing. That's the basics behind the motor for the *Star Sapphire*. I'm sure the engine for the pod performs a similar mechanical operation. We obtain our drinking water and water for the hydroponics garden through the same engine." Lexi explained the mechanics to Jareth, as she understood them from Tink's multitude of lectures over the years. "I don't understand specifically how it works. I only know Tink's theory."

Jareth mulled over the information as Lexi descended to the next sail. The pod broke the surface and the top hatch popped open. Eagerly, Jareth propelled down to the pod. "How was it?" He questioned Brannon.

Nodding and smiling, "Magnificent! I never imagined how beautiful underwater appears! I cannot wait to embark on treasure hunting! Wow!" Brannon gushed, climbing out of the pod.

Unable to contain his excitement, Jareth dropped down into the pod, sealing the hatch above him. Brannon joined Lexi up on the deck of the ship. "Need help?"

Shaking her head, "No, I'm good. If you want, try and find Noah and Kabe. They're collecting firewood on the third island for Tink."

"All right! Not often we discover an area where we find firewood. Tink talked about manufacturing a flying pod and needs to be able to heat metal to form the body."

Lexi laughed. "She just finished building one incredible mode of transportation and is already inventing another?"

"We must keep our Tink happy in her laboratory!" Brannon kicked his boots into propulsion, heading towards the third island. Brannon joined the crew fifteen years earlier, an orphan at Shasta Port in the Oregon Territory. Charles and Mary found him fishing at the dock, trying to find food. He fit right in with the *Star Sapphire*, the son Charles dreamed of.

After an hour passed, the pod reappeared at the dock. The hatch opened up with Jareth and Tink exiting. Unable to hear their words, they seemed engaged in earnest discussion.

Tink propelled up to Lexi several minutes later. "Jareth enjoyed the trial run immensely. He asked many questions about the design and the mechanics behind my engine." Laughing, "He loved traveling underwater and almost went berserk when I showed him the arms. Is everyone else collecting firewood?"

"Either firewood or touring the flora and fauna. It's not often we discover an island covered in trees. Did Jareth seem to understand the mechanics involved in your designs?"

Rocking her head back and forth, "To an extent, but we reached a point where my invention surpassed his knowledge. If you don't need my help, I'll find the wood gatherers."

"I'm fine, here. Just want to take advantage of the down time to inspect the sails and ropes since we aren't airborne. A little maintenance now,"

"Saves a catastrophe later," Tink giggled, finishing Lexi's father's personal motto. The girls grew up hearing the proverb regularly.

Tink took off for the third island while Lexi followed the rope up on the fore mast. The ropes appeared in good working order. Movement atop of rock cliffs across the way caught Lexi's eye. She clicked in the telescope lens on her monocular, focusing on the object. Jareth propelled quickly around the rocks and through the trees. Then, he disappeared.

Lexi changed lenses to zero in closer, but saw no sign of Jareth. Keeping an eye out for movement, Lexi continued her perusal of the sails. Once she finished, still no Jareth. She decided to explore that direction, to ensure his safety. On the ground, a faint trail appeared amongst the vegetation. Following it, she reached the rocks she observed him propelling over and around. As best she could, by memory, Lexi worked her way up to where she watched him disappear. Between two rocks lay an adult sized opening.

Clicking in a low light lens and a heat seeking lens, Lexi peered into the darkened cavern.

Two tunnels forked off the main entry. A glimmer of light showed around the bend. The other tunnel remained dark in mystery. Cautiously, Lexi snuck down, peeking around the corner, Jareth sat on a stool looking into what appeared to be a piece of glass. A man's face stared out at him.

"Sir, I strongly disagree. We need to ally ourselves with the *Star Sapphire.* Not only did they design a completely self-sufficient ship, but their mechanic is simply brilliant. Her invention of the hydro-pod and plans for the flying pod would

22

bring priceless technology, knowledge and artifacts to us. The botanist constructed a hydroponic garden aboard their ship, growing an incredible array of plants, herbs and trees. If we replicate their ship, achievement of our mission becomes so much more possible and probable!"

The man in the glass stroked his beard. "We need that hydro-pod! Obtain it by any means necessary!"

Jareth sighed heavily, shaking his head. "I refuse to steal it. I'm traveling with them to Mount Elbert Port. That gives me plenty of time to gain their trust and try to bring them in as members for the Society. We're stopping at several ports along the way. I'll contact you again, when I'm able."

"With their advances in technology, can you set up a communication station on the ship?"

"No. Their technology focuses on mechanics and botany. Communications isn't a priority." Jareth hesitated for a moment. "Their interests parallel ours. I believe I can convince them to join-"

The man in the glass interrupted. "Don't say anything about us without my authorization! Don't jeopardize our work!"

Silence stretched on for several moments. "Yes, sir. I'll contact you as soon as I can."

"Get us that hydro-pod."

The face disappeared. Jareth slammed his fist down, "Damn it! These are good people! I won't hurt them!" Frustration colored his voice as he leaned back in his chair.

"I better gather my fifty variety of seeds I require for my ship." He stood and walked over to an alchemy cabinet with a hundred small drawers. Lexi saw each one bore a label but was too far away to read them. Jareth began opening drawers and extracting tiny objects, seeds more than likely, and jotting down notes on a paper. He placed the seeds in tiny compartments inside his long duster coat. After watching him for several minutes, Lexi left the cavern and returned to the ship, taking a different route to avoid detection.

Mulling over the conversation, Lexi tried to reach a decision regarding Jareth. He passed on the information to someone regarding the hydro-pod. Now, someone wanted it. Badly. Jareth objected strongly to betraying the crew. Someone ordered him to obtain the pod. By any means necessary.

23

Lexi's first responsibility fell to her crew, her family and her ship. As captain, her primary objective revolved around keeping them safe. Should she confront him about the conversation? At this thought, she hesitated. They literally stood on his turf. He possessed technology they didn't understand or know how to operate. Weapon systems may be located on the islands, in which they wouldn't be able to defend themselves. He needed to travel to Mount Elbert Port and hoped to arrive there via the *Star Sapphire.* If a confrontation occurred, Lexi preferred it happen aboard her ship, where she and her crew knew their strengths and weaknesses. Jareth wouldn't make a move for some time. Surely, not until they travelled closer to the destination. At present, they were weeks away, if they flew directly.

Lexi decided to talk with Tink. They must decide where and how to place the pod upon the ship. As captain, Lexi possessed the ability to manipulate the arrangements making it near impossible to steal. Even though the pod maneuvered safely, the design didn't include for long distance travel. It would either need to be transported by another vessel or driven short distances.

Back at the dock, the wood gatherers returned and loaded their haul into the belly of the boat. Tink reached into the skiff to grab more wood. "Tink! What's your idea on where to stow the hydro-pod?" Lexi asked.

Tink shrugged her shoulders. "I design, fabricate, manufacture, operate, educate and repair. Someone else gets to figure out storage," she responded, grabbing an armload of wood.

"I love you Tink, but you're a pain in the ass," Brannon dropped a kiss on her head. "Need help figuring this one out?"

Lexi nodded, "It crossed my mind this may take some finagling. How much does it weigh, approximately?"

"You don't want to know," Tink replied ducking into the hull of the ship with the wood.

Brannon and Lexi exchanged a look. "Let's measure the dimensions. I bet we may need to park it in middle of the ship to support the weight." Brannon remarked as they turned to gaze at the pagoda housing the bridge, look out, and Lexi and Khara's sleeping quarters.

"Here's a thought. What about attaching a balloon to the pod to bear most of the weight, place it on the bow, with a pipe connected to the engine to inflate the balloon? Then, to unload it, we unhook the pipe and set it in the water, next to the ship," Lexi suggested, pointing towards the bow which covered the engine.

"That forms a direct line to the engine. With its own balloon, the hydro-pod bares most of the weight. Transporting the pod by balloon takes care of the issues involved with loading and unloading." Brannon contemplated the idea after he listed the positive aspects. "Works for me. We placed the cherry red balloon in the storage room of the pagoda."

Smiling, Lexi stated, "I'll grab the balloon if you want to construct a harness. Let's hook a pipe to the engine to inflate it." The two separated, picking up pieces and parts required to store the pod.

About twenty minutes later, Brannon laid out the harness while Lexi prepared the balloon and then hooked up the pipe, using a set up similar to the *Star Sapphire*. As Lexi glanced up from tightening pipes, she noticed Jareth watching from the dock. When their eyes met, Jareth asked, flashing his heart melting smile, "Need help?"

Lexi swallowed her mistrust, returned the smile and shook her head, "We're almost finished. I just need to start the engine, if I can figure out Tink's set up." She opened the hatch and climbed down. Lexi started the engine and then reversed the exhaust, filling the pipe and then the balloon. Poking her head out the hatch, she watched as the blimp rose up. "Let's tie off the balloon while it fills, then hopefully, we can walk the hydro-pod onboard."

Brannon tied it to the dock as Lexi landed next to him, securing another rope. They watched the balloon slowly lift the pod out of the water. Lexi and Brannon kicked the propulsion on in their boots, untied the ropes, and began to guide the balloon to the ship. Out of nowhere, a wind picked up, blowing the blimp away from the ship, pulling Lexi and Brannon off balance. Using their propulsion, they attempted to right them- selves. Jareth dropped a chest he carried on deck and joined them, grasping another rope, adding his propulsion, aided in righting the pod.

Kabe and Tink joined in. The five of them worked together to direct the balloon to the stern of the ship. Tink hooked up the pipe fueling the balloon while the other four fastened down the pod. "I must say, the cherry red balloon stands out beautifully against the violet balloon!" Tink nodded her approval. "You know what we'd really benefit from? A transport device. A big plate propelled similar to your boots, making transport of large, heavy objects easier. Hmmm. I'll make a note of it." She removed a notebook from a pocket and wrote an entry.

3

Lexi studied the map, charting their course to Huascaran Port, when Khara entered the bridge, coming up behind her, kissing her neck. Wrapping her arms around Lexi's waist, "Finally, I locate you. We're on dry ground, surrounded by lush vegetation and you hide onboard, studying aero-nautical maps!"

Smiling and turning her head, she pressed her lips to Khara's. "I want to study the changes added from Jareth's map. While we need to return to the trade route, I wish to steer clear of the pirate ship. Are you in ecstasy with all these plants?"

"Mmm, yes, I am!" Kissing her neck again, "Let's talk about another type of ecstasy."

Surprised, Lexi turned away from the map, her lips a hair's breath away from Khara's lips. "What do you have in mind?"

Khara's breath tickled against Lexi, "You know I want a baby."

"Uh huh."

"Invite Jareth into our bed."

Raising an eyebrow, Lexi pulled back a little, gazing into Khara's eyes. Khara preferred to share a bed with a woman, while Lexi enjoyed both. Opportunities to meet men worthy of procreating with proved extremely limited. Jareth displayed significant intelligence, numerous valuable skills, and possessed a pleasing disposition and appearance. A child fathered by him would prove exceptional. And Lexi preferred to keep him under a very watchful eye.

"All right," she leaned in and kissed Khara. "I'll invite him."

"We want to thank you for the hospitality of your

27

islands and the gift of the seeds. You provided us with numerous food sources new to us," Khara smiled shyly, looking up at Jareth under her eyelashes.

Lexi walked over to him, using her left hand, she ran a finger from Jareth's hairline, down his jaw and neck, trailing to the waistband of his trousers. He reflexively inhaled, Lexi slid her hand on the inside of his waistband.

"Do anything you want with me, to me. I'll do anything you want me to do. You don't hurt Khara. Khara loves the feel of a man ejaculating inside her. Whenever you're going to cum, cum in her," Lexi explained the rules in a deep voice, as her hand wrapped around Jareth's penis. His member grew while he listened intently.

With a sexy smile, "Never tell a man he can have anything he wants," Jareth replied, closing his eyes as Lexi stroked him.

Placing her lips next to his ear, she whispered, "You can have anything you want from me."

Needing no further encouragement, Jareth replied, "Drop to your knees and take me into your mouth. Khara, come here and kiss me."

Lexi fell to the floor, unlacing his pants, she pulled his phallus out and placed it in her mouth. She sucked his entire organ down her throat. He moaned as the warmth completely encompassed him. Khara met his lips, her tongue inviting herself in to his mouth. Very thoroughly, she kissed him. He slid a hand under her shirt, cupping her breast over her corset. Gently he kneaded the nipple into a tight bud while Lexi worked his manhood in and out of her mouth while stroking his scrotum. He buried his hand in her hair and then pulled her head back. She increased suction on his cock as he pulled out of her mouth, slowly.

"Undress and climb on the bed." Lexi gave him a sexy smile and walked over to Khara, kissing her deeply as she pulled her shirt over her head and dropped Khara's skirt to the floor.

Khara stood in an emerald bustier and black bloomers, her milky white flesh accentuated by her copper hair. The bustier pushed up the mounds of her breasts, barely concealing the nipples. Lexi untied her bloomers, letting them fall to the floor.

Khara released the ties on Lexi's shirt revealing a black

bustier. Her breasts, not as large as Khara's, but still enticing. Khara walked behind Lexi and unlaced her pants, allowing them to fall to the floor, exposing Lexi's nether region. Kissing her neck, Khara slipped a finger inside Lexi's vagina and stroked her clit. Lexi closed her eyes and moaned softly.

Jareth watched them while his member grew to an enormous size. He laid down on the bed. "Lexi, suck my cock. Khara lick her clitoris. Get her very, very wet," His voice took on a low baritone. Lexi smiled mischievously as she crawled across the bed, lowering herself down and taking him back into her mouth, swallowing him down into her throat. Khara giggled as she placed herself between Lexi's legs and Lexi lowered her nub down onto Khara's awaiting mouth. Khara flicked it with her tongue, causing Lexi to whimper while she engulfed Jareth's penis. He moaned as the vibrations of her throat engorged him, burying his fingers in Lexi's hair.

After several minutes, Jareth ordered, "Lexi, lay on your back. Khara, suck her clit and ready her for anal penetration. I'm going to cum in you." He grabbed her hips and shoved himself deep into her. She cried out as he plunged repeatedly inside.

Khara sucked hard on Lexi's clit and thrust her finger in her vagina and then her anus, in time with Jareth's thrusts. Jareth yanked Khara by the hips against him as he shot his sperm deep within. Lexi and Khara orgasmed at the same time as Jareth. He pushed Khara flat onto the bed, next to Lexi, landing half on top of her.

Jareth reached his left hand over to Lexi's womanhood. He slid a finger along her inner folds. Lexi widened her legs as he inserted a finger into her vagina. Gently, he pushed it in and out several times, moistening it with her juices. Then, he pulled his finger out and slid it to her anus. He circled it with the slickness. Softly, he pushed the tip of his finger inside her and looked at her face. She smiled. Slowly, Jareth worked the finger in and out. "Khara, lick her clit."

She jumped up and moved to Lexi's right side, flicking the button several times causing Lexi to buck. Jareth slid two fingers in her anus while Khara licked her tenderly. "Perform a sixty-nine with Lexi on top." The two changed positions with Lexi pulling Khara's legs apart and exposing her clit to the open air. Lexi blew on the nub before she licked her softly from the hood all the way to her ass. Khara moaned and pulled Lexi's clit hard into her mouth. Jareth knelt behind Lexi, sliding his cock on the outside of her vagina, lubricating it with her juices. He slid in and out several times, feeling Khara's tongue touch the tip of his phallus. Suddenly, he plunged his cock into Lexi's ass, burying it until his balls slapped against her clitoris. Khara licked the clit and his scrotum as he gently thrust into Lexi's ass. Lexi whimpered. He withdrew. He pushed in again, until he felt Khara's tongue. Khara whimpered as Lexi nibbled her nub too hard. Jareth slapped her ass. Hard.

"Don't hurt Khara," he reminded softly. "You lick her soft, very soft."

Lexi nodded, trying to relax her body. Jareth continued to push in and ease out of her rectum, slowly gaining in speed and thrusting harder. Khara's tongue softened on Lexi's clit, tenderly licking it while Lexi struggled to gentle her tongue on Khara. Lexi gave up, not trusting herself and fingered Khara's sweet spot, rousing her to orgasm. Khara sucked on Lexi, as she began to climax. Jareth held on to Lexi's hips as he pounded repeatedly into her. Lexi and Khara climaxed. Pushing Lexi off to the side, Jareth grabbed Khara and rammed his cock into her cunt, spewing his seed deep within her.

Khara fell asleep, hanging off the side of the bed. Jareth turned towards Lexi. She smiled. Jareth returned the grin, reaching out and stroked her tender nub. Lexi reciprocated by grasping his manhood, stroking it as he began to grow hard. Her juices flowed freely from his ministrations. She moved on top of Jareth, sliding down his cock. He grasped her hips, moving up and down slowly, massaging him with her vaginal muscles.

Slowly, Jareth picked her up and brought her down, controlling the speed. She rocked her hips to and fro, rubbing her nub against his pubic hair, bringing her to orgasm. He smiled as her body shivered with each wave. Grasping her hips, he started pounding inside, sending her into another orgasm.

"Do you want me to cum in Khara or let her sleep?" Jareth whispered in Lexi's ear.

"Inside me. She get's bitchy if you wake her for sex."

Jareth laughed softly, holding her hips stationary while he buried himself deeply within her folds, as he sought release. "So, is it okay if I wake you for sex?" Jareth whispered as he snuggled.

"Like I said, you can do anything you want to me."

He laughed again. "Good."

A couple hours after a little sleep, Jareth slid inside Lexi from behind. By the time Lexi roused, they both orgasmed, then returned to their slumber.

The next morning, Tink, Brannon and Kabe readied the ship for lift off. Excitedly, Khara worked in hydroponics planting new seeds. Jareth finalized a few projects, unsure when his next return to the islands might be. Lexi and Kabe studied the map, planning the best route to Huascaran Port.

Brannon entered the bridge. "Why don't we compare an old world map and see if we can find a spot to test out the hydro-pod? Find an old civilization to explore!"

"Attempting to locate some of the old cities and treasure hunting sounds like fun!" Kabe offered up.

Lexi flashed a wry smile. "I agree."

By mid-morning, ship and crew prepared to ascend, leaving the island paradise behind. Everyone except Lexi and Jareth stood at the railing, watching until the trees disappeared from sight. Lexi steered the ship while Jareth guided her between the buoys, returning to the open sea.

Moving behind her, Jareth nuzzled her neck, resting his hands at her waist. "If I wreck my ship because of your," Lexi hesitated briefly, "distractions, I'm going to be very angry."

Laughing, "There's nothing to crash into," he whispered in her ear.

The sound of someone bounding up the stairs reached them. Jareth moved away from her, turning to the map. Kabe burst through the door. "I already miss your islands. It felt fantastic to stand on actual dirt, see trees, animals, breathe oxygen derived from actual trees and plants, hear birds sing." Kabe sighed, "Paradise."

"I find it difficult to leave as well. It's hard to imagine large land masses covered the Earth, once upon a time." Jareth replied wistfully.

"Mother Nature and Poseidon fought valiantly. Unfortunately, Poseidon won, turning Earth into his Kingdom," Lexi

31

replied. "Now the skies and the ocean make up our world."

Kabe nodded, joining Jareth at the map. Comparing the compass heading to the path laid out, Lexi maneuvered the ship to place them on course for Huascaran Port.

Everyone gathered at the table for lunch. Khara laid out seared tuna, potatoes, broccoli, carrots and juice. As the food passed around the table, different conversations drifted about. Lexi waited until everyone dished up their plates.

"I want to make a proposal," Lexi stated after swallowing a mouthful of tuna. "Tink's new invention sparked excitement and ideas in several of us. I, for one, am quite intrigued with the idea of treasure hunting. What if we head directly to Mount Elbert Port, deliver our shipment and set off to search for treasure of some sunken city?"

A chorus of answers in the affirmative met Lexi's suggestion. Lexi glanced to Jareth. His eyes alighted with excitement. "I brought the perfect book along!" Jareth jumped up from the table, bolting out of the dining room. Everyone looked at each other, curious at Jareth's actions. In less than a minute, he returned, book in hand.

"This book tells about the Aztec Indians prior to the Spanish colonies. The Aztecs constructed temples to their gods and designed lots of statues, idols, jewelry and other offerings. Made of gold." Thumbing through the book, he found the page he searched for. "The archeologist drew a map to the temple in the city of Tenochtitlan." He showed everyone the chart. "By comparing this to an old world map and a current map, we may identify the actual location."

Kabe grabbed the book from Jareth and began studying the page. "In our library, we own a few books and atlases on this area, as well. It wouldn't take much gold to fund... other endeavors."

"With the books and charts we keep on board..."

"I brought numerous with me, as well," Jareth added. "By utilizing all the research materials we possess, we can identify where to find the cities. With the hydro-pod... The possibilities are endless!"

Excitement spread infectiously through the dining room After lunch, Kabe and Lexi plotted a new course directly to Mount Elbert Port. Even taking a straight line to the city, it required three weeks of travel to reach their destination. When Kabe's presence wasn't required on the bridge he worked with Jareth, who discovered a wealth of information within the *Star Sapphire* library. They compiled research and shared it with the crew each evening over dinner.

Tink vacillated back and forth between building another hydro-pod and her flying pod design. The main difficulty she faced with the flying pod lay in the building supplies. Brass proved too heavy for flight, so Tink experimented with numerous other materials.

In the belly of the airship, Tink arranged different spaces for each type of project. An array of metals lay in stacks only identifiable by her. Assorted nuts and bolts she kept sorted and stored in compartments. Her workshop housed the ship's steam engine. A separate opening in the furnace allowed Tink access for molding metals, fabricating and other activities. Another section held a vast selection of chemical compounds. Assorted switches, gadgets, buttons, levers and such covered every available surface.

Tink strolled through her wonderland, taking stock and assessing possibilities for the flying pod. Aluminum? She pondered the thought. Lightweight. Malleable to work with. Sturdy and strong. Pulling a sheet from the pile, she tested the thickness. Aluminum just might work. Acquiring it from a Chinese trader in Oruo a few months back, she exchanged it for some gears she constructed. Always enjoying a wide variety of supplies, Tink thought the trade beneficial. Gleefully, she took the sheet to the flying pod work area and started measuring.

Jareth and Kabe sat surrounded by maps in the library. Kabe scaled the map from the book into a larger size. Now, the two men poured over a detailed old world map Jareth brought with him from the island.

"This mountain peak and river seem to matchup with the old map," Kabe excitedly pointed out. "This forest here seems about right with this!"

"I think you're right!" Jareth drew on the old world map, marking the spot, matching up landmarks. He grabbed a ruler, measuring distances and compared it to the legend. "It looks like it rests about three miles inland from where the coast use to be."

"Now, let's match up the old world map to the new map!" Kabe unrolled his most recent chart created after the flood, with Jareth's upgrades added to it.

They compared the two. "The ocean waters cover most of what use to be known as New Spain. Let's find the highest peak in Mexico now, and compare it to New Spain from the old map. So few landmarks continue to exist since the world flooded." Jareth noted, studying the most recent chart.

By dinner time, Jareth and Kabe believed they identified the area where Tenochtitlan and the temple stood. Khara prepared a dinner of flounder and sautéed vegetables. Everyone took their seat at the table.

"We'll reach Mount Elbert Port tomorrow late morning. Our options include either stopping here for the night or reaching Tucson Port before dark and dropping anchor. What do you want to do?" Lexi asked the crew, taking a bite of flounder. The crew voted resoundingly to dock at port. Jareth, Kabe, Khara, Tink, Granny, Caroline and Noah disembarked while Lexi and Brannon secured the ship.

During their voyage, Tink designed and built the propulsion transporter to support the hydro-pod. Lexi secured the movable plate under the hydro-pod and locked it in place with the lock Tink fabricated. She deflated the balloon, allowing it to drape over the pod and disconnected the pipes, leaving it completely dead on the ship. The pod wasn't going anywhere.

Tink set out for the tinkering shops in the marketplace. While in transit, she devised a list of items she required for completion of her projects. Keeping herself busy during the voyage, she fabricated numerous objects to offer in trade.

Caroline and Granny shopped along the open marketplace. The rest of the crew set out for the Kraken, an establishment infamous for their beer, wine and stories of the sea.

Jareth pushed the swinging doors open and announced, "Four of your best beers! We come off the high seas with an unquenchable thirst!"

The barkeep laughed, "Yeah, I never heard that one before!" He set out four pints, surveying his latest patrons. "Jareth! You returned! Already? We expected your arrival in a couple more weeks!"

Jareth stared at the barkeep wide eyed, "Yes, we decided to take a short-cut and I'm in a hurry to pick up my new ship. Let me introduce you to my friends from the *Star Sapphire*. Kabe, the navigator, Khara the botanist and Noah, ship builder, retired Captain and Navigator. Crew, this is an old friend of mine, Frenchie, the Mexican."

After introductions, mugs raised high for a toast, they gulped down the beer, a welcome change to juice and wine. They exchanged stories of the sea and ports with other sailors. Jareth excused himself to use the restroom. Looking over his shoulder, he ducked into a door marked employees. He made his way through a maze of hallways, reaching a door with a combination lock on it. Keying in the code, he entered the room. A looking glass mounted on the wall dominated the room. Jareth activated it. After a few moments, Blaine's face appeared.

"Jareth! You're in Tucson? Already?"

Nodding, "The crew decided to head directly towards Mount Elbert Port. They intend to drop their cargo and I'll pick up my ship." Flashing one of his winning smiles, "I convinced them to search for the Aztec temple in Tenochtitlan!"

Blaine appeared surprised, inclining his head. "The Historians prefer to possess the hydro-pod ourselves."

Exasperated, "Blaine. We need to embrace the crew of the *Star Sapphire*. I worked with them extensively. Their knowledge, skills, equipment, library and maps offer substantial desirable assets to the Historians."

Shaking his head, Blaine stated, "Our only interest lies in the hydro-pod."

"She's building a second and began constructing a flying pod."

"Just bring us the hydro-pod." Blaine disconnected the communication.

Frustrated, Jareth slammed his fist down on the desk. "Dammit! I refuse to steal from them!" He stood up, then remembered to leave the item he acquired back at Aconcagua Port, a book entitled, *The Adventures of Tom Sawyer*, by Mark Twain. The Historians learned a copy of the book showed up in Argentina. They decided the book needed to be preserved. Jareth held the distinction of being the best acquistioner within the Historians.

Weaving his way back through the maze, Jareth returned to the crew. Lexi and Brannon joined them while he communicated with Blaine. He dropped a kiss on her neck, "Everything settled back at the ship?"

She smiled, "Yep. I want to trade Frenchie here, out of a keg of beer. But I'm not having any luck!"

Jareth laughed, "You serious?"

"Yes, I am."

He turned to the barkeeper, "How about a mature olive tree?"

Surprise spread across Frenchie's face, "Hell, yeah! Let me grab the keg right now!"

"How about in the morning?" Lexi countered. "It'll be easier to move in daylight."

"No problem. Say, ten o'clock?" Frenchie suggested. Lexi nodded in agreement. Olive trees held significant value, providing more than just a food source. Heavily sought after, olive oil carried a steep price. The leaves of the tree served medicinal purposes and tea. A keg of beer also gleaned notoriety as a high value commodity. Between the growing and processing of the hops and the kegs for storage, the value compared equally to an olive tree. The *Star Sapphire* owned two mature trees and two young trees.

After about an hour and a half, Tink entered the Kraken and sidled up to the crew. "Whew! I found all the supplies I needed and more! I ran into another tinkerer and we exchanged a number of ideas. I'm going to meet him tomorrow at the ship to show him my projects. He developed several inventions I'm curious about." She picked up Khara's beer and drank a couple gulps. "He created a communication system and an underwater suit. I'm returning to the ship. I want to prepare for his feedback."

"I'll come with you. I plan to hit the traders first thing in the morning," Lexi responded. She looked to Khara. Khara nodded. Jareth stood up, as well.

The four walked along the boardwalk towards the dock where the *Star Sapphire* lay moored. "It's such a change, walking on ground that doesn't move!" Khara giggled, stumbling against Jareth. He laughed and wrapped an arm around her waist, steadying her.

"How much did she imbibe? I can't remember the last time I saw her inebriated!" Tink laughed.

"Brannon and I showed up late," Lexi smiled. "I think Jareth holds responsibility for this."

"I didn't realize she drank that much," Jareth defended himself.

"It's fine. She needs to relax and let herself go, once in a while," Lexi chuckled. "It's a rare privilege to see her in this state."

The group boarded the ship. Tink bid them goodnight and skipped down to her workshop. Jareth picked Khara up and carried her, not trusting her to navigate the steep, narrow flight of stairs. Lexi laughed softly, following behind.

Khara fell asleep instantly, as Jareth laid her on the bed. Lexi unlaced her waist cinch and tenderly removed her skirt. She pulled the blouse over her head, leaving her in her corset and bloomers. "There's nothing worse than sleeping in a corset," Lexi remarked as she loosened the ribbons, releasing her imprisoned breasts. Dropping a kiss on her lips, Lexi pulled the covers over Khara.

Jareth smiled, gazing at Lexi. She picked up a blanket, crooking her finger towards Jareth. They continued climbing the stairs to the lookout at the top of the pagoda. Lexi laid the blanket on the floor.

She stripped down to her teal colored corset that heaved her breasts high, exposing her areolas but covered her nipples. And her bloomers. Untying the waist, the bloomers sunk to the floor. Her nether regions lay naked other than a small patch of hair dotting above her clitoris. She walked over to Jareth and kissed him thoroughly, then whispered in his ear. "I want you to screw me. Make me hurt. Please."

Wickedly, Jareth smiled at her. He turned her around and slapped her buttocks. Hard. She gasped. "Kneel down on the bench, your ass towards me. Face the window."

She heard Jareth moving around behind her and then he slapped her bottom with something thin, fibrous and coarse. It stung. She caught her breath. He spanked her several more times and she moaned. The next blow landed lightly between her legs, nipping her pleasure center. Squeaking in surprise, Lexi instinctively closed her legs. He whipped the cheeks of her buttocks hard three times.

"Open your legs."

Lexi complied, juices flowing, trickling down her thighs. He swung and again, hit her clit. She put a hand down to protect the sensitive nub. "Uh, uh. Now, you did it. Turn around and face me."

Licking her lips, Lexi obeyed him. He picked up her hips and placed her on the edge of the rough wood bench. Removing the sash from his waist, he blindfolded Lexi. He then tied her wrists and hooked them above her head. Taking her left leg, he stretched it out wide and secured it to the leg of the bench. He mirrored the action with her right leg.

Her bindings felt like the same material he spanked her with. Rope. Lexi smiled. He slapped her button, softly. She bucked. He struck it again and again as she grew wetter and wetter. Then, his tongue stroked her softly from her anus, along the folds of her labia and up to her sweet spot, flicking the hood. She whimpered. Slowly, softly, he licked her again and again from ass to clit. Perched on the brink, Lexi begged, "Please!" The rope hit the tender button over and over and over until Lexi screamed out her orgasm.

Jareth thrust his member straight into her ass, holding onto her hips, as deep as his cock travelled. Lexi bucked wildly as he continued to thrust in and out of her, the full length of his penis. Then he stopped. He rubbed the tortured area between two fingers. She moved up and down his member. He slapped her clit. "Hold still." She paused.

She felt something push against her vagina. It was a tight fit, especially with his penis fully distended in her rectum.

Sucking in a harsh breath, she forced her muscles to relax. His cock pulled most of the way out and then pushed all the way back in. She moaned in ecstasy, arching. The object in her vagina moved out and then in, as he flicked her clit, while she murmured her pleasure.

Reenacting this ritual over and over again, in slow motion, drove Lexi crazy. She whimpered, cried, begged, screamed and pleaded for him to plunge into her harder, faster. Finally, he honored her requests. Not only did he pound into her, but he sucked her nipple into his mouth and not so gently, bit her nipples, each one in turn. The two continued the sexual battle until Lexi surrendered, orgasming, as she bucked her hips

38

wildly against Jareth, sending him inside her as deep as possible, forcing Jareth to fall over the same cliff, drowning in orgasm, as well.

When Jareth regained his senses, caught between his teeth, he sucked Lexi's left nipple. Still bound, Lexi, covered in sweat, their juices soaked between her thighs, spittle flowed from her mouth, moaning in ecstasy, as she attempted to catch her breath. Jareth released her breast, pulled the object from her vagina and eased his member from her tunnel. She groaned, dejectedly. He laughed as he climbed off of her, untying the bindings, then removed her blindfold. Slowly she opened her eyes and smiled up at him.

"That is exactly what I wanted."

4

The next morning, Tink escorted her new friend aboard the *Star Sapphire* and showed him the hydro-pod. "Tink, this is incredible! How do you maintain enough oxygen for the pilot and navigator?" Shamus questioned, switching lens in his monocle to examine the seal between glass and brass.

"The propulsion system separates oxygen from steam and filters it back into the pod," Tink explained.

Shamus glanced up at her. "Genius!"

Tink propelled to the top and opened the hatch, allowing Shamus to enter. Surveying the control panel, Shamus identified each gadget. "Do you have a communication system to the ship?"

Shaking her head, "I lack the knowledge to design one." Shamus smiled, raising his eyebrows. "You created one?"

"I also invented an underwater suit," Shamus nodded smugly.

Jareth overheard their conversation as he stood outside the pod. Poking his head in the hatch, "You want a job on an exploration vessel? I'll provide you your own workshop, maybe even rival Tink's!"

Shamus' eyes grew wide, "That's my wildest dream! Yes!"

"Today, we sail to Mount Elbert Port where I pick it up from the builder," Jareth explained. "When I return to Tucson and we can set up your tinkering space."

Excited, Shamus turned to Tink. "May I tour your workshop? I want to see how to design my own. How much space will I have?"

"Probably similar in size to Tink's," Jareth answered after he mentally performed some calculations.

The two tinkerers rushed down stairs.

Granny located Jareth on the bow, surveying the ships docked at port, "Finally! I found you. On your new ship, did you allow for a hydroponic garden spot?"

A wide grin broke out across Jareth's face. "I designed a whole level below deck and six raised boxes for fruit trees above deck. There's a lotta planting to be done."

"Do you own enough seeds?"

Nodding, "I think so. I packed the chest I brought with me full."

"I'll accompany you and help you plant."

Caught off guard, Jareth responded. "Thanks, Granny! That would be tremendously helpful!"

Nodding, Granny continued, "I'll assist you in setting up the hydroponics system and ensure it functions correctly."

"There you are. This new ship of yours, you hire a crew already?" Noah walked down the bridge onto the deck, joining them.

Shaking his head, "Not yet. I plan to recruit in Mount Elbert Port and in Tucson when I return to pick up Shamus."

"Brannon and I will sail with you and help work out all the bugs," Noah stated, puffing on his pipe.

"I greatly appreciate your help, all of you," Jareth appeared a little overwhelmed with offers of assistance.

"A new ship is very exciting! It's been decades since we set up and outfitted the *Star Sapphire*," Granny exclaimed. "Do you want seeds from our garden?"

Shaking his head, "No. I specifically intend to plant items you don't grow, providing us with a larger variety."

Later in the day, the *Star Sapphire* docked at Mount Elbert Port, at the Williams Timber Company. The airship carried an order of lumber originating in Aconcagua Port. The company sent workers to begin unloading the shipment while Jareth and Noah walked to Dream Ships Boatyard. Tink set out for the market area, searching for a few items Shamus requested she obtain. Granny and Khara followed her, taking excess food, plants and seeds to sell or trade. Lexi, Brannon and Kabe stayed to watch the unloading of the timber.

41

Jareth gazed in awe at his new airship. The large emerald green balloon bore the cedar vessel above the water. The top underlayer of the ship, encased in glass, displayed the common design adding a garden aboard. In the center of the deck stood the bridge. Barely containing his excitement, Jareth entered the ship builder's office, carrying a satchel.

"Jareth, my boy! Good to see you! Ready to take command of your airship?" A heavily bearded man barked out behind a desk covered in blue prints. He pushed papers to the side, extending a hand to Jareth.

Smiling widely, "I saw it. The airship looks fabulous!" After shaking his hand, Jareth set the satchel on the desk. "Bob, this is a good friend of mine, Noah Canatolli, semi-retired captain of the *Star Sapphire*. Noah, Bob Roberts, owner of Dream Ships Boatyard. Here's the final payment. I think you'll be very pleased with the selection of seeds." Pulling out a sheet of paper, he handed it to Bob.

Leaning back in his chair, he read through the list. A smile spread across his face. "Fantastic." He picked up the satchel, glanced inside, then locked it in a safe. "Shall we check out your ship?"

The crew met at Katie's Cafe later in the evening. "How's your ship?" Lexi asked Jareth.

"Incredible! The steam propulsion engine operates at maximum efficiency. Once Tink and Shamus add their upgrades, he'll surpass us. Granny, Caroline and Khara will love his kitchen. Cedar shelves line the library! To ensure the safety of the communications area, we need to protect it from Tink, ensuring she doesn't take everything apart," Noah described, eating his salad.

Smiling, Jareth replied, "It's the most beautiful ship! The hydroponic garden seems so barren. Wait 'til we start planting! I need to stock the pantry while my garden matures."

"Stock your pantry from our pantry," Granny offered.

Kabe piped up, "If you want to build a pagoda like ours, Brannon and I can help."

Jareth nodded, "I love your pagoda," glancing towards Lexi, "especially the lookout." Lexi smiled softly.

Both ships remained in port for several days. The *Star*

Sapphire continued unloading cargo while Khara frequented the marketplace, selling and trading excess fruits, vegetables, nuts and seeds. She kept her eyes open for seedlings not present in her garden. Jareth worked on stocking his airship.

He prepared to leave port prior to the *Star Sapphire*. Noah, Caroline, Granny, Brannon and Kabe joined him to finish outfitting his yet to be named vessel. The two ships planned to meet up in the Gulf of Mexico. Jareth intended to pick up Shamus on the west coast of Mexico and fly overland, mapping out and matching up landmarks from the old map to the current chart. Lexi proposed to sail down the US west coast to the Gulf of Mexico and start surveying underwater landmarks. While en route, Tink wanted to finish constructing another hydro-pod. In his new workshop, Shamus focused on building underwater suits.

After Jareth flew out, Lexi entertained herself visiting local shops within the marketplace while the company continued to unload the *Star Sapphire*. Tucked between two buildings, several streets off the main thoroughfare, Lexi stumbled on a store advertising treasures dated prior to the flood. It took a moment for her eyes to adjust to the dimly lit interior. Rows of shelves held assorted items, some Lexi recognized, others completely befuddled her imagination.

Wandering through the shop, she found a section dedicated to old maps. Lexi unrolled and studied numerous scrolls until she found one piquing her interest. Hand drawn, the map depicted a city. As she studied it closer, she realized it portrayed the ancient city of Tenochtitlan. The very city they searched for! Lexi identified the cartographer and hunted for others made by the same person.

"Can I help you?"

Lexi jumped at the question. An old man stood beside her, peering through thick spectacles. "Oh! I love old maps. This one intrigues me. Do you have any others made by the same person?"

Nodding, "Ah, yes. Juan Martinez. I purchased these from his descendants. Apparently, he took part in early exploration of Mexico," the man stated as he dug through the pile, extracting five maps.

"I'll take them." After handing the clerk the requested coins, Lexi hurried through the streets, returning to the airship. She unrolled her newfound purchases in the lookout and studied them.

Khara entered a few hours later. "What treasures did you find?"

Excitedly, Lexi responded. "I found maps of Tenochtitlan, the temple and palace drawn by one of the Spanish explorers! The detailed drawings show many buildings, streets, and the moat surrounding the city!"

Khara raised her eyebrows in surprise. "What a find!"

"Once we locate the city, we now know where to plunder!"

She laughed, settling on the floor next to Lexi, picking up a map and studying it, then set it back down. Inhaling deeply, she turned to Lexi. "I'm pregnant."

Completely caught off guard, Lexi faced Khara. Khara giggled and threw her arms around Lexi, hugging her tightly. "I'm pregnant! I can't believe it! We're going to have a baby!" She pulled away and kissed Lexi deeply.

Still suffering from shock, Lexi remained speechless.

Khara broke the kiss, pulled back, beaming. "Will it be a boy or a girl? Will the eyes be green, brown or blue? Red, black or blond hair? I'm so excited! We're having a baby!"

It dawned on Khara Lexi hadn't responded. Pausing in her glee, Khara gazed at her expectantly. Lexi opened her mouth, then closed it. Then, opened it again. "Wow. So soon?"

Wrong response.

"Really?! I tell you I'm pregnant and your reply is, 'So soon?'! We talked about this! We wanted a baby!"

Lexi hesitated. Khara angry was a situation to be avoided, at all costs. "I just meant I'm surprised it happened so quickly. So much is occurring right now. What's Jareth's response going to be?" Sighing, Lexi drug her fingers through her hair.

Khara flicked her head, "He'll get over it. This is our baby."

"Really? There would be no baby without Jareth. And I guarantee you, he won't see the situation in the same light." Lexi paused, "Alright, we're having a baby. We're having a baby. We're having a baby!" Smiling, Lexi wrapped her arms around Khara, laid her forehead against hers and kissed her soundly. "Let's return to our quarters, Mama, and I'll show

44

you how happy I am."

Holding hands, they descended the stairs and entered their room. Kissing Khara tenderly, she untied the cincher at her waist and pulled her blouse over her head. "Lay down."

Khara climbed on the bed and laid against the pillows. The tops of her breasts spilled over her corset. Lexi kissed one and then the other, softly, sliding her tongue inside the corset to flick her nipple. Khara arched, moaning.

Slowly, Lexi tugged the ribbon, untying her corset, allowing her breasts freedom. Encircling one orb, Lexi kneaded the mound of flesh while she sucked the nipple, gently grazing it with her teeth.

Reaching under Khara's skirt, she slid her hand up her leg and in between her thighs, rubbing her through her bloomers. Lexi turned her mouth's ministrations to her other nipple, suckling it deeply within her mouth. Khara moaned and rocked against Lexi's hand. "Touch me, please touch me!" Khara begged.

Sliding her hand inside Khara's bloomers, her fingers felt out her clitoris, labia and vagina. Khara whimpered. moving against her touch. Slowly, Lexi rubbed the folds, purposefully avoiding her yearning nub. Struggling to make Lexi touch her where she needed to be touched, Khara groaned petulantly.

Unable to continue teasing, Lexi yanked her bloomers off, hooked her arms under her knees, forcing them up and open, she covered her sex with her mouth. Her tongue flicked and sucked her clit while her teeth nipped at her vaginal opening. Khara cried out when Lexi placed two fingers inside her, deeply, as she nibbled her sweet spot. Wave after wave flowed over Khara, but Lexi didn't stop, continuing her ministrations until Khara lay weakly on the bed, spent.

Several days after Jareth left port, the trader finally finished unloading the inventory from the *Star Sapphire*. Khara traded the extra food items and seeds from the pantry for items they needed like wine and flour. She intended to plant new seeds obtained through trading, while everyone else searched for the lost city.

Lexi declared them ready to leave Mount Elbert Port. She chartered a course down the Gulf of Mexico to the southern tip of the United States to Albuquerque and then on to Cuidad

Victoria, the capital of Mexico. Kabe believed the ruins of the city of Tenochtitlan lay south of Cuidad Victoria. Using the hydro-pod, Lexi and Tink planned to explore underwater, searching for the lost city while Jareth and Kabe identified landmarks along the continent as they flew over, ensuring they investigated the correct area.

The Gulf of Mexico lay in a tight channel between the United States and Mexico. Ship and airship traffic tended to run heavy. Lexi paid close attention, navigating high above the trade traffic. Settling in at the helm, she surveyed the mid-morning horizon, ensuring a safe distance buffered the *Star Sapphire* from other ships. She cruised at the highest altitude, with the balloon propelled by the steam turbines. Fewer ships sailed up here, those traveling further destinations. This wasn't an area normally frequented on their excursions, typically choosing to stay on the west coast of the Americas. She kept a close eye on her surroundings while vigilantly monitoring the gauges and map, maintaining speed to match the ships in front of her.

Tink busied herself working on the second hydro-pod. Procuring everything she needed while in port, she now assembled the parts. Only minor modifications differed this pod from the original design. Shamus offered input resulting in the propulsion system operating more efficiently, allowing for use at lower depths, creating more oxygen and better pressurization. Once she assembled the second craft, Tink planned to implement the changes into the first pod.

Taking a break from planting her newly acquired seeds, Khara delivered lunch to Tink at the bottom of the ship and Lexi, at the top. She found her sister buried within the cab of the pod, soldering a gadget into the control panel. Tink mumbled something akin to "Leave it over there," pointing with a glowing torch to her left.

On the bridge, Lexi proved more appreciative for her salad, as she stood pouring over a map, comparing it to land masses below.

"Are we lost?" Khara joked, setting down the tray.

Laughing, Lexi shook her head. "No. I'm adding more detail to our chart. It appears a volcanic eruption added a couple islands," pointing to a mountain range with smoke billowing from the top. "That appears to be a new volcano forming within those peaks."

Khara grimaced, "We aren't going to be too close to it,
"No. We're sailing several hundred miles south of here. The
wind currents tend to blow to the east and we're headed
south. It shouldn't affect us at all."

Sighing in relief, Khara replied, "Let's try to stay away
from active volcanoes, if possible."

Kissing her, "I'll do my very best to keep us far away
from volcanos actively spewing lava, ash and other debris."

Lexi wrote down the coordinates while the underground
pod sunk towards the ocean floor. Keeping watch on the depth
meter and compass, she drew a map of their course while Tink
piloted the craft.

"So, what exactly are we searching for?" Tink asked, expertly manning the controls.

"Mmm. Keep your eyes open for a city."

"A city. Well, that should be obvious."

Laughing, "If we search the right area. Between the volcanic eruptions, the entire planet flooding, shifting of the tec-
tonic plates, nothing stayed put," Lexi noted.

"What are you doing?"

"I'm trying to map our search area. That way, once Jareth
arrives, we won't waste time searching the same area twice."

"Ahh. This gadget," Tink pointed to a series of numbers
spinning, some slow, some fast, "tracks our distance in feet."

"Really? Perfect! Using those measurements, my map will
be semi accurate!"

The two spent hours underwater looking for any kind of a
landmark reminiscent of the time prior to the ice caps melting.
They returned to the ship to eat lunch and compare Lexi's map
with the old charts, hoping to find some overlapping areas.
After the meal, Lexi and Tink set out again, exploring where
they left off. They spent two full days investigating the area
to no avail.

On the second evening, Lexi sat in the library studying
the map of the city she obtained while at Mount Elbert Port.
Almost five hundred years passed since the Aztec inhabited
their capital. An active volcano stood within the vicinity.
This meant earthquakes probably occurred under the sea.

Rock, lava and sand potentially obliterated the site. When the polar ice caps melted, the sea level rose, covering the city. Tidal waves caused by earthquakes definitely washed over Tenochtitlan. Sand. Sand coated every surface, filled in every nook and cranny. Where buildings once stood, mounds of sand cloaked their existence. Numerous buildings circled the temple and palace. They should be of similar height, if still erect. The temple and palace towered over the buildings. Pouring over the old world map, she found where the cityonce stood. Comparing it to the new world map, she located where the city should lay. Then she factored in earthquake tremors and tidal waves originating from the volcanic area, which could have resulted in pushing the city further south.

Lexi contemplated the charts and effect of the volcano on the local area, reaching the conclusion they needed to focus their search more to the south of their current position. Tomorrow, she'd chart a course indicating the new location.

The next morning, Lexi shared her thoughts with Tink.

Nodding her head, "Makes sense to me. Especially after five hundred years!"

Pulling up anchor, Lexi piloted the airship south about fifty miles. They spent the day traveling to the new location. No land masses appeared on the horizon, in any direction. Based on her calculations, Lexi halted the ship in the area she believed the city occupied. Once she secured *Star Sapphire*, the three young women ate dinner in the lookout, with a glass or three of wine, toasting to the success of the expedition, the new baby and their future.

The next morning, moving slowly, Lexi and Tink set out in the hydro-pod. The ocean floor appeared smooth, with a sandy bottom. Sea plants grew, offering habitat to a wide array of fish and aquatic animals. Under water, life flourished along the smooth floor. They spent a couple hours surveying the seascape. As Lexi and Tink plodded forth, in the distance, sandy dunes rose up.

"Let's check out that tall mound over there," Lexi pointed out.

Tink steered towards the towering column. She circled it. "Yep, it's a mound."

"Can we brush or blow off some of the sand?"

Using one of the appendages, Tink scratched the top of pod, contemplating the predicament. Then, nodding, she protracted the arms from the pod. Waving them around, she moved some of the sand, revealing a stone. A square stone. The two women looked at each other. It appeared man-made. "If I turn the pod around, the force of the propulsion system will blow more sand away." Tink maneuvered the ship, pointing the exhaust towards the sand dune. It jumped forward. "Oops. I need to place the brakes on. Hmm. I didn't think to build brakes."

"An anchor?" Lexi suggested as they both turned around, observing the impact of the propulsion on the mound. Several feet of stacked rectangular stones appeared from under the sand. A corner of a small building!

Smiling at each other, the women squealed with glee. "We found it!" Lexi laughed.

"What should we do now? Go grab an anchor?"

"Can I take out the other pod? Let's transport anchors down in the pockets, throw it out and start clearing sand using the propulsion exhaust system."

Tink nodded, "Sounds like a plan. If Khara wants to come down with us, she could check it out, too."

They re-emerged from the water next to the ship and landed on the floating pad. Khara walked out onto the deck. "You returned sooner than I expected. Is everything all right?"

Lexi climbed out of the pod, excited. "We found it! Or at least, we think we did! We found a building! We need an anchor. And we're taking the other pod out!"

Disbelief flowed over Khara's face. "You found it?"

Giggling, Tink emerged from the pod. "We think so! "We're using the propulsion exhaust to blow the sand off the structure. An anchor will hold the pod in place."

"Want to come down and check it out?"

Shaking her head, laughing, "I'd rather stay above water."

Lexi scurried across the deck obtaining anchors while Tink raced down to her workshop to find chains. Khara followed Lexi.

"What exactly did you find?"

"Rectangular stones stacked on each other and affixed

together using some substance, creating a corner. Obviously man-made!"

She paused a moment as Lexi carried an anchor over to the pod and then grabbed a second anchor and placed it by the second pod. Tink ran up the stairs carrying a long chain.

"Wow! I didn't really think we'd find anything," amazed, Khara commented.

"Let's weld the chain to the body of the pod, then the other end to the anchor and place it in the pocket." Tink suggested, enabling the torch on her left arm and pulling her goggles to cover her eyes. Lexi followed suit, affixing the chain and anchor. Khara disappeared for a few minutes and reappeared, carrying a tray with two glasses of ice tea. Once finished, Tink pushed her goggles onto her forehead and grabbed a glass.

"Thanks! I needed a cool drink."

Lexi nodded as she reached for one, too, quickly gulping it down.

"Okay, are you ready?" Tink asked, setting the glass down on the tray.

"Yes!" She dropped a kiss on Khara's lips. "We'll be back! Which pod do you want me to take?"

"Take the first one. I want to make sure everything works appropriately on the second pod."

"Okay. I'll follow you. It might take a few moments for me to figure out how to operate it."

They each entered their pod. Lexi strapped herself in, started the engine and descended behind Tink.

Taking advantage of the opportunity to play around at the controls, she followed Tink to the bottom of the ocean. Once they reached the stone building, Tink turned her pod around, backed up to the object, then used the arm appendages to remove the anchor placing it on the ground. Following her movements with a lot less dexterity, Lexi finally lined her pod up and extracted the anchor.

The two worked for several hours, exposing the small structure. Comprised of large rectangular bricks, the building stood about three meters high, three meters wide. The sand blew away revealing an opening. But the pods proved too large to enter. Gazing inside, little could be ascertained. Tink motioned to Lexi to return to the surface. Lexi agreed. Using the appendages, they picked up the anchors and chain, stowing it in the pocket of the pods.

Tink led the way as Lexi played with the controls, spinning the vessel in circles and flipping upside down. She prac- ticed extending and retracting the arms, wiggling the fingers, picking up objects and moving them to other places. Breaking through the waves, the pods reached the surface. Moored next to the *Star Sapphire* stood Jareth's ship, with its large emerald green balloon. Tink and Lexi propelled to their airship and landed on the propulsion pads, then transferred the pods to the deck.

"Two hydro-pods! Terrific! Did you find the gold already?" Jareth asked as he walked up to Lexi and kissed her soundly.

Smirking, "We found a building, possibly a guard station," Lexi responded, pressing her lips to his, again.

"Are you kidding?" A gruff voice sounded behind Jareth.

Tink giggled, "No, we're not. We found a structure built of rectangular stones. Using the exhaust from the pods, we cleared the sand away. After we compare it to the charts Lexi found, we may possess a better idea of what it is and where it stood within the city."

Lexi stepped back from Jareth and eyed the gruff voice. The man appeared to be in his forties. He sported a full beard, covering his face, leaving only deep blue eyes exposed. A sailor's cap protected his head with salt and pepper hair peeking out, as he puffed on a pipe.

"Lexi, Captain Canatolli, meet my first mate, Mathew Fitzpatrick." Jareth introduced him. Lexi offered her hand and they shook. "Maps? You found more maps?"

Nodding, "I discovered a small shop that procured actual charts of the city drawn by one of the first explorers. It details the layout of Tenochtitlan. And the temple," Lexi explained. "We want to compare the map to the dimensions of the building in hopes of determining where in the city to search for the temple."

"Before you start pulling out maps, let's eat dinner first!" Khara interrupted the excited conversation taking place around the deck.

Everyone laughed at her proclamation. "Is dinner being served on our ship or on Jareth's?" Lexi asked, dropping a kiss on her lips.

"Ours. I'd already started preparations prior to their arrival but I made plenty for everyone." Khara invited the other crew.

"We stocked up on wine while in port. I'll grab a barrel," Noah announced, crossing the deck and swinging onto the second ship, using a rope.

"Dinner will be served in five minutes."

Jareth added three members to his crew, counting Matt and Shamus. His third person, Ricardo, appeared to be a fourteen year old boy. Substantially undernourished, his clothes hung like rags. Barefoot, he moved nimbly across the deck, staying out of everyone's way, but helping out anywhere possible.

As people took seats around the table, Ricardo helped Khara set out bowls of steaming food: fresh peas, mashed potatoes, jumbo shrimp and salad. Khara prepared more than enough food for both crews. She nodded to Ricardo to take a seat next to Granny. As the food circled the table, everyone dished up.

"Land sakes, child! Fill your plate! A doctor could use your body as a skeleton in his office! Every bone sticks right out!" Granny exclaimed, plopping a large spoonful of potatoes on his plate.

"Have you decided on a name for your ship?" Khara asked Jareth as she sat down.

Flashing his heart stopping smile, Jareth replied, "Yes, the *Mountain Peak.*"

"*Mountain Peak?*" Lexi questioned.

"I'm from the Montana Territory in the heart of the Bitterroot Mountains. The snowy, tree covered peaks remain one of my favorite scenes," Jareth shared, "I'm unable to live in the mountains, but at least, this way, I keep them with me."

"Ah, the mountains! One of the most exhilarating activities I experienced involved skiing down snowy mountain slopes. Those were the days!" Granny sighed deeply, reminiscing.

"Just shoot me now," Noah murmured, rolling his eyes.

Snickers floated around the table. Changing the subject, "What does Tenochtitlan look like?" Matt asked, spooning

52

peas into his mouth, moaning over the sweet flavor.

"Like mounds of sand under the ocean." Tink answered, peeling her shrimp and popping it into her mouth.

"How long did it take you to find it?" Jareth questioned.

"About four days. We realized we searched the wrong spot after about two days. We went back to the maps and factored in movement of plate tectonics from the earthquakes and sand erosion. After moving further south, we found the building this morning and decided to take out both hydro-pods to use to excavate the structure," Lexi explained. "Hopefully, we can identify the building from the maps and determine the location of the temple."

"How do you intend to identify the building?" Matt asked as he peeled his shrimp.

"We took approximate measurements," Tink responded.

"Matt, tell us about yourself," Lexi stated.

He swallowed his mouthful of food. "Well, Jareth and I have known each other for a number of years. We worked together on a couple excursions. When I heard he picked up his vessel, I raced to meet him at port. I'm excited about this expedition. I studied Old Mexico/New Spain and the cultures of its people, extensively. The maps you discovered I find intriguing. What's your plan for tomorrow?"

"I think we'll go down in the hydro-pods and let you look the situation over. Get your take on the site after studying the maps tonight." Lexi stated, nodding towards Jareth.

"Do you have any way to communicate between the two pods?" Shamus asked.

With a wry look, "We used hand signals," Tink responded. "I failed at developing any type of communication system."

"Well, I'll help with that. If you want to assist me, Tink, we can start after dinner while they pour over maps," Shamus offered.

Nodding enthusiastically, "I'd love to! Looking at maps bores me," Tink giggled.

"A communication system would be very beneficial between the pods," Lexi agreed.

"And underwater suits. I think the suits will aid in your search."

"Oh, definitely! The pods proved too big to fit inside the

building. But in one of the suits, entry appears feasible, allowing for further, in-depth exploration." Lexi stated.

"We need to determine who serves where the best," Kabe mentioned. "I, for one, volunteer to man the search from the safety of the *Star Sapphire* lookout. I prefer to be above the water." Laughter surrounded the table at his frank announcement.

"I want to try the underwater suit. I love swimming," Lexi volunteered.

"We all know how to swim, but I prefer the pod," Brannon stated, dishing up more potatoes. The true difficulty lay in locating water where the temperature proved cool enough to safely enter without thermal protection. But their parents insisted all the children learn to swim, for safety sake.

Jareth swallowed a mouthful of shrimp, "I swim and am excited to learn to operate a pod." Grimacing, "The control panel appears rather complicated. There's a lot of levers, buttons and switches."

Laughing, Lexi said, "I took one out today by myself. I played with the controls and figured it out fairly quickly." Taking a sip of her wine, "With a communication system, Tink can provide instructions as needed." Pausing a moment, "Tink and Shamus. Try to develop an interlink into an auditory enhancement to allow communication whenever necessary between you, the pods and the suits."

"We should set up a communication system between both ships and throughout them," Noah suggested.

"Not a problem. I'll instruct Tink, Kabe, Brannon and Ricardo on the system to speed up the installation process." Shamus offered.

"Tink and I can teach whoever wants to learn how to operate the pods." Lexi offered.

"Perhaps, we should spend tomorrow installing the communication system, teaching and learning operation of the pods and the suits. Then, treasure hunt the next day." Jareth suggested.

Nodding, Lexi agreed. "Good idea. As part of the instruction process, we can show you the site and what we found so far." Glancing around the table, "If we finished dinner, why don't we retire to the library and study the new maps I discovered?"

"I agree. Leave us to talk of something less boring," Granny declared. "Ricardo, you keep eating until you're full. You need to put a lot of weight on those bones. The rest of you are driving Khara and I crazy." Khara looked amused.

Laughing, everyone rose from their seats. "Tink, come check out my workshop and we'll grab the communication equipment," Shamus offered. Tink smiled in agreement.

Aside from Khara, Granny and Ricardo, the rest retired to the library. Lexi pulled out the detailed maps of Tenochtitlan and laid them on the table. Everyone gathered around her, gazing at the ancient scrolls. "It looks like it's written in Spanish. Anyone read Spanish?"

No one responded. "Ricardo?" Lexi questioned.

Being the closest person to the dining room, Brannon stuck his head out the door and yelled across the hallway, "Ricardo! Can you read Spanish?"

After a moment of silence, "Si, Señor. I speak and read Spanish," Ricardo responded from the dining room. He entered the library and walked over to peer at the charts. Softly, "Thank you for saving me from Granny. I couldn't eat anymore, if I tried."

Everyone laughed quietly. Lexi described the building and the measurements to Ricardo. He read the map and pointed to a small building in the lower right corner. "It sounds like you located the guard's station."

"Based on the small size, we thought so, too." Lexi replied. She pulled out her hand drawn map and the present day map. "Approximately, here is where we located the building," pointing to the map. "So, the temple should be around… here?" She drew a circle on the map using her finger. "Mounds of sand lay throughout this area. We must remove it to find the structures."

"How did you use the pods to remove the sand from the building?" Jareth asked.

"We welded a heavy chain and anchor onto the pods. At the site, we backed up to the building, threw out the anchors and used the exhaust from the propulsion system to blow the sand off." Lexi explained.

Kabe and Brannon laughed. "Ingenious!" Matt remarked. Studying the maps Lexi obtained, Kabe glanced to

Ricardo. "Would you help me re-draw these scrolls and translate them into English?"

Surprise colored his face and Ricardo responded, "Of course, señor. Whatever you need me to do."

"Great idea!" Jareth remarked.

That night, Lexi and Khara welcomed Jareth back to the *Star Sapphire*. Once they retired to their quarters, Khara kissed Jareth, gently encircling her tongue around his, teasing and tantalizing. Slowly, she trailed her mouth down his neck, unbuttoning his shirt, then unlaced his pants. As his pants slide to the floor, she grasped his penis in her hand and began stroking it, while his length grew and thickened. Lexi stood behind her, each nipple pinched softly between her fingers.

"I'm laying down. I want both of you to blow me, at the same time." The two women looked at each other and smiled, then kissed each other. Kneeling on the bed, they took turns kissing, licking and sucking on his balls and organ, in between kissing each other. Groaning deeply, Jareth whispered, "Khara slide down on me."

Eagerly, Khara climbed on him, inserting his member inside her and she began riding him, arching her back, allowing deeper access. Lexi grasped her hips and sucked harshly on her nipple, quickly bringing on her orgasm. Khara tried to slow the momentum but Lexi held her in place as Jareth raced, reaching his climax.

Lexi smiled as she eased Khara down on the bed, then inserted Jareth's phallus into her mouth. He growled a smile at her as she swallowed his length, locking her gaze with his. It didn't take too long for him to recuperate. Lexi slid down his penis and rocked her body back and forth, bringing herself to orgasm as Khara sucked her nipple deep into her mouth. Jareth grabbed Khara by the hips, positioning her vagina over his mouth and began licking her softly. She gasped as his tongue flickered over her clit and reached her hand down to Lexi's, rubbing it. The two women orgasmed together as Jareth continued to pump into Lexi. Khara lay down next to them as Jareth withdrew from Lexi and rolled on top of Khara, ramming his cock deep in her as he came.

The three lay entangled as they tried to catch their

breath.

5

The next morning, over breakfast, Shamus and Tink sported new auditory hardware. "We set up communication systems in the pods and suits. While the crew learns to pilot the underwater modes of transport, we'll integrate the system into the ships."

"Ricardo and I translated Lexi's maps and made two copies. Take them in the pods with you. It may aid in the search for the temple." Kabe handed a scroll to Lexi and one to Jareth.

"Fantastic! Thank you!" Lexi unrolled her scroll, scanning it. "It details distances between structures, what the building materials consist of, all kinds of pertinent data! This will be incredibly helpful."

Ricardo dropped his eyes to his plate, blushing at the praise. "Terrific!" Jareth studied his scroll.

"Who's interested in learning to pilot the pod?" Tink asked, biting off a chunk of apple.

"I am!" Granny responded enthusiastically. Jareth and Matt laughed, while the others groaned. Granny looked quizzically, "No, really. I'm serious. I thought about it last night. I want to go down in that contraption and see the temple. It'll be neat!"

Noah rolled his eyes. "Have mercy on us."

Brannon piped up. "I want to learn." Jareth and Matt voiced their interest, as well.

"Who wants to swim?" Shamus asked, his lips twitching. Everyone glanced at Granny. "How wonderful! Swimming with the fish! Sign me up. When I was younger, I use to dive for oysters, searching for pearls in the Orient."

Lexi hid a smile, raising her hand. Jareth and Brannon

also indicated interest.

Jareth looked to Ricardo. "Do you want to learn to operate the pod or the suit? As many people need to be trained as possible."

Ricardo looked up to Jareth. "Whatever you wish, Captain."

"Do you know how to swim?" Shamus asked.

He nodded. "I dove for fish and crab, often." Lexi shuddered softly. Diving in the ocean required a strong constitution. The water temperature ran close to scalding, in most places. Lexi never checked the temperature at Tucson Port but she thought it tended to run overly warm, due to volcanic activity in the region.

After breakfast, interested persons met on deck. Tink took Jareth, Matt and Brannon to the first pod and demonstrated the control panel, explaining the multitude of levers, buttons, knobs and switches. Lexi, Ricardo and Granny followed Shamus to the suits, lying on the deck.

"Constructed from a metallic fiber, the suits maintain a comfortable temperature. It's very strong material, waterproof and resistant to puncture. Located on the back of the suit is a pump. It extracts oxygen from the sea water, into the suit, providing breathing air and propulsion." Shamus described as he picked up the helmet. "The helmet screws onto the neck of the suit forming a water tight seal and allowing sight through the glass. The foot flippers aide in propulsion. The fingers of the suit allow for dexterity under water."

"Incredibly impressive. Can I put it on?" Lexi asked as she knelt down and felt the fabric of the suit. The material possessed a soft but thick, heavy, stretchy cloth. The stiff flippers provided little flexibility. The light weight helmet, comprised of the same material held a strong, circular shape with a glass face. Striations lined the inside lip of the helmet to attach it to the suit.

Nodding, "Take your shoes off, anything pointy, jewelry, knives, all hardware."

"I thought you said it was puncture proof." Lexi responded as she unbuckled her boots.

"It is. But we don't need to take unnecessary chances," Shamus explained. "Leave your ocular adaptation device in place but take off your arm braces."

"All right," Lexi unbuckled her arm brace and glanced over her shoulder. Granny stood on deck, in her bloomers and a blouse. Ricardo hid his eyes in his hands. Shamus appeared wide eyed, shocked. "It's best she goes with me. I'll keep an eye on her." Lexi sighed softly, running a hand through her hair.

Granny stepped into the suit, pulling the flippers onto her feet and up her legs, wiggling her bottom as she shrugged into the arms, inserting her fingers. Lexi removed her other arm brace and inserted her feet into the flippers and followed Granny's actions.

"Land sakes! How in the world do you see out of this thing?" Lexi stifled a laugh. Somehow, Granny placed her helmet on backwards. Ricardo tried to assist her as she flailed about the deck.

Shaking his head, Shamus ran to Granny. "Hold on! Wait! Let me assist you." Hastily, he rotated the helmet, detaching it from the suit, then he placed it on her appropriately. Lexi fastened the suit with a magnetic zipper and snap closure. She picked up the helmet, eyeing it before screwing it into position.

Shamus finished outfitting Granny and came over to check on Lexi. "Okay. You're ready. Let me start the pumps, then lower you into the water." He moved behind Granny and pushed the start button on the pump. Next, he initiated Lexi's pump. Air moved into the suit and blew out through the flippers. "Let's place you in the water."

Lexi and Granny jumped overboard. "Do you hear me? Respond by touching your head to the right side of your helmet." Shamus explained.

"Wow. This is neat!" Granny giggled as she tread water.

Lexi floated beside her, "Magnificent! Shall we swim, Granny?"

"I think we shall." Granny popped her head underwater and kicked her flippers, splashing Lexi.

It took a few moments for Lexi to overcome her body's reluctance to breathe underwater. Once she allayed her fears, she turned to Granny. "Are you okay?" Granny twirled about, performing somersaults. Laughing, "Can you breathe?"

She began executing barrel rolls. Lexi rolled her eyes. "I think you're adjusting fine." Lexi swam towards the bottom of the ocean.

"Wait for me, Lexi!" Granny called out, quickly swimming after her. "This is fascinating! Everything appears crystal clear! Look at the fish! The plant life! So, where's this temple?"

Lexi looked back as Granny swam after her, turning to and fro, gazing at everything. Lexi saw the two pods navigating above them. The pilots played with the controls, learning to maneuver the crafts. "Shamus, can we speak to the pods?" "Yes. If you move your head left, you gain the ability to communicate with anyone within one thousand meters on the same frequency. Straight back, you open a link with the ships." Shamus directed.

"Suit two to pod one and pod two. Can you hear me?" Lexi asked.

After a few seconds, Jareth responded. "Yes, we hear you. We're figuring out the controls. How's the suit? We watched Granny somersaulting!"

"The suits allow for maximum flexibility!"

"I haven't experienced this much fun in fifty years!" Granny giggled. "But I'm exhausted. I think I'll return to the surface and send Ricardo down. This is a young-uns job!" She swam towards the sky.

Lexi sank to the bottom and practiced grasping rocks and small objects in her fingers. After a few minutes, she made her way towards the surface, expecting Ricardo to appear soon. Sure enough, he dove down, swimming towards Lexi. "What do you think, Riccardo?"

Gasping, "It's difficult to convince your body it's alright to breathe!"

Lexi laughed. "I experienced that problem, too!"

"The sensations of swimming underwater, perfect sight and breathing almost overwhelm me!" Ricardo expressed in an awed voice. He swam beside Lexi, gazing around.

"I never dreamed this type of movement possible underwater," Lexi agreed as she skimmed along the bottom of the sea.

"Want to show us the structure you discovered?" Jareth asked over the communication link.

Looking behind them, Lexi saw the two pods moving through the water towards them. "Sure! Let's head in that direction, now!" Glancing towards Ricardo, "I'm not sure if the force of their propulsion will create enough of a wake to disrupt our ability to swim. Stay close to the bottom and off to the side."

"All right. I'll follow you." Ricardo dropped behind Lexi. "Watch out for us. I don't know if your propulsion affects us."

"I see the structure! Magnificent!" Matt announced.

The building appeared as they approached the area. Lexi and Ricardo swam around and entered through an opening. The cramped interior revealed a faded mural painted on the wall depicting two warriors fighting with spears. The colors dulled over time. Sand partially filled the interior, coming half way up the walls. Ricardo noticed a partially buried jug. "Lexi, should I pick this up?"

Lexi turned to see what he found. "Yes! What did you discover?"

Ricardo reached down and gently pulled a jug from the sand. Painted in a multitude of colors, it displayed various shapes. "Good job! Let's take it to the pod. They can place it in their pocket."

"Ricardo found a jug! It's still intact!" Lexi announced over the link. Ricardo exited the structure, showing it to the pods.

"I'll try to pick it up using my arm and place it in the pocket," Jareth replied. "Good job, Ricardo!" Jareth reached out with the appendage and flexed the fingers, attempting to take the jug. After several tries, he successfully grasped it and retracted the arm. He fumbled with it several times before it in placing it in the pocket.

"Whew! I know I made that look easy, but it required significant skill! The artist painted intricate designs on the vessel! The sand protected the colors and preserved the shape." Jareth held up the jug as he inspected it.

Smiling, "My calculations of the location of the city proved close, but incorrect. I thought we pinpointed the southeast corner. Instead, we established the northwestern corner, according to the measurements of the building. Given that, I believe the temple must be located approximately," Lexi

62

swam away, "over there. About eight hundred feet from here."
Matt looked towards the area Lexi pointed at from the
controls of the pod. He sat next to Tink. Working the levers, he
attempted to move in that direction, but resulted in ascending
and reversing the pod. He didn't activate the communication
link, but Ricardo guessed his comments would make Granny
blush. Tink tried to hide a giggle.

Jareth and Brannon propelled towards Lexi fairly smoothly. Ricardo kept an eye on Matt's pod as he swam towards
the others. Piles of sand spanned the area. "Why don't we
measure off and mark the perimeter of the city with buoys?"
Brannon suggested.

"Let's remove just enough sand to verify the dunes cover
structures," Jareth added.

"Before we start excavating, why don't we teach everyone how to use the pods and suits," Tink remarked. "Ricardo
needs instruction on operating the pod and you two wanted to
try suits."

"The suits allow for significant freedom of movement
and extreme dexterity. You're going to love it!" Lexi executed
a back flip.

Jareth laughed. "I can't wait to try it."

Brannon joined in, "I'm excited, too. It looks like fun!"

A sigh breathed over the link. "I need more time in the
pod. I'm not interested in swimming. Being underwater without the safety of a structure isn't my cup of tea," Matt commented.

"Let's return to the ship and trade places. Lexi may prove
to be a better instructor than I am," Tink suggested. "I'm an
inventor, a designer. Others determine how best to utilize my
creations."

Everyone made their way to the surface and exchanged
places. Lexi entered the pod with Matt. "Okay, do you want to
take us down?"

"Sure." He pushed a lever. The pod propelled up. "Oops."
He pulled a second lever and the pod moved to the left. "Not
that one."

Lexi pointed to the first lever. "Pull it towards you. That
starts our descent."

Matt nodded. The pod sank below the surface.

"Push that lever forward. It propels us forward as we descend." Lexi explained.

The hydro-pod hiccupped forward in short spurts, then evened out. After several minutes of descent, they almost reached the floor of the ocean, but Matt made no motion to slow.

"Go ahead and gently push the first lever forward. We're almost at the bottom."

Matt jerked the lever. The pod jumped and responded by leveling off, but continued forward. "Great. Let's head towards the city." Lexi held on to her seat. She made a silent note to herself to talk with Tink about straps to secure a person to the seat, for safety.

Gazing at the levers, Matt pulled on the first lever, sending the pod plummeting to the ocean floor again.

"No!" Lexi yelled as she flung her arm out, knocking his hands off the levers. His foot stomped on the acceleration pedal. The motor roared and the pod rocked back and forth, side to side, up and down. "Whoah! Remove your foot from the pedal!"

Matt jerked his foot back and raised his hands up, not touching anything. Lexi breathed in deeply and slowly exhaled. "Should we discuss the function of all the levers?"

He ran a hand through his beard, sighing. "There's just too many levers, buttons, switches and knobs."

Lexi looked out all the windows, searching for the swimmers, laughing. "Yes, Tink likes her gadgets. Let's allow Jareth and Brannon to pass by us. Then we'll move out further where more open area exists to practice maneuvering without any obstructions," Lexi suggested.

Meeting her eyes, "Thanks! I think I can get the hang of this contraption with practice," Matt responded.

After hours of working with Matt, Lexi realized only a remote chance existed that Matt could ever pilot the pod. "Perhaps, you're better suited as navigator and cartographer in the pod as we excavate the city. You may learn more of the operating techniques observing others," Lexi suggested.

With a wry look, "That sounds like a viable alternative. When we start working in the city, accurate and delicate maneuvering will be paramount," Matt noted. "It's rather apparent that I lack the coordination to operate the pod smoothly.

Do any of these gadgets say what time it is? I'm starving!"

Lexi laughed, pointing to the time piece. "This one does. It's dinner time! If we're late, Khara becomes unhappy. I strive to avoid Khara's unhappiness."

"Being a victim of marriage once upon a time, I understand, completely. Why don't you take the controls? Our arrival will occur faster and safer," he chuckled.

When they reached the ship, Brannon and Jareth sat on the deck, removing their suits, with Shamus supervising. Tink and Ricardo parked the pod on the propulsion pad and chained it down. Lexi followed suit while Matt observed carefully.

Everyone headed to the dining room.

"I'm not sure what I enjoyed more: the suit or the pod!" Jareth exclaimed, excitedly. "The sensation of swimming underwater with free motion... What an experience!"

"I agree! Once you overcome the fear of breathing underwater, there's so much to see, so much to experience!" Brannon added.

"I felt like a young girl again. As a youngster, I worked for a circus. Ohhh! To be able to perform acrobatics once more! To be as agile as I use to be!" Granny announced with a whimsical look upon her face. Noah rolled his eyes.

"The circus?" Shamus asked, surprised.

"Why, yes, dear. For almost a year, I flew through the air on the trapeze and performed funambulism for the Branberry Englestrom World Famous Circus," Granny reminisced, a dreamy look in her eyes. "Ah, those were the days!" Tink leaned over and whispered in Shamus' ear. He drew back and shot her a quizzical look.

"Lexi appointed me as navigator and cartographer within the pod. I'm afraid my piloting skills leave the general populace in grave danger," Matt remarked, in a sad voice, before breaking into a smile. "The control panel proved too elaborate for my brain to comprehend."

Laughter broke out around the table. "I love Tink, but I lack the capacity to operate most of her inventions. She certainly inherited her father's intellect." Noah announced. "And his ingenuity. I'll ride along" glancing to Lexi, "as navigator and cartographer, but the only vessel I'm qualified to operate is a flying ship."

"Hear, hear!" Matt announced, raising his glass of

wine. Noah clinked his glass, as well as Kabe and Khara.

"Those of you hungering for adrenaline feel free to utilize the pods and underwater suits!" Khara declared, shaking her head.

Lexi winked at her, raising her glass. "Here's to those of us who reach for the stars or dive to the sunken cities and to those who lift us up and guide us on." Resounding cheers and raised glasses met the toast. "It requires all of us to ensure the success and wellbeing of our endeavors. Our latest project manifests as the most trying and most beneficial to mankind we ever assumed. We strive to keep the history of Earth alive for future generations, to ensure past civilizations will never be forgotten."

"We need to tell him," Lexi stated forcibly, pulling her blouse off over her head. "He'll figure out soon enough. It's better he hears it from us, then someone else." She stood in their quarters, wearing navy bloomers and a matching corset.

Khara sighed deeply. "Not yet." She laid in bed, reclining against the down pillows, watching Lexi undress.

"Do you want Granny to tell him?"

"Tell who what?" Jareth asked, entering the room. "Mmm. You look nice," Jareth commented with his sexy smile, slowly eyeing Lexi head to toe. He turned his gaze to Khara. She dropped the bedspread, displaying her breasts. Jareth groaned. "What's Granny telling who?"

Lexi and Khara's eyes locked. Silently, the two argued. "So, I'm the who," Jareth responded as he watched them. "Now, what's the what?" Neither responded, raising his eyebrows, he inquired, "Should I ask Granny?"

"No!" Both ladies answered harshly. Khara jumped out of bed, naked and scurried into the dressing room, slamming the door.

Lexi and Jareth stared after her. He turned his gaze to Lexi. She dropped her eyes to the floor. *Khara should be the one to tell him*, she thought to herself. But, she lacked the fortitude to pass on the information. Jareth placed a hand on her chin and brought her face up, holding her gaze. Lexi inhaled deeply. "Khara discovered she's pregnant."

His hand fell away. He staggered back against the door. Disbelief and shock spilled over his face.

66

Looking at Lexi, he opened his mouth, then closed it, wordlessly. Roughly, he paced over to the far side of the bed and looked out the window. "How?" He paused. "I came in her. You told me to." His mind quickly performed the calculation, drawing the conclusion, "You planned this? You planned this!" His anger washed away the disbelief.

"We didn't think…" Lexi started, splaying her hands to her sides.

"You didn't think what? I'd stick around? I cared?" Jareth yelled, raking a hand through his hair, tearing it out of its tie. Shaking her head, "I know you care. We made plans together, this expedition," Lexi tried to sooth his anger.

"Two drop dead gorgeous women can do whatever they want as long as I get laid?" He turned to glare at Lexi, his face harsh with pain. "Do you even like me? Actually want me? Or just my sperm?"

Lexi inhaled a shaky breath. "Yes, we like you, we want you. You're handsome, intelligent, ambitious. You hold the same values sacred we do." Lexi reassured him quietly. "It's incredibly infrequent we find a man like you. We chose to take advantage of the situation."

"Don't tell me. Let me guess! You're pregnant, too?" Jareth accused, slamming his hand against the window, turning to face Lexi.

"No, I'm not pregnant," Lexi replied. "I take specific herbs to ensure pregnancy doesn't occur."

"So, now what? Are you done with me? Have I served my purpose?" Hurt crept into his anger.

Lexi looked to the ground, and then met his eyes. "I hope never to be done with you."

"What in Poseidon's hell does that mean?" Khara screeched, exiting the dressing room, hurrying straight to Lexi.

Lexi reached a hand to Khara's cheek, trying to assuage her fear, "I love you for your gentleness, your wit, your beauty, your touch, creating and maintaining our home." The other hand she extended to Jareth, attempting to gentle his anger. "I love you for your adventurous spirit, your humor, your intelligence, your touch." Inhaling deeply, "I need both of you to be fulfilled. I never experienced such happiness and satisfaction like when I'm with you, the three of us, together."

Lexi's feelings drained the anger from both of them. Khara rested a hand on Jareth's chest. "You intrigued me from the beginning. The more I learn about you, the more I wanted your child. You make me feel protected. You bring so many possibilities for the future with you, more than I ever imagined. You satisfy Lexi in ways I can't and don't want to. Lexi is my heart, you fill in all the spaces, completing us. It takes the three of us," tears rolled down Khara's face. "I always felt like something was missing between Lexi and I. We need you to complete us."

Jareth inhaled deeply, cleansing the hurt and pain, but he remained speechless. Lexi stepped in closer and raised her lips to his. Shaking his head, he pushed her away, "What about me? What I want? I dream of adventure. I hold responsibility for..." Raking his hand savagely through his hair, "I'm responsible for so much. You never considered me or my feelings about a child."

Fear strangled Lexi's heart, the pain cutting deep. "Jareth," Khara whispered softly, reaching out to him.

"No. I need time to think." He turned around, exiting the room.

6

The crew experienced on the job training from this point forward. Lexi and Ricardo commandeered the underwater suits. Brannon and Granny operated one pod while Jareth and Matt piloted the other. Matt and Kabe communicated back and forth, plotting their route and discoveries. Kabe remained on the *Star Sapphire*. Tink and Shamus monitored commu- nications and dealt with questions concerning operation of technology. When their expertise wasn't required, they con- structed more waterproof material and objects. Whenever Tink discovered a free moment, she worked on her flying pod. Noah commanded the two ships above the ocean with Kabe's assistance while Khara and Caroline cared for the gardens and prepared meals.

The pods carried multiple buoys to mark the boundaries of Tenochtitlan. While they prepared for departure, Lexi and Ricardo donned the suits and dove into the ocean, making a beeline for the city.

They swam towards the buoy indicating the building al- ready discovered. The swimmers intended to scout the bound- aries while the pods moved to the next dune to extract sand.

"Do you want to head left and I'll head right?" Ricardo asked as they reached the buoys where Ricardo found the jug. "Why don't we stick together, at least until we locate the perimeter. Just in case any unforeseen issues arise."

"Okay, probably a good idea." The two turned to the left. "We need a way to blow sand off dunes to determine if we discovered structures or sand dunes." Lexi commented.

"I'll hold you. Use your flipper propulsion to move the sand, at least a little to ascertain if bricks lie underneath." Ri- cardo suggested as they studied a dune.

Lexi laughed. "Okay. How should I be positioned?"

Ricardo moved behind Lexi, placing his hands under her arms, holding her torso. Pointing her flippers towards the sandy covered mound, Ricardo replied, "Start kicking your feet. The propulsion should expel the sand off the structure." Lexi slowly moved her legs, engaging the propulsion system which vented hydrogen and sodium from the ocean water the suit consumed and modified. This caused a flow to emanate from her flippers towards the dune. As the sand dispersed, a corner brick appeared, then a partial wall became visible.

"We're on the right track!" Lexi proclaimed, as a man-made corner peeked out from the debris.

"We need the buoys."

"I sure it's evident a structure exists. Let's move on. Once the pods arrive, they can mark it." The two swam to the next accumulation.

"I'll hold you while you blast away." Lexi moved behind Ricardo, grasping him under the arms. "Start kicking your legs to instigate propulsion." He complied, moving his lower limbs softly, at first, ensuring Lexi could manage the force. "Here's a brick! We should use this tactic with each pile. You prove to be far more effective in removing sand than me. It must be your strength." Lexi laughed. After a few minutes, a corner pillar peered through the mire. "Let's move on. The next knoll appears to be over there. The city laid in a circular pattern surrounded by a moat. The next point is not situated in a straight line."

Ricardo followed Lexi to the sandy hill she surmised as the next building within the city. Before they finished their excavation of the dune, the pods arrived. "Can you drop buoys indicating those last two buildings?" Lexi asked as she let go of Ricardo.

"Of course, Cap." Brannon replied as he steered to the building. Jareth and Matt started in the opposite direction. The pod turned, dropped anchor and began using the propulsion system to expose bricks made by man centuries earlier.

The work proved to be strenuous, but mindless. Lexi thought about the scene with Jareth the night before. Kicking herself for blindly following Khara, she wished more discussion occurred, more thought entered into the decision to have a baby. Honestly, she didn't think a pregnancy would occur

70

quickly. It seemed easier to go along with Khara than argue. Fear blossomed at the thought of losing Jareth. Lexi realized she relied on him, enjoyed his company, craved his touch. She understood Khara's position. Rarely, a man of Jareth's caliber crossed their path. In today's world, it proved difficult to meet eligible bachelors. Lexi found no way to fix the situation.

Hours later, Lexi and Ricardo expressed exhaustion, having swum at least half way around the perimeter of the city, exposing numerous structures. The crew broke for lunch to compare notes from the underwater crew to the above water crew and collate the original map.

Once everyone arrived at the airships, they moved to the dining room, to discuss the activities and results produced thus far.

"We marked and cleared three structures identified by Captain Canatolli and Ricardo." Brannon stated after everyone dished up helpings of sautéed shrimp and vegetables.

"And we placed buoys at two structures on the right side," Jareth announced. His typical energetic demeanor seemed rather subdued.

"Hopefully, within three days, we'll outline the perimeter." Lexi remarked, peeling her shrimp. "Honestly, I'm too tired to continue in the underwater suit. I prefer a pod." Lexi acknowledged.

"I'll swim." Brannon offered.

"As will I," Jareth responded.

"I want to help Khara prepare dinner," Granny stated. "Someone can take my spot."

"I'll take Brannon's spot," Shamus stated. "I want to learn to operate a pod."

"Shamus and I will take pod one. Ricardo and Matt, pod two." Lexi replied with a tired smile. "Continue where we left off on the left side. The two swimmers scout ahead, identify structures. We'll continue where Brannon and Granny left off." No one offered any contradictory actions. After finishing lunch, everyone emerged on deck to embark on the pronounced crew assignments.

Brannon and Jareth donned underwater suits and set out to the city. Ricardo performed a system's check on the pod prior to descending. Shamus executed a full control panel analysis and then propelled towards the bottom of the sea. The two pods kept in close proximity to each other until they reached the sunken city. Lexi and Shamus broke right while Ricardo and Matt swung left, following Brannon and Jareth. At the fourth sand dune, Shamus backed the pod up to the mound and dropped anchor. He initiated the propulsion system, blasting the sand away. After several minutes, man-made bricks appeared. They continued to expel debris until a corner peeked through. Recognizing this as a man-made structure, Lexi deployed a buoy marking the spot. They moved to the next accumulation. After an hour, it became apparent this wasn't a building. No bricks appeared under the mound. Shamus and Lexi continued to the next dune.

"Do any of you intend to eat dinner tonight?" Khara's voice demanded over the ship link.

Lexi and Shamus turned towards the clock. "We didn't realize it grew so late! We'll ascend immediately." Shamus stated.

"I'm sorry, Khara. We lost track of time. Jareth and I are heading to the ship straight away!" Brannon declared.

Within half an hour, the expedition crew landed uponthe deck of the *Star Sapphire*. After securing the pods and stowing the suits, a single file line dropped below deck to the dining room. Over dinner, the crew discussed advancements made. On the left, five more buildings were identified. On the right, three structures. Plans developed regarding tomorrow's expedition.

Tink and Shamus decided to trade positions to allow Shamus to provide maintenance for the communication system between ships.

"Has Jareth spoke to you?" Khara asked, drying a dish and placing it in the cupboard.

Shaking her head, Lexi replied, "Not a word."

Khara sighed, dejectedly. "We really screwed up."

Lexi raised an eyebrow, saying nothing as she placed silverware in a drawer.

"You need to talk to him," Khara spoke softly.

"And say what?"

Khara spun around, bracing herself against the sink.

"We're sorry! We were wrong! Anything! Do you want to lose him?"

"No, I don't want to lose him! I just…" Lexi hesitated. "I don't know if there's anything to say. We violated his trust. We purposefully made an important life choice without involving him, effecting the rest of his existence. A baby changes every single part of your life, every choice, your priorities. Everything." Lexi hung her head.

Khara turned around and finished drying the dishes, placing them in the cupboard. "Go talk to him."

"Do you assume any responsibility whatsoever for the situation we find ourselves in?" Lexi asked. "You always create these situations and then expect me to fix it. You take whatever you want and when it goes to hell, I make it all better! This time, I don't know if I can fix it." Lexi turned on her heel and stormed out of the kitchen.

Up on deck, she kicked her boots and flew to the top of the balloon where she sank cross-legged, watching the sun sink on the horizon. Taking several breaths, she exhaled loudly, trying to blow out all her negative emotions. Her favorite hiding spot since a child, she loved the endless view of sky and water.

A whistle interrupted her calming meditation. Lexi turned towards the sound. Jareth sat atop his balloon. He waved. Lexi laughed, stood up and propelled to him. "Can I share your balloon?"

He nodded and held out a bottle, wordlessly. She took the bottle and swallowed down a couple gulps. The whiskey took her breath away. "Thanks. You plan better than I do. I didn't think to grab alcohol." Her voice came out wispy, in response to the strong drink.

Snorting, he raised the bottle to his lips.

"I'm sorry. We realize we really screwed up. We made a very short-sighted decision and didn't take into account you at all," Lexi offered, softly. Jareth returned the whiskey. She guzzled, shivering as it burned her throat.

"It's not that I'm against having a baby or having a baby with you two," Jareth gulped the whiskey, replying after several moments of quiet. "I'm angry because you planned it without consulting me."

"I understand totally. We are completely in the wrong."

Lexi took the bottle and swigged a mouthful. "We don't want to lose you."

Jareth tipped her chin up, locking eyes. "Both of you?"

"Both of us."

Searching her eyes, he judged the truth for himself. "The two of you provide me with everything I ever dreamed of. The perfect lady, Khara makes a home, grows our food, so incredibly beautiful." He reached over and curled a tendril of Lexi's blond hair around his finger. "You're fearless, adventurous in life and bed. Whether it's my deepest fantasy of underwater cities or sexual delights, you're right beside me. You're gorgeous. Raising a child with you two? With your family? I couldn't hope for a better life. For me or my child."

Lexi reached up, drawing his lips to hers, sinking into his kiss. As the sun slipped below the horizon, they shed their clothes. Jareth moved behind Lexi sliding his penis deep inside her as he held her against him, one hand cupped her breast while the other caressed her clit. They moved together as the balloon offered more bounce to their actions. The stars popped out above them as they tumbled over the waterfall.

After breakfast, Jareth and Lexi arrived on deck prior to anyone. They donned underwater suits. Once finished, the other members of the crew spilled onto the deck, preparing to engage the pods.

"We're ready to head down. We'll continue to detect structures where you left off yesterday. Mark them behind us," Lexi ordered as she finished sealing her suit.

"Hopefully, today, we finish locating the perimeter of the city," Jareth stated. He closed the underwater suit and placed the helmet upon his head. Tipping his head, he activated the communication link, "We'll meet you below!"

He and Lexi dove into the sea, swimming to the bottom. Upon reaching the perimeter marked the previous day, they swam to the next mound. Jareth held Lexi as her flippers propelled sand from the dune, exposing man-made bricks. After they determined a structure lay under the heap, they surveyed the surroundings.

"I realize that accumulation falls outside our survey of the city, but we should attempt to uncover it, ensuring a structure isn't buried there." Lexi stated, pointing to a dune laying

74

independent of the circle of Tenochtitlan. "If nothing else, it helps pinpoint the boundaries."

Jareth looked towards the dune she indicated. He agreed. It lay in close enough proximity to the perimeter they must determine if it fell within the border. Jareth enjoyed holding Lexi as her propulsion system blasted sand from the mound, exposing nothing. They moved on to a dune approximately ten meters inside the previous pile. Lexi held Jareth while he activated his propulsion system, removing debris. While dissipating, bricks appeared, marking the boundary of the city.

The two swimmers fell back from the perimeter. The pods descended to the site. Ricardo and Matt marked with buoys the structures identified by Jareth and Lexi. Brannon and Granny worked on the opposite end, exposing structures under piles of sand.

The three teams worked until late morning. Matt's internal clock indicated lunch time. He communicated over the link they planned to surface. "The last thing we want to accomplish is to anger Khara," Jareth exclaimed, chuckling, shaking his head.

The two pods immediately ascended towards the airships. Lexi and Jareth swam slower. As they reached the *Star Sapphire*, they observed the pods parked upon the propulsion platforms. Lexi and Jareth climbed on deck, shed the suits and strolled to the dining room.

"We made good progress this morning, identifying the perimeter of the city," Lexi announced to the members of the crew remaining aboard the airship. "We discovered several new structures."

"Terrific! What type of buildings?" Noah took a seat at the table.

"Not sure yet. Right now, we're only uncovering enough to identify them as man-made." Jareth clarified further. "We want to determine the perimeter of the city prior to searching for the temple. After we identify the boundaries, then we begin the search for the temple."

It took three more days to finish circumventing the perimeter of the city.

7

Lexi used the propulsion on her boots to jump from the *Star Sapphire* to the *Mountain Peak*. Nothing like a midnight booty call, she smiled to herself, crossing the deck under the quarter moon. Passing by the communications room, Lexi heard voices. Thinking it may be Jareth, she paused. It was Matt.

"Damn it, sir. I attempted operation of the underwater vessel!" His voice, mired in frustration. "The controls prove too complex and I lack the coordination to safely pilot the pod."

Lexi recognized the voice from Jareth's communication room on his island. "You possess the capabilities to pilot an airship but can't operate a hydro-pod?"

"The inventor likes her gadgets, levers, bells and whistles. She designed the control panel too complex. I spent the last week on board the pod, observing Ricardo operate it. But, it's beyond my abilities!" Matt cried out in frustration. "Hell, I can't pilot their ship, either. Tink retro-fitted the helm with her enhancements. In fact, I'm delaying Tink from installing her gadgets in Jareth's ship. If she makes the installations, then I'll prove unable to pilot the *Mountain Peak*."

With her back against the wall, Lexi listened for the response. After a brief hesitation, "Ask Jareth to request Tink install each gadget individually. Learn the function as it's installed, making it easier to become proficient. Then, you may gain the knowledge required to operate the pod."

Matt groaned. "And if I fail to learn, I'm out of a job."

"Any chance Jareth will change his mind and acquire the pod himself?"

"No. He's in love with the two women, Lexi and Khara. His loyalty lies with the Canatolli family. He found his niche

76

here with them." Matt declared.

"The Historians need that hydro-pod!" The voice demanded.

"I'll do what I can, sir." The link severed. "Why don't you sail down here and take a look at the control panel. I doubt you possess the capability of operating the damn thing!" Matt muttered.

Lexi lightly and quietly jogged to Jareth's quarters. Softly, she opened the door and ducked into his room. Shedding her clothes, she climbed into bed, reaching for him. He moaned tiredly, then lustily as she wrapped her fingers around his cock, quickly bringing him to full size. Climbing on top of him, she slid down, piercing her g-spot and then rocked back and forth, stimulating her clitoris on his pubic hair. By the time Jareth gained his senses, Lexi achieved her first orgasm.

He tossed her under him and proceeded to pound into her, hard. She whimpered in ecstasy with each plunge. She met him, thrust for thrust while they raced towards the cliff of their orgasm. Arriving together, their final drive pushed them both off the edge.

Once they caught their breath, Jareth, asked, "I'm not complaining, but what brought that on?"

"Mmm. I couldn't sleep, too aroused. Khara hates to be woken up, especially for sex." Lexi kissed him. "I thought I might find you," she kissed him again, "More obliging."

"Always obliging for a beautiful woman." He whispered, turning in to her kiss. "Now, can you sleep? We plan to swim miles tomorrow morning. Or is it this morning?"

Lexi laughed. "I think it's this morning." She cuddled on his chest and fell asleep.

Just before dawn, he woke up, sliding into Lexi. By the time she gained her senses, she experienced her first orgasm.

"What's the plan today?" Brannon asked, biting into a pear as everyone dished up.

"I vote we start extracting sand from the temple," Jareth announced. Affirmative responses surrounded him from the crew. "Let's start at the front entrance. Once we clear it, swimmers move inside and begin to remove debris within while the pods expose the outside. We need to document each item we

77

find and where within the temple we discovered it."

"Bring the items to me and I can sketch them. I suppose I could venture down in the pod and see the interior of the temple once it's been cleared and draw it, too," Khara volunteered.

"Khara is an artist. She draws, paints and sculpts," Lexi replied.

"We need to create and maintain a written record of our findings!" Matt noted. "The historical ramifications of our expedition will educate people for generations to come! We'll preserve a little bit of this culture, saving it from the sands of time." After a moment, "No pun intended. Okay, perhaps a small pun."

"My invention of a small camera may prove invaluable. I'll work on the design today. See if it's possible to fabricate a water proof unit," Shamus suggested.

"A camera?" Khara questioned.

"The device records a scene on a film. Using chemicals, I produce a paper copy, reflecting the colors. We take pictures of the temple and you can utilize them for your drawings, indicating where we locate items," Shamus explained.

Khara's face expressed her wonder. "Intriguing. You piqued my curiosity about your camera and pictures. Once everyone takes off, show me your invention."

"I doubt we'll progress too much today. A lot of sand needs to be extricated just to locate the entrance. It'll require a couple days at least to reach the interior well enough to observe anything of detail," Brannon remarked. "Granny, do you plan to accompany me?"

Shaking her head, "No. Shamus' talk of his camera brought up memories of when I worked as a model for an artist friend. Of course, that happened before I met your grandfather." Granny giggled, Noah groaned. "At that time, society considered the pictures rather risqué! One of the paintings my friend created hung in the French Louvre."

For several moments, everyone seated around the table remained frozen, not knowing how to respond. Then, Jareth jumped up. "Well, imagine that! I call an underwater suit!"

Following his example, Lexi replied, "I intend to operate a pod. Ricardo, you may either don a suit or ride with me. The work conducted around the temple requires extreme precision, to ensure the structure remains undamaged."

Ricardo nodded enthusiastically. "I wish to ride with you. I plan to observe how you operate the pod in close proximity to the temple."

"Right now, the suits may prove to be more in the way, than helpful," Matt pointed out.

"What if we use one to act as a scout? Check out the building, maneuver around quicker and easier?" Lexi offered.

Jareth responded, "I think one suit will be fine."

According to the map, the entrance to the temple faced east. The crew focused their efforts in locating the opening.

Jareth stayed out of the direct path of the propulsion systems from the pods blowing billowing clouds of sand away from the targeted area. Using hand signals occasionally, he directed the pilots to change course, optimizing the work process. By lunch time, the front facade of the temple appeared exposed for the first time in centuries. An arched entry led into a cavernous room. Two smaller domed openings lay on either side of the entry, allowing for viewing within. Obscured by sand, the interior remained hidden. With careful operation and maneuvering, the pods may possibly gain entrance. However, one wrong move would prove fatal to the entire project.

"Lexi operates the pods well enough to move one inside," Brannon volunteered as they took their seats at the table. "I know I lack the skill to steer a pod in such close quarters."

"Thanks for the vote of confidence!" Lexi sighed. "Yeesh. I desire a lot of practice prior to attempting that," mentally practicing the task. "Rather a tight fit, negotiating the pod must be perfect. At this point, the temple lacks open space to operate the pod."

Everyone quietly munched their lunch while contemplating the problem. "A pipe made from the underwater suit material," Shamus proclaimed, raising his fork with a carrot on the tip, up in the air.

The majority of the crew looked at him quizzically. "Attached to the exhaust system of the pods!" Tink exclaimed.

"Screw the pipe onto the pod once you reach the site!"

"The appendages manipulate the exhaust whichever direction required!"

"Or by the people in the underwater suits!"

Tink and Shamus whooped and clapped hands while the rest of the crew attempted to digest the plan they formulated.

"For those of us unable to keep up with one genius, let alone, two, explain to the rest of us what you're discussing. Slowly, please," Noah prompted.

"We build a long flexible pipe from the underwater suit material. Either a person or the pod, using the appendages, direct the pipe where it needs to point to expel sand from the temple," Tink explained.

"The material is flexible and lightweight, but strong and waterproof."

Lexi considered the idea. "Build the pipe in small sections. Then, we attach or detach pieces as needed."

"Just like how the helmet latches to the suit!" Jareth exclaimed, catching on to the idea.

"The pods transport the pipe and remove through the pocket once we reach the temple," Ricardo added softly.

"Do you possess enough of the fabric?" Noah asked.

Shamus nodded his head. Excitement became infectious around the table. Shamus and Tink divided up design and manufacturing tasks, speaking in technical terms only they understood. Once they developed a plan, both jumped up, running in opposite directions. Tink sprinted for the bowels of the *Star Sapphire* to her workshop while Shamus bounded upstairs, heading to his workshop aboard the *Mountain Peak.*

"I don't know what they decided, but I think they formulated a plan," Matt remarked, sitting back and puffing on his pipe. "If only they told us what to do."

Laughter erupted from the rest of the crew as a few nodded, agreeing. "Why don't we return to the temple and clear sand from the rest of the outside of the building? We may discover other openings to utilize in blowing out debris," Ricardo suggested hesitantly.

"That's a good idea," Lexi stated. "In fact, let's focus the temple as the epicenter and continually move sand to the outside of the city. Who wants to operate a pod and who wants a suit?"

For the next two days, Tink and Shamus built the flexible

blow pipe with multiple attachable parts to extend the reach. The rest of the crew removed sand from the perimeter of the temple, locating numerous openings. They developed an efficient process and honed their skills in operating the pods and swimming in the suits. Ricardo proved to be an intricate part of the crew. He displayed a quick intelligence, dexterity and strength. Shying away from no task, he frequently volunteered for less enjoyable occupations. He mastered the skills to expertly maneuver the pod and proved to be the most proficient in the underwater suit.

Finally, Shamus and Tink declared the flexible blow pipe ready to be tested. Lexi and Tink took one pod while Brannon and Shamus operated the second. Jareth and Ricardo donned underwater suits. As everyone submerged and headed towards Tenochtitlan, Lexi suggested over the link, "Let's try the flexible blow pipe outside the city first, just in case there's... issues."

"It's perfect! There won't be any issues," Tink replied.

"Captain's prerogative," Lexi announced, as a flood of failed experiments assaulted her memory.

Tink groaned, but Shamus replied, "No problem. Here's an open spot. Let's remove the pipe, hook it up and go from there."

Prior to leaving the surface, the crew stowed the pipe into the pocket. Lexi utilized the appendages to open the pocket and remove the pipe. She then tried to attach it to the exhaust. "Hmmm. It's difficult to line up the striations correctly."

Ricardo swam over and assisted the appendage in placing the pipe on straight and helped to screw it on. "Alright, it's firmly affixed to the exhaust."

Lexi increased the propulsion. The flexible blow pipe flew out of Ricardo's hands, flinging him through the water, head over heels. "Whoa! Cut the propulsion!" Jareth cried, swimming after Ricardo. "Ricardo! Are you okay?"

Ricardo righted himself and nodded after a brief hesitation. "I failed to appreciate the force of the propulsion."

"None of us realized the magnitude of strength created by the exhaust system," Lexi shot a sideways glance to Tink. "We'll both hold the pipe, along with the appendages of the pod," Jareth declared.

"Alright." Ricardo and Jareth took up opposite sides of the flexible blow pipe and Lexi grasped it with the appendages.

"Okay. Everyone ready?" Lexi asked. Once receiving affirmations from all parties, she slowly engaged the propulsion. Initially it appeared fine, but as the propulsion increased, Jareth and Ricardo began to waver within the water.

"Add propulsion from your suits to steady you," Shamus suggested.

Kicking their feet, their self propulsion provided a counter balance, offering better control. Taking commands from the pods, Ricardo and Jareth practiced maneuvering the pipe and directing the propulsion towards specific areas.

"Okay! I think we're ready for the temple! What do you gentlemen think?" Lexi asked, thrilled with the progress and effectiveness of the latest contraption.

"Onward ho!" Jareth proclaimed.

"Let's unhook the pipe so it doesn't hit anything in route to the temple," Ricardo suggested.

"Mmm. Good idea." Jareth and Ricardo unhooked the pipe and swam away with it.

At the temple, Lexi lined the pod up with the main entrance, securing it with the anchor while Jareth and Ricardo hooked the pipe to the exhaust, then stretched it inside. Lexi slowly added propulsion, as they maneuvered the pipe, targeting specific areas and blowing the sand out another opening.

Brannon steered the second pod towards the area the sand evacuated and began moving it outside the perimeter of the city.

"Magnificent!" Tink pronounced as they worked together, removing the particles from the interior.

"Is it lunch time?" Jareth asked. "I need a break! This requires prolonged strenuous activity."

Lexi decreased propulsion, allowing them to rest. Peering at the chronometer, Lexi declared, "Actually, it is close to lunch time. We made fabulous progress! Great job everyone! Let's stow the pipe and ascend!"

When Lexi and Tink exited the pod, Jareth and Ricardo lay prone on the deck of the ship, still in their suits. "Ahh. The poor tykes appear all tuckered out!" Tink giggled. Lexi smiled and unfastened Jareth's suit while Tink worked on Ricardo's.

Shamus unscrewed their helmets.

"Whew. Thanks. We required a few minutes rest," Jareth replied, sitting up and shaking off the suit.

"Manhandling the pipe proves to be a rather arduous occupation," Ricardo stated as he shed his underwater gear.

"Well, I pronounce the flexible blow pipe a qualified success!" Jareth announced.

"It worked well?" Noah asked.

"Extremely well! We suffered a tsunami at first and Ricardo hurdled through the water. But with two people using their suit propulsion and the appendages holding the pipe, they directed the flow and cleared sand from the temple at an impressive rate!" Lexi announced. "Brannon used the second pod to remove the sand from the city, out of our way."

"We're starving and dying of thirst. Let's head to the dining room and continue this discussion." Jareth asked, gaining his feet. "Whew! I'll be stiff and sore tonight!"

"I believe I will, as well," Ricardo replied. "We must work less time. Directing the pipe proves quite grueling."

Lexi nodded. "I doubt I'll withstand as much as you two." "I'll suit up! I served a brief stint as a fireman before the great flood. I'm an expert at manhandling a pipe!" Granny announced.

"By the grace of Poseidon," Noah muttered shaking his head. Matt coughed heavily, attempting to cover a chuckle.

"Lunch is served!" Kara announced, providing the well timed and deeply desired interruption.

After lunch, Lexi and Brannon donned the underwater suits while Jareth and Matt took one pod and Ricardo and Granny jumped in the second. They stopped off at the same spot to allow the swimmers the opportunity to learn to control the pipe using their suit propulsion system. Even though they observed Ricardo and Jareth, Lexi and Brannon both flew around until they mastered the technique.

They arrived at the temple, set up and began extracting sand from inside. Lexi happened to glance at the pod and noticed Jareth and Matt appeared to be embroiled in a heated argument.

Unsure if it would work or not, she tilted her head, opening the link to the pod.

"Dammit, Matt! I told him I'm not stealing a pod! I believe Lexi, her crew and ship pose a tremendous asset to the Historians. It remains in our best interests to work with the *Star Sapphire*, indoctrinate them into the Society than to steal their equipment!" Jareth proclaimed angrily.

"Well, that's not how he wants it done," cajoled Matt.

"What's he going to accomplish with a pod no one else possesses the knowledge to operate?" Jareth retorted.

Matt shook his head. "I pointed that out to him as well. He's intrigued with the concept. You know how he responds when an idea sticks in his head. He refuses to move on from the pod. He said he intends to take your ship."

"Like hell! He lacks authority! I paid for half of it!"

"And the Society paid for the other half."

"Which is why I'm working on this project, ensuring the Society benefits from the greatest archeological find of the century! Which only happens with the assistance of the *Star Sapphire* and her crew! No one is stealing the pod!" Jareth announced.

The communication link fell quiet for a few minutes.

Lexi angled her head to sever the link when Matt offered a suggestion. "What if you convince Lexi to park one of the pods on the *Mountain Peak*? Then, we tell him one pod resides in our possession."

Irritated, "No reason exists to abscond with a hydro-pod! We are on assignment. The Society ordered us to excavate the Aztec city. If one of the pods turns up stolen, that severely hinders our assignment and the completion of the project. We strive to work for the greater good of humanity. The greater good is best served by us working with the *Star Sapphire* to uncover the city. I believe the Society will agree. What do you think?"

"He ordered us to obtain the pod."

"Think for yourself! Don't just blindly follow orders from some greedy old blow hard!"

"It feels like quitting time. I'm exhausted!" Brannon observed over the link.

The conversation abruptly halted. "It's pretty close. Let's call it a day." Jareth responded. "The interior looks really good!"

"We're beginning to expose some of the detail from the walls and floor. Intricate patterns and surprisingly, some colors survived years of being buried under sand," Brannon remarked, letting go of the pipe and stretching out his fingers as Jareth cut propulsion.

"You alright, Lexi? You're very quiet." Matt observed. Lexi looked up and smiled tiredly. "Yes. I'm just exhausted. It really takes a physical toll on you, operating the pipe." She stretched her hands above her head and flexed her body. "Give me a moment, then I'll start stowing away the pipe."

After a brief respite, the swimmers put everything into the pockets. Then, the crew returned to the surface. Lexi con- templated the situation. She didn't understand entirely what the Historical Society represented or Jareth's involvement. She realized they wanted one of the pods. Or at least, someone within the society wanted a pod. Did she trust Jareth?

For about the hundredth time, she wished Khara wasn't pregnant. That complicated everything. Ample opportunity presented itself to Jareth to steal a pod and he seemed disinclined. What about when they concluded exploration of the city? Would he change his mind? To complete the excavation of Tenochtitlan required a substantial amount of time. Sand wouldn't move itself. Well, it would. But not quickly...

8

Ricardo located Lexi in the lookout, as she considered a bank of clouds forming on the horizon. "I spent a lot of time studying the maps you discovered." He laid out three of the scrolls on the draft board, securing them. "Here, is the room we opened up today. See this mark on the wall? I think it leads to a chamber or tunnel."

Switching mental gears, Lexi turned her attention to the scrolls. "What? How did you reach that conclusion?"

"This mark corresponds to," he hesitated, finding the correct scroll and locating the mark in the upper left hand corner. "This mark here. I think the icon indicates this scroll relates to that mark."

Lexi analyzed the two scrolls, identifying the marks. A gust of wind ruffled the paper. Lexi groaned. "Hold that thought." She clicked the communication link to both ships. "I think a storm appears to be blowing in. We may want to head to a higher altitude."

"I noticed the same clouds you did and reached the same conclusion," Jareth responded from the bridge of his ship.

"I'm already in our bridge and readying to fire up the engines," Brannon replied.

"Okay. I'm in the lookout. Call if you need me for anything." Lexi said, disconnecting the link. Returning her attention to Ricardo, "Let's lay out all the scrolls." The lookout appeared like a perfect place to compare the maps, with benches along all four sides. "Start here with the one of the city, then the one of the temple. Next, the first floor of the temple, then the second floor of the temple."

Moving the second floor scroll further down the bench, Lexi placed the scroll of the room with the mark on the wall next to the first floor map. After laying that one out, she positioned the scroll with the mark in the upper left hand corner. "Have you discovered any other scrolls with similar markings?" She asked Ricardo.

He smiled at her. "Yes! I see what you're doing. This is how I arranged them, too. I'll lay them out and then show you the connections I realized." He laid the scrolls down, one by one.

Lexi walked to the communication link. "Kabe, report to the lookout if possible." She felt the engines fire up and the balloon inflated from the hot air piped from the belly of the airship.

"See this mark on the scroll? And see it on the next one? Then, here is another mark, and on this map, a corresponding mark." He showed her a pattern moving through one scroll to the next and onward through all five scrolls.

Kabe opened the door hastily and closed it against the wind. "What have we here?" He questioned, taking in the scrolls spread across the benches.

Smiling, "Ricardo found a pattern of marks from one scroll through the rest. Explain it to him," Lexi replied.

Ricardo started again, pointing out the initial mark and following it and the others as it flowed through. Kabe became excited. "I need my tablet! I'll be right back!" Don't move anything!" He squeezed through the door, allowing the wind as little impact as possible.

"Great job Ricardo! You definitely discovered something!" Lexi praised the young man. He smiled shyly, ducking his head.

Kabe returned within moments, carrying a large tablet and numerous pencils. Darting back and forth between the scrolls, he sketched on his pad. "Ruler. I need a ruler."

"I'll grab it!" Lexi replied. As she exited the room, she noticed the ship gained altitude. The dark storm clouds grew bolder on the horizon but above them lay blue skies. She bolted down the staircase and into the library. Khara saw her race by and called out to her.

Lexi grabbed the ruler from a drawer. "Ricardo located a secret tunnel leading to a chamber under the temple within the scrolls I obtained at Mount Elbert Port!"

"What?! Really?"

"We're studying his findings in the lookout! Join us when you can."

"Okay! The soup is almost finished, then I'll come check it out!" Returning to the lookout, Lexi squeezed in the door and handed the ruler to Kabe. He measured the scale from the scrolls and performed a few calculations, then sketched on his pad.

Ricardo and Lexi peered over his shoulder, attempting to stay out of his way.

"Here you are!" Jareth stepped inside the lookout and glanced around at the maps lying everywhere. "What are you working on?"

"Ricardo spent time researching the scrolls I found. He believes he discovered a hidden chamber under the temple. Kabe is drawing a scale map of the chamber based upon the scrolls," Lexi explained. "Have we reached a safe altitude from the storm?"

He nodded as he walked over and observed the layout of the scrolls. Lexi took his arm and directed him to the first scroll. She explained the flow of the scrolls and pointed out the pattern of markings indicating the chamber. Just as she finished the demonstration, Kabe gleefully shouted out.

"Here it is!" He held out the map he constructed. Lexi and Jareth moved to his side, gazing at the map. "There appears to be a hidden staircase behind the north wall. The staircase descends under the temple into a series of tunnels. The tunnels lead into a chamber approximately fifty feet below the temple. Another tunnel enters the chamber from one of the buildings lying on the perimeter of the city."

While gazing at the drawing, Jareth asked, "Will the tunnels and chamber contain sea water?"

Kabe shrugged his shoulders, "I'm just the cartographer. I imagine it depends on the construction. More than likely, I'd assume so. Shamus and Tink could probably produce an educated speculation."

Jareth walked over to the communication link, "Shamus and Tink, please report to the lookout aboard the *Star Sapphire*." He returned to Kabe's side. "We cleared this room already. I failed to notice anything indicating a hidden passage. How do we open it or trigger it?"

Raising his hands up, "I'm just the cartographer," Kabe responded.

Lexi and Jareth looked at each other and then turned to Ricardo. He knelt down, examining the first scroll. Marking a spot on the scroll, he moved to the second, then third and down the line. "I believe I located the area where the mechanism may lie. See this symbol here," pointing to the wall on the first scroll, "and here, here and here? It appears before a new entry way. Perhaps, it indicates a lever."

"Or a trap." Lexi remarked, noting the symbol he found.

Shamus entered the lookout with Tink close behind.

"Ricardo discovered a hidden chamber under the temple from the scrolls I obtained. Kabe drew a scale map of the route to the chamber. We believe this symbol indicates either a trigger to access the hidden areas, or a trap." Lexi summarized succinctly.

"Wow. We retire to our workshops for a few hours and you find a secret treasure chamber!" Shamus observed, surprised.

Tink grabbed Kabe's map while Shamus studied Ricardo's findings from the scrolls. Then, they exchanged places. After several minutes, the tinkerers both cried out, "Incredible!"

The others in the room started firing questions as them. "Whoa! Wait a sec! One question at a time! Ricardo! Excellent work!" Shamus held his hands up, quieting everyone as Khara came in. "First question goes to Ricardo for the amazing discovery!"

"Thank you, Shamus. Do you think sea water filled the corridors and chamber?" Ricardo asked.

Shamus and Tink looked at each other. "It depends if the construction sealed the areas." Tink responded.

"The construction of an underground chamber and corridors necessitates superb workmanship and materials. Taking the weight of the initial structure and dirt into account, the architect and builders designed accordingly," Shamus surmised.

"They built pyramids with hidden tunnels and rooms."

"They possessed the knowledge..."

"With the moat surrounding the city and the one tunnel exiting in a building near the moat..."

"Located in close proximity to the coast with tropical storms and hurricanes, where striking land occurs commonly…"

"You'd think the architects designed to include safety from flooding…"

The two reasoned back and forth, then turned towards their audience. "Yes, we believe a significant possibility exists that the structures are waterproof," Tink stated.

"How do we access the area without flooding it?" Jareth asked.

"Open and close the door quickly?" Shamus responded, grimacing.

"Will oxygen remain in the corridors and chamber?" Lexi inquired.

Shamus and Tink looked at each other. "The sealed area protected the oxygen as long as it maintained water free status." Shamus commented.

"Unless someone became trapped and breathed it all," Tink replied.

Lexi sank down cross legged on the floor, spreading out Kabe's map. Everyone followed suit, surrounding the map. "Our first step requires us to determine how to gain entrance to the hidden staircase."

"We must minimize water leaking into the corridor, if dry," Jareth stated.

"Once we ascertain access to the passage, we fabricate something to allow ingress while holding back the water as much as possible. I'm thinking we devise a shield of some sort. Made out of plastic or metal. The characteristics of the shield need to include strength to withhold the pressure created by the force of the water." Tink said.

"Use a sheet of plastic with a hole cut large enough for someone to access. Line the hole with a tunnel fashioned from waterproof material. A person crawls inside, closes a hatch, crawls through. At the end of the tunnel presents another hatch. The second hatch allows exit from the tunnel. No water escapes!" Shamus declared.

"Terrific idea! Your plan minimizes water leaking into the tunnels." Tink giggled.

"What about carrying oxygen, at least initially, until we determine the breathability of the air?" Lexi pointed out.

"The underwater suit maintains oxygen within for respiratory use. Keep the suit on and intact until you determine the chemical characteristics of the air inside the corridor," Shamus explained. "Light a match inside the tunnel. If it flares, oxygen exists."

Tink focused on the original scroll where the mark indicated the secret entrance. "Determine if the door slides side to side or down and the size of the entry way. We need the measurements to construct the shield and waterproof tunnel."

Lexi nodded, "Alright. Would the communication link work in the tunnel?" Lexi asked.

Shamus thought for a moment, then shook his head. "I doubt it. The walls and dirt provide too thick of a barrier."

"I'm sure no light enters into the corridor. We need small portable lights." Jareth observed.

"Who's entering the secret entrance?" Shamus asked.

Lexi raised her hand, "I'll go!"

No one raced to volunteer. Lexi gazed at Tink. "Don't look at me! Crawling through a dark, narrow tunnel which may or may not contain oxygen?" Shaking her head, "I'm an inventor, not an explorer."

"If I fit inside the tunnel, I want to investigate the secret corridor," Brannon announced.

"Same with me," Jareth stated. "Us tall, broad shouldered gentlemen may prove too large to gain entry."

"I'm willing to embark on the endeavor," Ricardo offered.

"Terrific! We found our explorers!" Tink giggled.

The next morning, Ricardo and Lexi floated in front of the wall concealing the staircases. "On the scroll this area bares the mark," Ricardo stated, activating the communication link, "which may indicate the location of the secret entrance."

Carefully, they ran their hands across the area, closely examining the wall. After about a half hour, Ricardo discovered an anomaly, "I think I found the mechanism! My finger fits in a loop within this indentation. If pulled, the wire engages the door, sliding it."

"Good work! Now, let's find the doorway. Then, we determine which way it slides," Lexi commented. The trigger lay about a third of the way along the wall. "I believe it extends towards the corner."

"I concur," Ricardo replied. It took a while to locate the entrance. Situated a foot off the floor, the entry way appeared short and narrow. Three feet high by two feet wide. Definitely a tight fit.

Lexi clicked the communication link. "Shamus, Tink, we found the trigger and doorway." She provided the dimensions. "Perfect! We'll start fabricating the shield and waterproof tunnel. You know, someone must embark on a supply run. We lack some of the components to produce additional waterproof fabric."

"It's almost lunch time. Let's discuss supplies then. Shall we head up?" Lexi stated to Ricardo. He nodded in agreement. The hydro-pods effectively cleared sand away from the small building where the tunnel surfaced on the other side of the secret chamber. A window opening lay opposite the entry. The pods operated at a lower propulsion to effectively manage the pipe with only the appendages. Due to the small size of the building, the pods cleared most of the sand from the interior partially exposing the floor.

"Before we return to the surface, do you two want to examine the interior and try to locate the trap door and lever? You know what to look for and may find it quickly," Jareth asked.

Lexi looked to Ricardo and he nodded. "We're swimming over now."

"The trap door appears to be in the floor, according to the scrolls. The mark indicated the release in the northeast corner. I'll search for it while you locate the dimensions of the door," Ricardo suggested.

"Works for me," Lexi stated as she swam into the building. Using her feet propulsion, she blew the rest of the sand out the doorway, clearing the floor. Within half an hour, they discovered the lever and the measurements of the entry.

At the dining table, the crew gathered around, conversations abounded regarding supplies, discovery of the secret entrances and Granny's stint as a miner. "Back in the day, before the flood, we used parakeets to test for poisonous gases. If the bird dies, the miner cries!" Noah just shook his head, as

Granny responded in a singsong tone.

"Let's focus on what we must obtain to move forward at this point. Shamus, do you possess enough material to fabricate a shield and waterproof tunnel?" Lexi questioned while dishing up seared tuna.

Shamus grimaced. "Since the doorways appear small my stores include enough plastic for three. But I only have enough fabric for one tunnel. I believe we require additional waterproof suits. Once explored, I may wish to enter the tunnel."

"I want to visit the secret tunnel! It reminds me of the old mine. Perhaps, we'll discover gold!" Granny exuberantly volunteered.

"Lexi and Ricardo must ensure the clearance area of the doorways and corridors. I'd like to investigate, as well." Brannon remarked.

"Me, too." Jareth stated.

Nodding, Lexi agreed, "Entry through the temple appears tricky. The doorway stands a foot off the floor, three feet by two feet, probably rounding a corner, and immediately drops down a flight of stairs. For larger individuals wearing an underwater suit, maneuvering around inside the tunnel might prove difficult, if not impossible." Lexi pointed out, mentally picturing the logistics of the situation.

"Is there a procedure to extract water out of the tunnel? Like a reverse propulsion system?" Jareth asked.

Tink and Shamus looked at each other and nodded. "The intake on the pods. The propulsion system extricates water from the ocean and removes the oxygen, utilizing heat for running the engine, releasing sodium and hydrogen into the water. By rigging pipe to attach to the intake, we instigate removal of the water from the tunnel."

"Using the intake system requires significant care to ensure the safety of the person and the tunnel. An ample supply of oxygen should be built up within the suit in case any issues arise." Shamus commented.

"Can oxygen be carried in a bag or tank or something? In case no oxygen exists in the tunnel?" Lexi asked.

Shaking her head, "I don't like this. Too many risks arise associated with entering the tunnel. Why don't we focus on the temple and buildings?" Khara stated.

Caroline agreed. "It sounds too dangerous, too problematic. The possibilities of something going wrong appear immense! You don't know what lies behind the secret doors."

"That's why we're planning for all the possibilities. Imagine what's down there!" Lexi tried to reassure them.

"There may not be anything. This might all be for naught. You risk your life for what?" Khara retorted angrily.

"Or we may discover a room filled with gold!" Lexi replied with a beguiling smile.

"It won't matter if you're dead."

"Worst comes to worst, we flood the tunnel," Shamus responded. "I think the potential for successfully accomplishing access to the secret tunnel remains high. We're planning every precaution and testing our developments prior to implementation."

"I think it's ridiculous!" Khara growled out.

"Sounds like the pregnancy hormones kicked in," Granny observed, flopping mash potatoes on her plate. "I'm with Lexi. We may hit the mother lode!"

The rest of the crew experienced their survival instinct bursting forth and became very busy with their plates. After a few minutes, Lexi returned to the subject of the tunnel. "Shamus, will the shield be ready for implementation by morning?" With a mouthful of food, he nodded. "Okay, why don't we take it out tomorrow? Let's test it where we evaluated the pipe. Ensure maneuverability."

Khara slammed her fork down and stood up from the table, then stomped into the kitchen. "Seven more months. We better prepare and button down the hatches," Granny shook her head, sadly.

Coughs, chokes, and suppressed giggles circled the table. No one dared breathe, in case Khara heard. Finally, Tink caved, collapsing into hysterical giggles. "Only you, Granny. Only you!"

The next morning after breakfast, Shamus carefully loaded the three and a half foot by two and half foot plastic sheet with the waterproof tunnel collapsed down to six inches thick. He placed it in the pocket of the pod. "Okay, I'm ready. Are you?"

Ricardo and Lexi fastened their underwater suits, indicating their preparedness. Once they reached the training grounds, Lexi opened the pocket and removed the shield. She disconnected the device, expanding the tunnel to its full size. It waved around in the force of the current, holding no specific shape.

"Hmm. That's interesting. I wonder what shape it'll take in the corridor," Lexi observed.

"I think it will respond the same as on board the ship, but probably depends upon the properties of the air," Jareth replied, "or water within the tunnel."

Lexi removed her flippers, placing them in the pocket of the pod. She swam to the tunnel and studied the latch. "Are we ready?"

"All systems go!" Tink called out from pod two.

"Ready in pod one," Jareth declared.

Lexi opened the hatch. Water rushed in, expanding the tunnel fully. She grasped the sides of the opening and propelled inside. Kicking gently with her feet, she moved through to the other end.

"All's good!" She reported. "I'm at the other opening. Proceed to extract the water and observe the results."

"Yes. Ricardo, if you hook it up, we'll study the effects," Shamus remarked.

Ricardo nodded and removed the pipe from the other pod, attaching one end to the intake and the other end to the tunnel. "Engage the intake slowly." Tink flipped a switch and gently water flowed out of the tunnel, collapsing it around Lexi. It formed to her body. Lexi tried to move, but became entangled.

"Maybe allow some water back in," Lexi suggested.

Tink flipped the switch and water flowed in. "That's good." Lexi opened the second hatch and exited the tunnel.

"Hmm. All the water in the tunnel will flow out into the staircase," Brannon observed.

Discussion ensued revolving around pumping water and carrying it out from the other end, utilizing a waterproof bag to catch the water. The crew debated pros and cons, brainstorming possible solutions.

"Gelatin."

The debate halted as everyone turned towards Brannon in pod two. "Close the first hatch after extricating some of the water. Lexi adds gelatin to the tunnel prior to opening the second hatch. The water becomes solid. Lexi picks up any escaping gelatin and puts it back into the tunnel, closing the hatch. On this end, we open the first hatch, removing all the gelatin and sucking the water out, awaiting her return."

Everyone looked at Brannon in silence. Then, Jareth responded. "Oh, you're serious? Crawling through gelatin?" Grimacing and shuddering, "Gelatin?"

After several moments, Tink giggled. "I think it's a possibility!"

Shamus rocked his head back and forth and turned to Tink. "I agree. I believe it may work."

"Who wants to ask Khara for gelatin?"

"Granny!"

"We'll head up and grab the gelatin while Ricardo and Lexi play in the tunnel." Jareth and Brannon turned their pod and quickly began ascension.

Ricardo opened the hatch and attempted to enter the tunnel in the same manner as Lexi. But his broad shoulders failed to fit. He twisted sideways with his arms straight out in front of him. Softly kicking his feet, he eased into the tunnel. It was a tight fit.

"Tink, see if you can suck out the water and close the hatch with the appendages," Lexi recommend.

"Okay." Tink extended the appendages and picked up the pipe, fastening it to the hatch. It took her numerous tries as the appendages lacked the dexterity required to perform the minute movements.

"We assemble the pipe prior to entering the tunnel. Then, you close the hatch," Lexi suggested. She moved to the front hatch and attached the pipe, then moved back. Tink closed the hatch and secured the lock. Flipping the switch, she gently siphoned the water out, collapsing it.

Cheers extended over the link. "This is gonna work!" "Now, Ricardo and I can both traverse the staircase." Within ten minutes, pod two returned with gelatin.

Lexi laughed as she opened the hatch, expanding the tunnel with water. She entered the tunnel and Ricardo squeezed in as well, after he attached the pipe. Once inside, Tink closed the hatch, flipped the switch and gently drained some of the water from the tunnel. Not as much water flowed out with two people crammed in the space. Prior to opening the second hatch, Lexi removed the gelatin from the waterproof pouch, sprinkling it within the tunnel, mixing it as best she could, given the restricted movement. She opened the hatch and exited, with Ricardo following behind. Lexi closed the hatch. Tink opened the front hatch, filling the tunnel with water. Lexi retracted the tunnel by pushing it closed.

"It works!"

"Swimming through gelatin produces an odd sensation," Ricardo remarked.

"Shamus, will communication be possible through the plastic? Once we exit the tunnel and collapse it?" Lexi asked.

Nodding, Shamus replied, "Yes, the link works through plastic."

"So, we enter the corridor and descend the staircase, then report back to you what the situation entails on the other side?" Lexi questioned.

Again, nodding, "Sounds like a plan!" Shamus responded.

Presenting a wide smile, Lexi replied, "Let's try it!"

The crew gathered up the collapsible tunnel and moved to the temple. Inside, Lexi and Ricardo affixed the shield over the hidden opening. Tink placed the pod outside a window where they observed. Jareth pulled the second pod up to another open spot where he and Brannon watched. Ricardo found the trigger and pulled the loop, resulting in a portion of the wall sliding over, revealing an opening. Lexi opened the hatch. Water flowed in, expanding the tunnel. Using a light affixed to her wrist, she illuminated the tunnel and the staircase.

"No water appears on the stairs!" Cheers broke out over the communication link. Lexi grasped the sides of the tunnel and propelled herself in, arching around the corner, then swam through the tunnel as is rested upon the stairs, leading down. "It's a tight corner. Ricardo. You may want to lay on your side until you swing around the corner. Facing towards the right allows easier access. I'll try to squish up, providing you as much room as possible. Can you hear me?"

"Yes, we can." Jareth reassured her from the pod. Lexi reached the end of the tunnel and scrunched.

The tunnel wriggled as Ricardo entered and struggled around the corner.

"I made it. I'm in. Close the hatch," Ricardo said, groaning from his exertions. Lexi and Ricardo felt the tunnel collapse as water drained out.

"Okay. I'm adding the gelatin. You alright, Ricardo?"

"Uncomfortable, but fine."

Lexi added gelatin and moved around, mixing it. Once it gelled, "I'm opening the hatch." She opened it and using her hands, walked herself out and down the stairs. She reached the bottom and stood up. "I'm standing at the end of the stairs. Can you hear me?"

Scratchy and broken, "We barely understand you. Can you breathe?"

Lexi took several deep breaths, then, removed her helmet. She exhaled first and tentatively inhaled a small, shallow breath. The air smelled, old, stale, like dirt. The walls, lined with rock bricks, showed dirt poking through the cracks.

"Lexi?!" Tink's voice sounded shrilly in her ear.

"Yes, I can breathe."

Ricardo spilled out behind her and reached his feet. He removed his helmet and breathed deeply. "Whew!"

"Let's pick up the gelatin and stuff it back into the tunnel," Lexi said.

The two barely fit side by side on the staircase. They shoved gelatin back in, closing the hatch. Then they collapsed it, pushing it back to the opening. "Okay! At the bottom of the stairs, a closed door way blocks the passage. We must determine how to access the next hallway. We'll let you know what we discover."

Lexi searched the casing surrounding the door, trying to ascertain where it opened and how. Meanwhile, Ricardo studied the right side of the staircase looking for the trigger. "Air flows through this crack, where the door intersects the wall. I found a loop, similar to the one in the temple. Should I pull it?"

Lexi looked back at him and replied, "In for a penny, in for a pound." He pulled it. The door slid off to the left, exposing a dry, dark narrow walk way. Lexi illuminated it. The dirt floor extended around a bend, with the walls constructed of

98

bricks.

The air, breathable, Lexi inhaled deeply, initiating the communication link. "It seems fine. We're continuing on."

"Be careful!"

Lexi cautiously walked down the path, shining her light all around. Stone slabs comprised the ceiling. "This construction appears incredible! No water leaked in at all! The earth flooded, but this corridor remains dry!"

Ricardo followed. "It is amazing."

The pathway disappeared around a corner. Lexi cautiously peeked around, shining her light. Unable to see the end of the tunnel, no immediate hazards seemed apparent.

Continuing, the trail dropped deeper underground. Suddenly, Lexi gasped and stopped. At the end of the tunnel her light shone upon a pile of material, and a bony hand.

9

Ricardo peered over her shoulder. "A body."

Lexi took a deep breath. "The skeleton laid here a long time. No odor of decay lingers." She knelt, moving the clothes, revealing a full set of remains. A cloak covered the body. A loin cloth hung low around his hips. Leather moccasins encased the bones of his feet. A gold necklace comprised of gems and nuggets adorned the neck. A beaded leather head band encircled the skull, tangled in long black hair.

"We need the camera to document this!" Lexi exclaimed.

"I'll return to the entrance and see if Shamus brought it and a waterproof case," Ricardo volunteered.

"Perfect! I'll attempt to find the trip wire," Lexi stepped over the body. Using her light torch on her wrist, she surveyed the door. Similar to the last one, it slid to the right. She ran her hand over the wall noted on the map and touched the loop. As she tugged, nothing happened. It seemed jammed or stuck, like the lever failed to engage.

Lexi tried to physically slide the door. No luck. A long spear lay next to the skeleton. Shaking her head, she knew she needed to wait, at least until they snapped pictures of the scene. Lexi found nothing else to aid in forcing the door.

Ricardo jogged down the stairs. "They sent the camera through. They're excited to see the pictures! Did you make any headway with the door?"

"Yes and no. Yes, I found the trip wire. The door slides similar to the previous one but it appears stuck. Maybe you can open it." Lexi suggested.

He nodded. "Shamus told me how to take pictures." Ricardo twisted a couple knobs and peered through a small opening, then turned the lens making adjustments. "Alright, that looks good!" He snapped several pictures. "Jareth asked us to bring some items back. He wants to ascertain the time period of the remains."

Lexi picked up the necklace and headband, placing them in the waterproof bag the camera came from. He handed the camera to her. "Where's the trip wire?" Lexi pointed out the spot.

He tugged the line. "Hmm. I can't move it either," Ricardo exerted himself, attempting to trigger the mechanism. Do you think it's locked from the inside?" He raised his eyebrows and cocked his head,

"It may be."

"Should we try from the other entrance?"

Lexi turned her cheek toward the left side of the entry way, slowly sinking to the floor. "I'm trying to ascertain if air flows from the chamber." She felt around the door except along the top but didn't encounter any breeze.

"I'll lift you onto my shoulders to reach the top of the door," Ricardo offered, bending down to allow her access.

Laughing, she climbed on and he eased to a standing position. Lexi placed her hands on the walls to steady herself. Cool to the touch, the walls felt dry. She leaned from the left to the right, "Ah! Air! Magnificent!"

Ricardo sank down to the floor as Lexi climbed off his back. "One mystery solved. Shall we return to the entry?"

Lexi nodded. "We won't gain entrance from this direction."

They retraced their steps up the stairs and to the opening. Lexi triggered the communication link. "The door appears jammed. We aren't able to open it. Air leaks through from the chamber."

"Hmm. What are your thoughts?" Jareth asked as Lexi peered out the transparent plastic shield.

"Try from the other opening? No implements exist in the corridor to use other than a spear held by the skeleton. After a few centuries, I'm unsure of its strength. I don't want to break it."

"Almost an hour and a half remains before dinner. Let's set up at the other entrance and see what we accomplish prior to ascending. Khara seems extremely unhappy right now. Being late for dinner may prove hazardous to our health," Brannon observed. Tink giggled.

101

"Alright, we're coming out." Lexi placed her helmet on her head.

"I'll close this doorway, just in case we experience water issues," Ricardo stated.

Nodding, "Good idea. We need to assume every precaution to preserve the corridors and chamber." Lexi finished suiting up, then extended the tunnel back down the stairs. With no water in it, she carefully climbed up using her hands and feet. Groaning, "Entering proved easier than exiting." Finally, she reached the temple entrance. "Ricardo, I reached the entry."

"Here I come. How do we close the hatch? Let me see if I can reach it. If not, you may need to exit and allow me to go in first." The tunnel jiggled with his exertions. "Uhh. I latched it. My body lacks the agility to bend this way." Punctuated by groans, he made his way upstairs and maneuvered around the bend. "I agree. Entering is definitely easier!"

Lexi slowly opened the hatch a crack. Water poured in, quickly filling the tunnel. But it remained encased within the shield. Opening it all the way, Lexi stuck her head out and used her arms to propel herself back into the temple. Ricardo followed.

Gazing into the tunnel, in unison, "How do we pull the other end?"

"For the next excursion, let's tie a string onto the far end hatch," Lexi suggested. "Is there rope in one of the pods? I'll swim back in and tie it on to pull it closed."

"Use the intake pipe. Perhaps, it'll collapse the tunnel while extracting the water," Tink suggested. "If we slowly drain it, maybe the tunnel folds up!"

Lexi and Ricardo hooked the pipe to the pod and Tink carefully extricated the water. "Is it working?" Shamus asked. Looking through the transparent plastic, Lexi replied "I can't tell yet." After several moments, "It is working! I see the other hatch!"

Once all the water drained out of the tunnel, it collapsed fully. Ricardo triggered the mechanism, closing the door. Lexi disconnected the tunnel. "Yeah! It worked! Off to the next secret corridor!"

The operation moved to the small building on the outskirts of the city where they located the second entrance earlier. Lexi set up the shield. Once in place, Ricardo opened the trapdoor which led down a flight of stairs. Water flowed in. "After you," He waved his arm.

Following the same ritual as in the first corridor, they entered. At the bottom of the stairs, Ricardo located the trigger. Lexi checked around the edges of the door and discovered air. "I feel air flowing in." Tripping the door, it slid to the right and the path led west. It appeared similar to the previous tunnel, the walls constructed of brick and the floor, dirt. Lighting the hallway with their flashlights, Lexi surveyed the walls and ceiling closer than before. No dampness permeated the bricks or dirt. "It's difficult to believe the skill of the builders survived centuries!"

Arriving at the doorway leading to the chamber, a skeleton blocked the entry way, same as the other corridor. This skeleton wore attire similar to the other guard. Ricardo located the mechanism to open the door. Air leaked along the top. Groaning, Ricardo attempted to release the catch but the door held fast. "This one appears jammed, as well." Dejectedly, they returned to the entrance and informed the crew. "Better return to the ship, we're late for dinner," Brannon said.

As they entered the dining room, Khara spun around. Her features rigid with anger, "You're late! I was scared to death! I didn't know if a cave-in buried you alive, trapped you in a tunnel or drowned in gelatin!" She ended in a shriek, waving her arms around.

Lexi walked over to her, "We're sorry. Everything is just fine. The final door to the chamber refused to open. In either tunnel." Lexi brushed her cheek. Khara turned and stalked away. Lexi grimaced.

"Well, tell us about the tunnels. Did your shield hold?" Noah asked, ignoring Khara.

The underwater team filled in the rest of the family over dinner. Lexi brought out the headband and necklace. The crew passed it around the table, gazing at the beautiful gems and remarking on the workmanship.

"I'll develop the film tonight and pass around the pictures in the morning," Shamus announced.

"How are you planning on gaining entrance into the

chamber?" Noah asked.

"Dynamite!" Granny suggested. "When I worked in the mines in California, I set up charges to expand the tunnels."

"There is no way on earth or under earth, that I'll allow you in the same room as dynamite." Noah declared.

Putting a quick end to this discussion, "Dynamite fails to be an option. We risk collapsing the tunnels and chamber," Shamus responded.

"How thick is the door? Is it wood or stone?" Tink questioned, dishing up a large spoonful of vegetables.

"The doors seem to be constructed of stone." Lexi replied.

"The other doors operate on a sliding mechanism. The trigger feels like a loop made of wire. When you pull it, the door slides to the right, receding into the brick wall." Ricardo described. But the triggers on the final doors fail to work. When you pull on it, nothing happens."

"What about cutting through the door with a torch?" Jareth asked Tink and Shamus.

"What type of stone is it?" Tink asked.

Lexi and Ricardo look at one another and shrugged their shoulders. "The type made of rock?" Lexi answered. "No idea."

"The second tunnel spans wider and permits easier access than the first, allowing Jareth and Brannon entry. And of course, Tink and Shamus could enter through either tunnel," Ricardo described.

Laughing and shaking her head, Tink replied, "Iharbor no desire to enter a small tunnel underground, under the ocean, crawling through gelatin. I'll operate a pod."

"Tomorrow, I'll check out the door, determine what type of stone and develop solutions for entry," Shamus volunteered with a smile.

"I'm ready to go in." Jareth swallowed his wine.

"Me, too!" Brannon responded, eagerly.

"Shamus, why don't we discuss what items you require and I'll accompany the ship to retrieve supplies while you deduce options for gaining entrance into the chamber," Tink offered.

Shamus nodded in agreement.

"What type of supplies do you need?" Noah asked.

"The materials to manufacture more waterproof fabric for suits and another tunnel."

"More pipe for the intake and exhaust propulsion systems."

"Gelatin."

Surprise crossed his features, "How does gelatin figure into your inventions?" Noah asked.

Ricardo explained the gelatin process. Matt choked on his laughter, Kabe stared wide eyed at Ricardo and Noah looked bewildered.

"I know lots of interesting things to do with gelatin." Granny commented as she chewed her salad.

The next morning, Shamus passed around the pictures he developed of the bodies within the tunnels.

Caroline shuddered and quickly passed the photos on to Noah. Lexi's father studied the layout of the skeleton, clothing and adornments. "Fascinating! Any indication of a struggle? Dried blood?" He glanced towards Lexi and Ricardo. They shook their heads. He passed pictures down the line.

"Can you remove the body and jewelry?" Matt asked as he studied the photos.

Shaking her head, Lexi responded. "Not yet. We don't possess a waterproof bag large enough for the body or the spear. We decided not to move anything else without talking with everyone first. There's no worry about anything disappearing," Lexi flashed a wry smile.

Matt and Noah commanded the *Mountain Peak* and set course towards civilization with Kabe, Tink and Caroline. Khara and Granny stayed above board on the *Star Sapphire* while everyone else returned to the city to gain access to the secret chamber. Ricardo guided Shamus into the tunnel, showing him how to access each section until they reached the inaccessible door. Lexi worked on sand removal from around the city while Jareth and Brannon monitored Ricardo and Shamus in the tunnel. At lunch time, they discussed the progress.

"What's your opinion, Shamus? How do we access the chamber?" Lexi asked, filling her plate.

Sighing, "It appears difficult. The trigger doesn't seem attached to the door. The mechanisms lay internally within the stone or in the chamber. It's inaccessible from the passage."

Shamus plopped a spoonful of potatoes on his plate. "Made primarily of granite, cutting through the door will be difficult. To gain access, we must move equipment in, maintain the structural strength of the doorway, while minimizing damage to the interior chamber."

"If the trigger fails to attach to the door, are you sure it's the actual trigger? Before the flood, I constructed houses with secret tunnels. Sometimes, we made false triggers to confuse people." Granny poked through her peas and carrots, removing the carrots.

Jareth cocked his head, trying to control a smile. Ricardo and Lexi looked at each other. "We didn't search for another trigger," Lexi commented, hesitantly raising an eyebrow.

"Before you start blowing up the tunnel, I'd check for another trigger," Granny suggested, eating only peas.

"Terrific suggestion, Granny! We'll start there right after lunch. So, you use to build secret passages in houses?" Jareth commented.

"I'd rather hear about the circus," Shamus replied.

Shaking her head, Khara begged, "Don't encourage her!"

The crew spent the rest of lunch with Granny regaling them about her times building houses in the Oregon territory, helping settlers migrating west. She described cutting down trees reaching almost to the clouds with cross saws as big as the dining table. Using a pulley system and horses, the settlers stacked logs, constructing the cabins. Explaining construction of the interior walls, in detail, she described the gears, cogs and wheels utilized to trigger secret openings, revealing hidden rooms and passages. Her audience, listened, enthralled with her story, unsure of her authenticity.

After lunch, Lexi and Jareth donned the underwater suits and entered the tunnel through the small building. The team decided to use this tunnel as the access proved easier. They spent two hours searching the walls, shining their flashlights across every nook and cranny.

"By the green meadows, I think I found it!" Lexi squealed. She knelt on the passage floor, illuminating a spot about eighteen inches off the ground. Jareth sank beside her, adding his light to the area. A little rock stood out against the layered bricks. "It moves." Lexi pressed it. A grinding noise occurred near their heads and extended towards the door. It slid left, revealing a dark opening.

Jumping to their feet, Lexi and Jareth peered through the doorway. They shined their lights inside. The room appeared to be roundish with stone walls. Wooden shelves held rows of books. Objects glittered on shelves and throughout. A red plush velvet covered chair stood in the center with a skeleton seated. A golden crown encrusted with jewels encircled the skull. Deep purple crushed velvet cloak encased the bones and a bony hand clutched a scepter.

On the floor, at his feet, lay two more skeletons. One bore a red cloak and the other, minimal clothing covered the remains. As they entered, they shone their lights. Bolts of bold colors of fabric lay stacked upon the shelves.

Jareth cautiously made his way to the bookshelf and began reading the titles, excitedly. "How did these books come to be here? In this chamber? The *Bible, Quran, Vedas, Torah, Tripitaka*. Dictionaries of English, Spanish, Arabic, French, Chinese, Japanese, Russian, German, Italian, Portuguese, Greek! A World Atlas! Mythologies of Egypt, Greece, Rome. Philosophies of Socrates, Plato and Aristotle. Shakespeare, Chaucer, *Beowulf, War and Peace, Kama Sutra*. Someone tried to preserve the basic tenets of societies!" Wonder filled his voice as he read the binding of each book. "Some of these titles the Historical Society doesn't possess!"

Lexi jerked her head, nonchalantly, "Historical Society?"

"Yes, Matt and I are members. We locate and obtain books and objects to preserve for future generations. The Society found thousands of books. But this," shining his light across the shelves, "This is a treasure trove! Who procured these texts and preserved them through the flood?"

Shining her light on the figure sitting upon the throne, "He appears to be a ruler. Long black hair, probably Indian. I didn't think any Indian rulers remained in power in Mexico."

"*War and Peace* published in the 1860's, just prior to the flood. In Russia! How did that book get here?"

Shaking her head, Lexi replied softly, "I have no idea."

Jareth moved away from the bookcase and walked around, gazing at the items within. "These objects range from ancient to just before the flood." Confused, "How?"

Lexi just shook her head. "We need more light. What do

we do first? Catalog everything? Take pictures? Take pictures first." Lexi answered her own question.

"Pictures, yes. I didn't think to bring a camera, did you?"

"No, I didn't either. Let's head back and prepare everything we need," Lexi suggested.

He nodded in agreement. "I want to stay here, surrounded by these books, but I suppose plenty of time remains to read." Over lunch, the crew hailed Granny a hero as Lexi and Jareth described the treasure room. Shamus boosted the communication link to the *Mountain Peak*, advising them of the discovery and ordered more of the components necessary to fabricate the waterproof material. Shamus prepared the camera and constructed waterproof carrying cases from his remaining supplies.

The next morning, Shamus and Ricardo entered the chamber to photograph and document the findings. Brannon operated one of the hydro-pods outside the small building, clearing debris while Lexi and Jareth focused on extracting sand from the center of the city.

"We need to discuss this Historical Society and their desire to obtain a hydro-pod," Lexi declared, blowing sand towards the perimeter.

Surprised, Jareth turned to Lexi, open mouthed, speechless. "Yes, I'm aware of your conversations regarding the acquisition of our vessel. I assume Matt brings others with him?" Continuing to stare at Lexi, Jareth didn't respond. "Answer me!" Lexi growled angrily.

Jareth sighed, "He may. But I refuse to steal the pod. Matt lacks the ability to operate it. Ricardo and Shamus demonstrate loyalty to you. The people Matt brings back won't know how to operate it and we won't teach them."

"Tell me about this Historical Society."

"The Historical Society obtains and protects literature, technology and art created prior to the flood, preserving for future generations and society. My mother and her family served the Society for generations," Jareth explained.

"And the man demanding the pod?"

"Blaine Whitcomb," Jareth replied. "He serves as the president. But the rest of the members will disagree with his order. You, your family, your ship, your equipment provide far more of an asset to the Society than just a hydro-pod."

"And if we fail to choose to join the Society?"

Hesitating, Jareth scratched his head. "We negotiate an agreement where the Society purchases the findings from us." Raising an eyebrow, Lexi turned to Jareth. "Does the Society maintain agreements, or do they send their," Lexi hesitated, "best acquistioner to obtain the items?"

Jareth had the gall to look embarrassed. "They execute agreements with a few businesses. And I continue to advocate strongly for some sort of working relationship with the *Star Sapphire*. Are you willing to work for the Society?"

Lexi laughed. "I hesitate since their main objective appears to be to abscond with our equipment. I refuse to worry constantly about someone stealing from us. My family and my ship are the most important things to me. Does the Society own your ship?"

He shook his head. "I traded a large amount of a wide variety of seeds to the builder," he paused and sighed. "And I borrowed money from the Society, an advance on future… opportunities. This project more than covers the amount fronted to me."

Lexi huffed in frustration. "So, they own part of your ship." Turning the pod, Lexi focused on clearing sand from the next building. "Will they attack us?"

"No! The Society abhors violence. The reality is, the Society lacks the ability to excavate Tenochtitlan without us. They require your hydro-pods and pilots. They need Shamus' underwater suits and us to use them. As the project progresses, the necessity of Tink and Shamus' genius to problem solve obstacles quickly becomes apparent. Without us, they lack the ability to remove the treasures without damaging them."

"Once the *Mountain Peak* returns, we need to set up a meeting and reach an agreement."

Jareth nodded. "I concur. We'll see who returns with Matt. Negotiating with most of the members won't pose an issue. Their main objective surrounds finding and obtaining historical items."

"What if Blaine shows up?"

He laughed. "Blaine doesn't leave the safety of his home."

Lexi looked at Jareth. "I am trusting you with my family, our well-being and livelihood."

"Your family adopted me. Khara carries my child. My livelihood intertwines with yours. I'm in this with you. You and I will protect our family, our livelihood." Jareth grasped her hands and raised them to his lips. "I give you my solemn word. I stand with you. I won't betray you."

10

Lexi woke to a *tink tink tink* noise emanating from the communication speaker. She eased out from under Jareth. He rolled over, stretching across the bed. Donning a robe, Lexi returned a *click click click* response over the system. She softly opened the door and climbed the stairs to the bridge. Picking up the microphone, she spoke, "What's up, Tink?"

Responding quietly, "We picked up three passengers. I overheard some of them discussing with Matt the best way to liberate one or both pods from our possession."

Several inappropriate words fell from Lexi's lips. "I already anticipated we may experience issues with Matt's friends' avarice." Sighing, "Are you in transit back to us?"

"Yes. I obtained everything we needed and more. We arrive tomorrow afternoon." Tink's voice crackled over the speaker.

"Alright. Both hydro-pods will be in use underwater, until dinner time. What is the best way to disable them, rendering them non-functional and difficult to ascertain why?"

Tink hesitated a moment, pondering the question. "From the interior, under the control panel on the navigator side, reach up under the left. A small rubber hose hangs down. There's a screw near a red wire. Slide the hose on the screw. That shuts down the whole system."

"What does it do?" Lexi asked.

"The hose comprises an integral part of the carbon dioxide intake unit. The extraction process requires carbon dioxide for the propulsion system to operate, leaving the pods dead in the water, literally."

"I'll take care of it. You and I are the only ones who know about this. Be safe."

"You, too."

Lexi ended the transmission, then returned upstairs, sneaking into her bed. Jareth lay wrapped around Khara. Lexi slid into bed softly, pulling up the blankets. Turning over, Jareth reached for her, parting her legs and entering her from the rear. Lexi moaned softly as he pushed between her tender, moist folds. He grasped her hips, forcing himself deep. She moved her hips as he plunged into her. He rolled over top of her, turning her head to kiss her as he pounded her into the mattress. They orgasmed at the same time, then fell back to sleep.

At breakfast the next morning, Lexi asked Jareth, "How do you want to proceed at this point?"

He swallowed his food then stated, "We need to catalogue all the items we discover. I'll go down in an underwater suit. Who else wants an underwater suit?" He looked around the table.

"I'm taking a pod," Lexi declared. "Writing isn't my forte."

"I'm preparing for the incoming supplies by producing some parts beforehand, to speed up the assembly process," Shamus peeled a peach.

"I read and write in both English and Spanish," Ricardo stated.

"Ricardo, you're with me," Jareth decided.

Brannon nodded with a smile. "I'd rather operate a pod."

"Do you want to start bringing items up?" Lexi asked.

"I think we'll leave everything in the chamber for right now. I want to see who Matt returns with. I intend to use the items as bargaining chips," Jareth replied.

"Bargaining chips? Why do we need bargaining chips," Khara asked, suspiciously.

Lexi sat back in her chair, gazing at Jareth, waiting for his response. The room filled with silence, as the attention focused purely on Jareth. He inhaled deeply. He glanced at Lexi.

"You explain it to them."

"Why do we need bargaining chips?" Khara asked, a little louder, emphasizing "why".

Again, he inhaled. "I'm a member of the Historical Society, an organization pledged to obtain and protect items created prior to the flood. Several members joined Matt while in port."

"What are their intentions?" Confused, Khara looked at Lexi.

"I'm not sure. It depends on who he brings."

Khara whipped her head around, facing Jareth. "What do you mean, 'it depends who he brings?' What might they do?" Khara's anger grew exponentially. "What is going on? Are we in danger?"

Jareth ran a hand through his hair. Soothingly, "Its fine. Really. One faction of the Society wants to obtain an underwater pod. Most of the members I can reason and work with."

"Are you kidding me? They intend to steal one of our pods? Are we in danger of an attack? What about Mom and Dad? Tink? Kabe? Are they alright?" Panic overrode her anger.

"They're fine. I talked to Tink last night," Lexi reassured Khara. Jareth looked surprised. Realization dawned on him. Their midnight sex. "Tink contacted me to warn us about a discussion she overheard regarding plans to acquire a pod."

"I side with you, the *Star Sapphire*. I knew nothing about anyone planning to hijack a pod," Shamus tried to reassure Lexi and Khara.

"I am merely a port orphan. I promise you, I am not part of any secret society," Ricardo commented.

"You're a lot more than a port orphan, but I believe you don't belong to this society," Lexi commented.

Ricardo raised his eyes, met Lexi's and then looked at Granny. "I lost my family a long time ago. You accepted me. I am loyal to you and the *Star Sapphire*. Anything you ask of me, I will do." He grabbed Granny's hand, clasping it between his.

"My loyalties lie with you. I am loyal to the *Star Sapphire*. I pledge to protect you, all of you. Within the Society, I hold a lot of," Jareth hesitated, "influence. I made it abundantly clear I won't allow anyone to pilfer the pods. I refuse to allow anyone to harm any member of the *Star Sapphire*. That includes Shamus and Ricardo. As far as I'm concerned, we're all part of the *Star Sapphire*."

Silence filled the room. Then Granny spoke, "In the Civil

113

War, I became a turncoat. I started out as a Confederate, but fell in love with President Lincoln. My, that beard and top hat. Every gal's dreamboat!" She fluttered her hand in front of her face, fanning herself.

Unbelievably, Khara burst out laughing first, tears filling her eyes. "Oh, feet upon the earth! Granny!"

It took several minutes for the laughter to die down, as Granny looked around, bewildered. Shaking her head, "If you saw him for yourself! Oh, my! I'm getting all worked up!"

Another raucous bout of laughter filled the room. Lexi tried control the situation, once the laughter died out. "Alright. Granny, let's save the story of you and Abe for another time. We all want to hear it, but right now we need to focus on the issue at hand."

"I'm scared, Lexi. I don't want to be alone with just Granny and Shamus," Khara said softly.

Lexi shot an angry look at Jareth. "Alright. I'll stay onboard."

Brannon said, "Lexi, I'll stay and ready the cannon. If Noah doesn't give the sign, I'll sink them."

"Wait a minute! We don't need to sink anyone!" Jareth replied.

"Like hell. Our family is being threatened. Noah, Tink and Kabe know the signal. If they don't answer, we blow your ship out of the sky," Lexi announced.

"I promise you. No danger has come or will come to your family," Jareth responded, worry clouding his eyes.

"What do you suggest at this point?" Lexi stated.

Jareth hesitated. "I'll contact the *Mountain Peak*, once they enter sight. Matt and your family members will verify everything's fine."

"Fine. Brannon and I remain onboard. Jareth, do whatever you want. Shamus and Ricardo, take whatever placement you wish. Any move towards Granny or Khara results in immediate death. I am not kidding." Lexi pronounced.

After a moment's hesitation, Jareth replied, "I'm taking the underwater suit and going down. Everything will be fine. I assure you."

Shamus stated, "If it's alright with you, Lexi, I want to work in Tink's workshop preparing for the new supplies."

Ricardo looked from Lexi to Jareth and then to Granny, asking what he should do. "I'll do whatever you ask me to do, Lexi."

Lexi paused. "Take a pod and go down with Jareth. Someone needs to back him up."

Ricardo nodded. "Of course."

Granny chimed in. "I'll go with Ricardo. Since everyone else plans to stay onboard, it sounds like underwater is the place to be."

Breathing in deeply, Lexi counted to ten and exhaled slowly. Granny proved to be a royal pain in the keister. "Sounds like we developed our plan. See you at lunch." Lexi stated, looking pointedly at Jareth.

He ducked his head and crooked a finger towards Ricardo. They exited the dining room and headed upstairs, with Granny following.

Shamus nodded and left, retiring to Tink's workshop. After the dining room cleared, Lexi looked to Khara. "Do you want to go above board with us?"

She hesitated, then shook her head. "Shamus poses no threat. I need to work in the hydroponics garden."

Lexi nodded, then replied, "Lock the door. Contact us on the bridge every fifteen minutes."

Khara rolled her eyes. "Really?"

"Really." Lexi deadpanned back. "Brannon, head to the bridge. Perform a radar check for any ships within the vicinity. I'll help Khara down here until she's ready to retreat to the hydroponics garden."

Brannon nodded. "Of course." He turned on his heel and climbed the stairs.

Lexi started picking up dishes and clearing the table.

Khara watched for a moment and then said, "You don't need to do this. I'll clean up the breakfast mess."

Glancing at her, Lexi replied, "Your safety means a lot to me. If you're scared, I'm taking care of you." She entered the kitchen carrying a load of dishes and returned a few moments later and gathered more. Khara picked up dishes with leftover food. Lexi filled the sink with water, placing plates and silver- ware within.

"You don't need to wash dishes, Lexi."

"I might as well help while I'm down here." Lexi

replied with a smile. She scrubbed a plate and placed it in the next sink to rinse. Khara shook her head, rinsing and depositing them in a drainer. Together, they finished the dishes and cleaned the kitchen. Khara instituted preparations for lunch. Once she certified the kitchen satisfactory, Lexi escorted her to the hydroponics garden.

"There's plenty of work to occupy me in here. I'll be fine." Khara responded, looking at the vast rows of plants.

"Lock the door behind me. Call every fifteen minutes or I'll bust in here with weapons loaded." Lexi stated, bluntly.

"Overkill?"

"When it comes to you, I don't take half measures. Your safety means everything to me." Lexi replied, kissing her softly.

"What about Granny?"

"I'm sure, in her youth, she trained as a ninja pirate soldier inventor doctor. She can take care of herself. Or start spinning a yarn long enough to distract an army from a war." Lexi responded, wryly.

Laughing, Khara kissed her. "I love you."

"I love you, too."

She paused for a moment. "Jareth?"

Sighing deeply. "I want to believe him. The next twelve hours will prove most revealing. But I won't risk you or the *Star Sapphire* in the process." Lexi responded, vehemently.

Khara nodded, smiling weakly. Lexi left the room, "Lock the door behind me and call in fifteen minutes."

Once she exited, Lexi entered Tink's workshop to check on Shamus' activities. She wandered around until she located him. He stood at the brass section, fabricating a helmet for the underwater suit. He welded a piece of glass into the brass, un- aware of her presence. Once she finished the weld, Lexi asked, "How's it going?"

Shamus almost bounced off the ceiling. Lexi swallowed a laugh. "Doing okay?"

He nodded, shooting her a self-conscious smile. "Yeah. Everything we need to make helmets, we already possess. With the helmets ready to go, when the *Mountain Peak* shows up, I'll start on the suits." He paused slightly, "If we aren't embroiled in a civil war."

Lexi grimaced. "As soon as they sail into sight, we'll contact them. Hopefully, Jareth proves correct and everything remains fine." The worry shone through her statement.

"I promise you, I'm on your side. If you need me, don't hesitate to ask. I promise I won't go near Khara. I pose no risk to you or your family." Shamus spoke from his heart.

Tears tried to come to Lexi's eyes, but she refused to allow them. "Thank you." She left the room and climbed the stairs, leading to the bridge. Lexi utilized the time, breathing deeply, regaining her composure. She tried to trust Jareth. But this involved her family. Her home. Her ship. Her life. She wanted to trust him. He provided her with every reason to believe in him. Taking another deep breath, she cleansed her soul, then entered the bridge.

"Anything on radar?"

Shaking his head, "No, not yet."

Lexi nodded. "Okay. I'll keep an eye on the horizon.

"I'm as worried as you. My parents and siblings travel on that ship as well. It's taking all my self control not to kick Jareth's ass for bringing this to us." Brannon angrily replied.

Swallowing down her own mistrust, "Jareth defended us up to this point." She sighed deeply. "The next few hours will prove whose side he chooses. Let's armor up and prepare the ship to wage attack, if needed."

"What do you want me to do?"

The next two hours, Brannon and Lexi hooked up three water cannons to the deck. Lexi moved the other pod to the first propulsion base, next to the ship radar. The radar bounced off the exterior of the pod, increasing the magnitude of its reach. The *Mountain Peak* appeared on screen, but well out of range of communications, without the boost from the communications array while docked at a port.

"Continue to track the *Mountain Peak* and monitor if another ship trails behind. Once it enters range, make contact. Inform them Shamus must question Tink regarding the manufacture of items for the pod. We'll await their response." Lexi maintained her self-control, keeping the fear out of her voice. But Brannon knew her well enough to recognize it.

Lexi started thinking about defense, and offense. After leaving Aconcagua Port, the pirates employed a large bow to shoot arrows at the balloon of the *Star Sapphire*. Deciding to build a similar apparatus, Lexi fashioned an arrowhead from a broken anchor. Rigging it to the propulsion system of the ship, the projectile could be launched at a target. Returning to Tink's happy place, she found an aluminum rod about five feet long and a few pieces of aluminum and fabric. She checked on Shamus.

Wrapped up in helmet manufacturing, he remained unaware she visited the workshop. Checking on Khara, she appeared elbow deep in dirt, thinning and pruning different plants. Lexi returned above deck. Using the torch in her arm brace, she fastened the broken anchor, fabric and aluminum, fabricating an arrow. Next, she attached it to the propulsion system feeding the second underwater pod.

Lunch time arrived. The pod and Jareth landed at the ship. Lexi assisted them to dock. Without discussion, everyone descended downstairs for lunch. Khara served a shrimp salad and fruit, since Lexi insisted she remain in the hydroponics garden.

"How did things progress in the cavern?" Lexi asked, forking a bite of lettuce into her mouth.

"Fantastic! I started inventorying the books in the secret chamber. I made it through all the religious texts and language dictionaries. If nothing else, the foundations of numerous societies will be maintained through the millennium."

"Ricardo, how did you perform?"

"I cleared the sand away from the rest of the buildings near the temple. Now, we need to focus on the outer ring of the perimeter."

"How are things onboard?" Jareth asked.

"Shamus built helmets for the underwater suits, Khara worked in the hydroponics garden. Brannon and I extended the range of the radar and built an arrow to shoot out the balloon of an airship," Lexi responded.

Jareth blanched, but didn't respond to her statement. Instead, he asked, "Has the *Mountain Peak* shown up on radar yet?"

"Yes, but it hasn't entered into communications range." Brannon responded, after looking to Lexi.

Jareth requested, "Please don't shoot my ship down."

"As long as my parents and siblings appear unharmed,

there's nothing to worry about. Once the *Mountain Peak* reaches communication status, we'll initiate contact. If family fails to reply…" Lexi trailed off.

"I assure you, everything is fine," Jareth responded.

"Then, you've no reason to worry, correct?" Lexi retorted.

"Lexi," Khara pleaded.

"Once I hear our family is safe, and back on board our ship, then I'll relax." Lexi replied. "What's the plan this afternoon?"

No one replied, immediately. Shamus responded after a hesitation, "I'll be down in Tink's workshop. I almost finished the helmet for the next underwater suit."

Everyone looked towards Jareth. "I'm returning to Tenochtitlan in an underwater suit to continue the catalogue of items."

Brannon looked to Lexi. Lexi nodded to him. "I'm staying here."

Ricardo stated, "I'll pilot a pod, if no one objects."

She nodded in acquiescence.

Granny announced, "I intend to accompany Ricardo. The two of us make a pretty good team when it comes to operating the pod."

Lexi groaned inwardly. After second thought, anyone stealing a pod, stuck with Granny, served as its own punishment. She'd ask Brannon to monitor the pod on radar, if possible.

Lunch grew into a very tense ordeal. People escaped once it seemed alright to do so. Lexi remained behind until Khara locked herself in the hydroponics garden. Making her way into Tink's workshop, she observed Shamus continuing to work on a helmet.

"Is it possible to monitor the hydro-pods on the radar?" Lexi questioned Shamus.

He pushed his goggles up and contemplated her question. After a few moments, he nodded. "Yes, if we optimize the radar to scan for hydrogen emissions, it would indicate the pod. Do you want me to program the radar to perform that function?"

Lexi nodded, "Given the present circumstances I want to try to keep an eye on all of our equipment. Is there any way to

119

track the underwater suits as well?"

Shamus hesitated a moment, deliberating. "Yes, if I calibrate the radar to scan for hydrogen in any emission, the suits will display as well. The pods and the suits expel hydrogen. Nothing else emits that compound in measurable amounts."

"Can you recalibrate the sensors in the radar now?" Lexi asked.

Looking at his current project, weighing priorities, Shamus nodded. "Yep, let me grab the necessary tools and I'll meet you on the bridge. I'd be so pissed if one of my underwater suits swam off."

"No kidding." Lexi stated, deadpan.

Shamus met Lexi above board within five minutes. He worked in the bridge calibrating the radar system. Brannon whooped as the underwater suit and pod showed up on the radar. Once he completed his task, Shamus disappeared below deck to finish the helmet while Lexi and Brannon monitored activities above water.

Lexi surveyed the horizon, three hundred sixty degrees from their center. Brannon wandered out, "The *Mountain Peak* entered communication range."

Lexi sighed and returned to the bridge, peering at the radar. It indicated the *Mountain Peak* flew into range to converse via radio. Taking a deep breath, Lexi triggered the device. "*Mountain Peak*, this is the *Star Sapphire*. Do you hear us?"

After a few moments, a reply came back. "Yes, *Star Sapphire*. We receive your broadcast."

"Terrific! Shamus has a question for Tink regarding the hydro-pod propulsion system he's preparing prior to your arrival. Can Tink respond?" Lexi held her breath, awaiting reply. "Yes, hold on. We'll locate her and radio back." Lexi recognized Matt's voice.

Lexi glanced to Shamus. After a couple minutes, Tink responded. "Hidey Ho, *Star Sapphire!* How are things?"

"Very well! I love your workshop. Much more organized than mine," Shamus commented. "I'm preparing the propulsion system for the hydro-pod. Do I connect the sodium-hydro-oxygen to the extraction system and then tie the extraction system to the expulsion system to the

120

exhaust?"

"No. You need to ensure the sodium-hydrogen ties into the expulsion system. The oxygen pours into the internal pulmonary system allowing for free transfer of oxygenation." Tink explained.

"Do I tie into the internal respiratory system or the linkage to the autonomic propulsion re-uptake anti-reduction expulsion system?" Shamus questioned.

"Hmm. Go ahead and tie it into the internal respiratory system linked to the expulsion system." Tink responded, in geek speak.

"Gotcha! When will you be rendezvousing with us?"

After a brief hesitation, Tink responded, "Matt thinks it will be about two hours. Mom is worried about Granny and Dad can't wait to not be around her."

Lexi breathed a deep sigh of relief and responded, "Khara planned an awesome reunion dinner. How many are aboard?" "We picked up four extra. An anthropologist, archaeologist, occultist and a strategist." Tink stated.

Lexi contemplated the pending arrivals. Brannon responded. "We'll make sure to place extra seats at the dinner table! We anxiously await your arrival. See you in a little while."

"Ready to return to my workshop!" Tink responded. "See ya soon!"

After signing off, Lexi breathed easier. Other than the strategist, the new passengers sounded unassuming. Activating the internal communication system, Lexi informed Khara everything appeared fine on the *Mountain Peak* and to expect four extra people for dinner. Returning to the deck, Lexi checked sails and ropes, making repairs as needed. Working uninterrupted for about an hour, Brannon shouted at her from the bridge and waved her in. Lexi floated about fifty feet in the air, surveying the underside of the balloon. She propelled to the bridge, dropping onto the stairs.

"What's up?"

He hesitated and pointed at the radar. "Another ship showed up on the radar. I watched it for about fifteen minutes. It appears to be mirroring the path of the *Mountain Peak*."

11

Surprise crossed her face as she ran to the radar and studied it. "Why am I shocked?" Lexi watched for a moment, noting the pod and underwater suit displayed on the radar. "Don't mention the ship to anyone, for now. Once the *Mountain Peak* arrives, reset the radar to display a shorter distance, not indicating the other ship. Show Kabe how to change the settings and advise him."

Nodding, "What about Jareth?"

Shaking her head, "No, not yet. Let's see how things progress this evening." Lexi propelled back to the underside of the balloon but returned to the bridge about every twenty minutes. The second ship obviously followed the course of the *Mountain Peak* at a distance where it remained unseen.

Brannon stuck his head out of the bridge. "The pod and suit appear to be returning to the ship."

Giving him a thumbs up, Lexi dropped to the deck and assisted them to land. Opening the hatch, Granny popped out. "We saw an octopus! I tried to catch it with the arms but that thing swam fast! I ate one in Tokyo once. The texture appeared a little chewy."

"You went to Tokyo, Granny?" Ricardo climbed out of the pod.

Smiling, Lexi shook her head. She helped tie down the hydro-pod and deactivated it. Jareth landed on deck and Lexi assisted him in shedding the underwater suit. "The *Mountain Peak* should arrive anytime. My family appear fine. They brought four extra passengers aboard, an anthropologist, archeologist, occultist and a strategist."

"I wonder who the strategist is," Jareth remarked. "What's your plan?"

"To directly inform them we refuse to allow them to steal our equipment. We need to work out some sort of equitable arrangement immediately," Lexi replied.

"It sounds like they're sending the typical crew to document the new find." Jareth remarked.

"Strategist?" Lexi asked.

"Muscle for issues of a physical nature, protection." Brannon yelled down from the bridge, "Ship on the horizon!"

Lexi and Jareth turned to see the *Mountain Peak*. The emerald balloon stood out against the blue sky. "Let's head to the bridge. Check on your family." As they walked upstairs, Jareth surveyed the arrow set to fire. He sighed heavily. On the bridge, he activated the communications system. "*Mountain Peak*, we see you on the horizon. How was your voyage?"

"*Star Sapphire*, our voyage received favorable winds, making it quick and fruitful. Do we drop anchor where we rested before?" Matt replied.

"Ask Tink how she wants to proceed with unloading the supplies acquired."

"Hi, Jareth! I'm so glad to be home! Um, let's use the propulsion pads to transport supplies from one ship to the other." Tink suggested.

"You could place one of the pods onto the *Mountain Peak* to keep the weight off the *Star Sapphire*." Matt offered quickly.

Lexi grabbed the microphone from Jareth, but he put an arm out to stop her. "That's alright. We'll park them in the ocean for now. Which team came with you?"

"Team four."

A cloudy looked crossed Jareth's face briefly, then he replied, "Great! I can't wait for Gertrude to observe our treasure trove! See you soon." Jareth disconnected the communication system. "Damn! They brought Terrence." Lost in thought for a moment, he turned to the radar. He glanced to Lexi. "Is there a way to extend the range of the radar?"

"What do you suspect?" Lexi made the adjustments to the radar.

"They brought another ship."

Lexi nodded, "They did. Brannon spotted it after the *Mountain Peak* appeared within communication range. He's monitoring it closely. I'll transport the pods to the ocean's surface," Lexi replied.

"Throw the suits inside the pods. I imagine you discovered a way to disable the pods?" Jareth replied.

Smiling, "Yes, Tink told me how to last night."

Dropping his head, he shot a sidelong glance to Brannon and Lexi. With a smile, Jareth said, "You guys are good."

Lexi climbed downstairs and picked up the underwater suit. Opening the hatch, she set it down inside. After disconnecting the pod, she propelled it to the ocean surface. She found the hose Tink described and hooked it on to the screw, then chained the pod to the ship, ensuring its safety. She dealt with the other pod and suit in the same fashion. Once finished, she returned to the deck as the *Mountain Peak* pulled along-side the *Star Sapphire*.

Walking over to one of the propulsion pads, she engaged it and moved it to the *Mountain Peak*. Brannon followed suit with the other pad. Their parents, Kabe and Tink stood on the deck. Tink kicked her boots into propulsion next to her parents. Lexi navigated the pad, stopping it next to them. "Get on, quickly." She stated quietly. Kabe jumped on and took the controls from Lexi.

Caroline laughed, "What? Why?"

Tink spoke quickly, "Get on, now!" She pushed them towards the pad.

Noah looked back at Tink and then to Lexi. He took Caroline by the arm as they stepped up, "What's going on?"

"The Historical Society intends to steal one or both of the underwater pods. Another ship followed this one. We secured the pods and the suits. We need you on our ship. Mom, go below deck with Khara and Granny," Lexi quickly filled her stunned parents in on recent developments.

"When did this come about?" Startled, Noah inquired.

"I overheard them on the ship last night and contacted Lexi to warn her," Tink replied.

Sighing, "I found out while we stopped at Jareth's island. Jareth assures me he harbors no intention of stealing the pod. Matt lacks the ability to operate it. The rest of his crew sides with us." Lexi informed her father, as Kabe piloting the pad to their ship.

"Do you think you should have mentioned this before

now?" Noah questioned.

"I decided to allow Jareth the benefit of the doubt. If he plotted against us, why would he guide us to his island?"

Shamus and Ricardo ran up to them as Caroline descended the stairs. "What would you like us to do?"

"Wait here. I imagine Jareth plans to disable his ship. Let's see what action he takes next," Lexi stated.

Noah examined the arrow mounted through the propulsion system of the pod. "Very nice." He opened a hatch. Inside lay a number of swords. "Boys, if we need them," he nodded towards the blades, "don't hesitate."

Jareth stood on the deck of his ship, next to Brannon.

Matt and a man unknown to Lexi, walked up to them. She propelled over, landing next to Jareth. "Gentlemen. We need to discuss our working arrangements as I refuse to allow you to steal our equipment."

A man Lexi assumed was Terrence, stared at her wide eyed. "We're aware of the ship following you. Now, who holds authority to enter into binding agreements for the Historical Society?" Lexi stated.

"I do. I'm in charge of this operation on behalf of the Society," announced an elderly chap, crossing the deck holding a cane. He wore a charcoal top hat perched upon riotous gray curls. Decked out in a pinstriped suit with a white shirt, ruffles at the neck and cuffs. Lexi guessed his cane probably held some sort of device. A pair of goggles adorned his hat with several adaptive lens' attached. His shoes appeared normal. "My name is Professor John Hastings, the archeologist of the team." He presented his hand.

"Captain Alexandrea Canatolli of the *Star Sapphire*. I'm in command of this expedition." Nodding towards Brannon, "My first mate, Brannon Mac O'Connell." Lexi shook his hand, as did Brannon. "Prior to attempting to steal our equipment, I recommend highly you travel to Tenochtitlan and the secret chamber we gained entrance to."

"Professor, we discovered the find of the decade, of the century! I already started cataloguing books from the library! It includes dictionaries from over twenty languages, the holy texts from many religions including the *Quran*, the *Torah* and more!" Jareth's enthusiasm bubbled over the tense proceedings. "Somebody transported important texts and art-work from numerous civilizations, preserving them. I found Tolstoy's *War and Peace* down there. Someone stored these items just prior to the flood."

"Really? Is there any indication who?" Professor asked, excitement lighting his eyes.

"The five skeletons might provide a clue," Lexi stated.

"Five skeletons!" A middle age woman broke in to the conversation. She wore a long dress of light green layered, flimsy, flowy material of a flowery pattern. Adorned upon her head lay a flappy hat with big flowers. She carried a parasol in gloved hands.

"One guards each of two entrances, appearing male. Three in the chamber, two adorned as females, one male, seated upon a throne," Lexi described. "Jewels, a crown, apparel indicates Indian, Aztec."

"When can we explore the city?" Asked a young man. He wore a top hat and a navy suit with a bow tie around his neck. A pocket watch hung from his vest. A thin mustache accented his thick lips. Choppy brown hair, worn a little too long covered his ears.

Lexi and Jareth looked at each other. "The hydro-pods allow us to transport one in each and we currently possess one extra underwater suit. Only someone wearing an underwater suit can enter the chamber. The pods prove too large to access the buildings where the tunnels lead to the room."

"We photographed the chamber and developed the pictures. Want to study them now and head down first thing in the morning?" Jareth offered. "That remains dependent upon reaching an agreement, ensuring the safety of the *Star Sapphire,* her crew, and equipment."

"Of course, of course!" The Professor stated, waving his hand, distractedly. "Now, let's study your pictures. Do we just step on this thingy majiggy?" He stepped on the propulsion pad.

"Yes, but-" Jareth started.

"Professor, our orders dictate we acquire a hydro-pod," Terrence stated.

Lexi took a ragged breath.

"Actually, our mission states we acquire and preserve knowledge and technology created prior to the flood. That

126

pledge demonstrates far more importance than Blaine misappropriating a new toy. This discovery proves to be the most significant find in the history of time. We require the hydropods and underwater suits to recover these items. As the highest ranking voting members currently present, the decision resides with Jareth and I. Jareth, do you vote we steal the hydro-pod?"

"No!"

"Professor, do you vote to steal the hydro-pod?" Professor took two steps and turned around, "No, Professor, I do not." He took two steps back and turned back around. "We voted against stealing the pod. Now, step aboard this pad mibob. Let's traverse to the other ship to study the photographs and peruse the catalogue thus far!"

The other two members of the team stepped on the pad. Terrence and Matt's boots contained propulsion units. They elected to propel over to the *Star Sapphire*. Brannon operated the pad. The riders adjusted their balance while increas- ing altitude and propelled towards the airship.

"What a most interesting mode of transport!" Squealed floppy hat lady. She grasped her hat securely to her head, wobbling a little as she gained her equilibrium.

"Gee, thanks! I originally developed the idea for bearing the weight of the hydro-pods while the airship flies. Now, we find all sorts of uses for them!" Tink giggled, as she flew around the pad.

Brannon set down on the deck of the ship and the passengers stepped off. "Wonderful! Wonderful! Now, let's see these photographs!" Professor clapped his hands together.

Jareth looked to Lexi. She shrugged her shoulders. "Let's adjourn downstairs to the library. Shamus! Will you grab the pictures of the site, please? Once in the library, we'll introduce everyone and discuss each person's role." Lexi suggested, leading the way.

Everyone trooped behind her and entered the library. "I'll grab Granny, Mom and Khara," Tink stated. She entered the hydroponic garden and disappeared. A few moments later, they exited through the kitchen and walked into the library.

The *Star Sapphire* crew introduced themselves to the newcomers. Professor repeated the information he provided on the *Mountain Peak.* His primary focus of study included ancient civilizations and performing archeological digs. "This proves to be my first opportunity to accomplish an excavation underwater!" Lexi noticed Granny paying particular attention to the professor.

The lady wearing the floppy hat introduced herself as Miss Gertrude Ramsay, the anthropologist. She specialized in world religions and linguistics. Gertie, as she preferred to be called, barely contained her excitement. "I can't wait to lay my hands on the dictionaries and holy texts!"

The young gentleman, Joseph Baker, the occultist, concentrated on magic, deities, demons and the like. "I'm rather out of my element. I typically work within a library but this unique opportunity provides for untold finds!"

Terrence King, served in the Union Army, as a free black man. When the flood hit, he befriended a scientist fellow and kept him safe during the initial pandemonium. Through him, Terrence joined the Society, offering protection and muscle on excursions.

Shamus handed the photographs to Professor with Gertie peering over his shoulder. They oohed and awed over Tenochtitlan. Individual prints of each building demonstrated the detail and craftsmanship allowing them to withstand the ocean overwhelming the ancient city. The photographs of the temple left the team awestruck. Their excitement became palpable while they deliberated the photos documenting the chamber. Gertie studied rows of books lining the shelves while Professor examined the skeletons. Joseph paid particular attention to the jewelry and scepters.

"What is the procedure for entering the chamber?" Joseph asked, barely containing his excitement.

Jareth explained the process, giving full credit to Brannon for the gelatin. "Ingenious! Simply ingenious! I appreciate the lengths you took to preserve the tunnels, the chamber, the treasures!" Professor exclaimed.

"There's no other way to enter the chamber?" Gertie asked, gazing longingly at the shelves full of books.

Shaking his head, Jareth replied, "Not that we discovered so far. If you think of any ideas, we'd love to hear them. Are any of you interested in swimming to the site in a underwater suit?"

Professor raised his cane, volunteering. "I'm quite excited at the prospect! The suits provide adequate oxygen?"

"Swimming down proved to be an exhilarating adventure!" Granny spoke up.

"You tried it?" Joseph asked, amazed.

"Why, yes! I haven't entered the chamber, yet but I utilize the underwater suit any time possible. I enjoy swimming with the fish! I frequently co-pilot the pods, as well," Granny added. "I find the city an amazing discovery of an ancient civilization."

"Now that we obtained supplies, I'm building additional suits, allowing more people to traverse at a time," Shamus declared.

"First thing in the morning, we ascend to the city, for your perusal. Perhaps, you know of some technology or better option to access the chamber?" Jareth stated.

"Gertie, Joseph, will you ride in the underwater pods? You aren't claustrophobic?" Lexi asked.

Hesitating, "I refuse to deny I'm rather anxious about traveling within a pod underwater, but seeing Tenochtitlan will make the discomfort worthwhile!" Gertie exclaimed. "Who acts as our guide?"

"I'll swim in an underwater suit. Lexi and Brannon, conduct the tours in the hydro-pods," Jareth stated.

Resounding "no" came from all around.

Brannon stated rather forcibly, "I'm staying aboard the *Star Sapphire*."

Lexi and Noah paused and then stated, "Agreed."

"Ricardo pilots the other pod. He demonstrated significant skills in operating the pods and the suits." Numerous responses of "Agreed" encircled the room. "We eat breakfast together and then propel to the city, working until lunchtime," Lexi explained. "Typically, we trade around with the pods and suits. The suits tend to be quite exhausting. At lunch, we'll determine if one of you wishes to swim."

"Speaking of food, dinner's ready," Khara mentioned.

"I am rather famished," Professor commented.

"Let's adjourn to the dining room. Khara hates it when we're late for dinner," Lexi commented, with a smile.

Khara and Granny prepared seared ahi, mashed potatoes, fresh green beans and a salad made up of assorted vegetables. "Your produce tastes delightful! Quite the assortment, so fresh!" Gertie complimented Khara.

Smiling, she thanked Gertie. "I'll show you the hydroponics garden after dinner. Mama Caroline and Mama Mary designed it. Papa Charles and Tink added their genius to it by feeding filtered water and increasing access to sunlight into the garden."

"Which explains why your deck appears transparent! Of course!" Gertie laughed. "I look forward to the tour!"

After dinner, Khara played tour guide to Professor, Gertie and Joseph, showing them the hydroponics garden. She explained the process and identified all the varieties of plants. Granny tagged along, taking Professor aside, showing off her fruit tree orchard. Tink supervised Kabe, Brannon, Matt and Terrence sorting supplies and moving what needed to be transferred into Tink's workshop. Shamus started manufactur- ing the waterproof fabric for another underwater suit in his workshop. Lexi, Noah and Jareth met on the bridge.

"What do you think the threat level sits at this point?" Noah asked Jareth, lighting his pipe.

"Pretty low, actually. Terrence won't move against Professor and I, no matter what his orders," Jareth replied. "Even though Professor's vote scenario seemed hokey, it actually carries a lot of significance. The way the Historical Society hierarchy works, two high ranking members reserve the right to override the President if it's a matter of Society philosophy. The team's visit to Tenochtitlan will result in erasing all doubt regarding this being the most important find in the annals of the Historical Society. Once the team agrees, I want Captain Briscoe of the *El Camino*, the ship following the *Mountain Peak,* to check out the city. When he sees the site, the logistics, the treasure, he'll reinforce our position."

Puffing on his pipe, "Do you believe the risk to the pods diminished?" Noah asked.

Jareth nodded, "Yes, I believe so."

Noah looked at Lexi. "I'm sleeping on deck tonight. If the pods remain in the ocean, I'll sleep next to the railing."

"That's my girl!" Noah smiled. Jareth rolled his eyes and mumbled under his breath.

Tink and Lexi parked the pods on the propulsion pads and disabled them. The team, including Terrence, inspected the pods, remarking on the craftsmanship. Lexi laid out a bedroll between the two vessels. Kabe, Brannon and Noah set up a watch schedule. Brannon showed them the radar settings for the longer range. The ship held its position about an hour away.

Through the night, they maintained supervision over the radar and scanned the horizon using heat sensing lens while Lexi slept in between the pods. The night passed quietly and uneventfully.

12

The next morning, everyone met at the dining room. Excitement spread through the Society team. Professor wore a safari suit but decided against a hat. The helmet erased the need. Gertie wore another dress made up of voluptuous layers of material with a hat larger than the hatch. Joseph rounded off the team adorned in trousers and a billowy, flowing blouse and a derby hat. Breakfast passed quickly with the team and crew ascending to the deck. Jareth showed Professor how to put on the underwater suit while Lexi and Ricardo readied the pods. Lexi noticed Terrence paid close attention to the ministrations performed prior to cast off. Once prepared, Lexi called Gertie over and she crawled up the ladder and through the hatch.

"You may need to remove your hat. I don't believe it fits through the opening," Lexi commented, hiding her smile.

"Oh, my. Are you sure?" She tried to duck in, but the brim proved too extravagant. "Hmm. If I bend this, or maybe, try," she muttered to herself as she worked her way around and somehow entered the pod, with the hat in place, for the most part.

Lexi turned away, fiddling with the controls to keep herself from laughing outright. "Go ahead and take your seat, Gertie."

"What, oh yes, dear." She spun around. "Look at all these gadgets, levers, and buttons! No wonder Matt lacked the ability to steal it." She plopped in the seat. "I'm staying away from the panel!"

Lexi sealed up the hatch and started the propulsion system. "Okay, Gertie. Are you ready?"

She squealed, "Yes! Let's traverse to Tenochtitlan!" Lexi moved several levers and the propulsion pad, along with the pod, levitated from the deck. With a few more actions, the pad propelled forward, clearing the railing then descended into the water. Gertie squealed, partly in fear, partly in excitement as the pod sank into the water.

"Oh my, my, my!" Water rose over the windows. "I see perfectly underwater! No water leaks inside! Oh, it's marvelous!" She continued to make little high pitched noises as Lexi piloted the pod.

"Ricardo, how goes it?" Lexi asked over the communications system.

"We're fine, following behind you." Lexi heard the laughter in his voice and squeals of delight emanating from Joseph. "Professor, what do you think of the underwater suit?" Lexi asked.

"Superbly magnificent! This invention proves to be the most incredible thing I've ever experienced! Once you overcome the fear of breathing underwater, it's glorious!" Professor described. "Exciting! Exhilarating! The freedom of movement!"

Lexi led the way to the city. Before they reached the perimeter, Gertie squeaked with glee. The outbuildings appeared and the temple rose in the distance. "The perimeter of the city lies here. Prior to the flood, a moat encircled these buildings." Pointing to the right, "This building houses one of the entrances to the chamber." Lexi pulled up and peeked through the window. "The trap door lies in the floor. The stairs lead down to a door, through a tunnel and into the chamber."

Propelling around the city, Lexi showed Gertie the buildings they'd uncovered so far, leaving the temple until last. Gertie failed to contain her delight over the detail still intact on the temple. They gazed through the windows, noting the interior craftsmanship. Lexi pointed out the second entrance to the chamber.

"Lexi, Ricardo, the Professor and I reached the city. We intend to enter the tunnel. Want to observe?" Jareth asked.

Gertie and Joseph answered in the affirmative. Lexi and Ricardo piloted the pods to the entrance in the small building. Professor and Jareth swam inside. Lexi activated the appendages, extracting the shield from the pocket. "My word! What a fantastic concept!" Lexi passed the shield to Jareth. He affixed it over the trap door. Once secured, he pressed the trigger, allowing the door to slide open.

The shield expanded into the tunnel. "Okay, now we enter. Afterwards, Lexi closes the hatch door, and extracts most of the water before we add gelatin," Jareth explained.

"Alright," the Professor responded, anxiety crept into his voice. Jareth crawled into the tunnel, the Professor waved to us and followed. Once inside, Lexi closed the trapdoor. Then she hooked the pipe onto the intake unit of the propulsion system.

"I'm activating the intake unit. Are you ready?"

"Yes, we're set."

Lexi flipped the switch and slowly increased acceleration. "Due to the thickness of the structure, we lose contact with them in a few minutes," Lexi stated.

"That's good, Lexi." Jareth stated, his voice scratchy. Lexi turned the system off and unhooked the pipe, while Jareth continued to explain the process. "Now, I add the gelatin and mix it around."

"Once the gelatin gels, they open the far end and climb out. Any water leaking out should be fairly solid. They pick it up and throw it back inside. Then, fold it up. Until they're ready to exit."

The Professor's face appeared at the hatch and waved. "I'm standing in the tunnel without my helmet! I breathe air! The tunnel is tall enough and wide enough for me to stand upright. We're traversing to the chamber! We'll see you in two hours!"

"Bye, Professor. Don't have too much fun!" Lexi replied, smiling. "Shall we continue to explore?"

"Yes, we shall! How did you move all the sand?" Gertie asked. Lexi explained and demonstrated their process. "Ingenious! Using the propulsion system from the pods to remove the debris! Ingenious!"

They spent the next two hours sidling up to buildings, allowing Gertie to examine the construction, peering through windows and doorways, glimpsing interiors. Lexi took time to demonstrate the functions of the hydro-pod. Using the propulsion exhaust, she cleared obstructions from a building still encased in sand. After blowing away debris from the bricks, a

134

vase appeared. She utilized the appendages to pick it up, placing it in the pocket. After several moments, Lexi opened the pocket from inside the pod and handed Gertie the vase.

Gertie almost hyperventilated as she studied the container, running a finger along the design. "Do you know how old this is?" Lexi shook her head. "Centuries! It's been buried for centuries! The hydro-pod found it, picked it up and placed it in the pocket!"

They returned to the little building. "Jareth, Professor, do you hear me?" Lexi asked over the communications system.

A crackling noise sounded in response. "I think they're in the tunnel," Lexi explained to Gertie. The trap door opened and the hatch on the shield exposed Jareth, then Professor. Once they exited, Jareth pulled the shield closed and secured the trap door.

"The treasures stored in the chamber leave me speechless! Better than any of my wildest dreams! Books I only heard of, thought lost to the flood waters! The basic foundations of numerous societies preserved!" Professor gushed. "Gertie, Joseph! You won't believe the objects encased in the secret chamber under the lost Aztec city of Tenochtitlan, beneath the ocean! Jareth and Lexi found it!"

Lunchtime conversation revolved around the objects within the chamber. The society members discussed the wonders they observed and the marvelous feats of invention allowing for it. "The hydro-pod design clearly demonstrates a fascinating piece of technology!" Joseph remarked. "What a remarkable idea to create the appendages. Very useful for picking up items of interest! And the pockets!"

"I agree! But all those levers, switches, knobs and buttons!" Tittered Gertie. "Never in a million years could I operate one!"

"I completed another underwater suit. Three people may swim into the secret chamber, now. But we must determine how to fit three in the tunnel. To elongate the tunnel, I propose we add more underwater fabric." Shamus suggested. "It wouldn't take long."

Lexi nodded, "Let's do that."

Shamus scarfed a few bites then jumped up. "I'm on it!"

"I don't wish to rock the boat, no pun intended, but I want

Captain Briscoe to observe the city and your equipment immediately. He'll understand the importance of your involvement, both the hydro-pods, and the necessity for each substantiated by the most monumental find of the century! Without at least two hydro-pods, it's near impossible to perform the necessary maneuvers required to excavate and recover the items! The importance to society, history, nations, is immeasurable!" declared Professor.

Lexi raised an eyebrow and gazed at Jareth. He met her look and nodded. "Alright, contact him. While Shamus modifies the shield, there's time to wait, pending his arrival. Gertie, Joseph, do you want to utilize the underwater suits?" Lexi noticed Terence stood up from the table, exiting the dining room. "You must, you must! The chamber treasures make the sensation completely worthwhile! Once you witness the discovery, we need to develop a plan for preserving these important pieces of history!" Professor encouraged. "Alas, I fear, I'm too weary to swim again."

"As an archeologist, you'll be amazed at the ingenious invention of the hydro-pod and its usefulness in the science," Gertie stated. "I for one, am completely entranced with the vessel!"

Quickly, the diners finished lunch. Up on deck, Lexi instructed Gertie and Joseph on the underwater suits, helping them to dress. Jareth instructed Professor on the inner mechanics of the hydro-pod. Terrence tried to listen in, sticking his head in the hatch while Jareth explained the controls. A whistle blew off the port bow as a yellow balloon sank down in their vicinity. The *El Camino* arrived.

Brannon stepped off the bridge and hollered to Lexi, "Captain, we received a hail from the *El Camino*. Captain Briscoe requests permission to come aboard."

Lexi nodded. "Permission granted."

About ten minutes later, the Captain propelled aboard the *Star Sapphire* using propulsion boots. Lexi rose to her feet and met him as Jareth exited the pod. Lexi noted Jareth forcibly pushed Terrence towards the meeting with the arriving Captain.

"Captain Briscoe, I'm Captain Alexandrea Canatolli of the *Star Sapphire*," extending her right hand.

Nodding, "I'm Captain Briscoe of the *El Camino*. The *Star Sapphire* appears to be a fine ship. I love your pagoda design for the bridge and lookout."

Lexi smiled. "Thank you. My quarters and a lounge area also lie within the pagoda. Over here, we parked the hydro-pods," leading the way to the propulsion pads where the two pods hovered, tied down.

"Very nice design. They're water tight?"

"Of course," Lexi remarked.

Shamus propelled from his workshop on the *Mountain Peak*, landing on deck carrying the elongated shield. "I finished the tunnel!"

"Terrific! We're ready to descend to the city," Jareth stated.

"Captain Briscoe, Its important that I, too, descend in a hydro-pod," Terrence interjected.

Lexi scoffed at him, shaking her head. "Not at this juncture. The expedition centers on archeology. It is far more important for the archeologist to observe the mechanical effectiveness of the hydro-pod than," Lexi perused him head to foot, "a bodyguard."

Nodding his head, Captain Briscoe agreed. "I require Professor's input regarding this matter, not yours." He won points with Lexi by placing the emphasis of the expedition on the archeological nature.

"Ricardo, pilot the other pod and Professor. Captain Briscoe and I propose to use this one. Lexi, Gertie and Joseph, swim down in the underwater suits." Jareth instructed. "Terrence, wait on either the *El Camino* or the *Mountain Peak*."

Terrence inhaled sharply, but turned and kicked his boots to propel to the *El Camino*. Captain Briscoe looked at Jareth, questioningly. "Terrence made his intentions abundantly clear he plans to abscond with a pod. He's not welcome aboard the *Star Sapphire* when Lexi and I descend. The crew stays busy with their own chores. They don't need to concern themselves with him."

Captain Briscoe nodded. "Well, let's observe this underwater city creating so much excitement within the Society."

Lexi donned her suit and the swimmers entered the water. Both experienced momentary anxiety regarding breathing underwater until they took a small gasp and realized they attained fresh oxygen.

"Oh, my! Why, this, this is wonderful! The freedom of movement! Look at the fish! The plant life! Everything appears remarkably clear!" Gertie squealed with glee.

"What an experience! I never realized how much life existed under the ocean!" Joseph commented, spinning around.

Smiling, Lexi led the way to the city while the two gazed in wonder at the secrets hidden below the sea. Once they reached Tenochtitlan, Gertie and Joseph swam off in separate directions, inside buildings, peering at architecture, mosaics and murals unseen in decades. "Are you ready to explore the real treasures?" Lexi asked, trying to rein them in.

"Yes! Of course!" Gertie swam to Lexi.

Joseph hesitated, torn between examining the temple and discovering the hidden objects.

"If you like, we can enter through the tunnel in the temple. There's a tight corner to turn initially. But both of you remain of small stature and shall fit."

Both exuberantly agreed. Lexi informed the pods and they putted to the temple, behind the swimmers. Lexi led the way through the temple, allowing Gertie and Joseph to investigate the many wonders within. When they eventually reached the room with the secret entrance, Gertie and Joseph watched intently as Lexi placed the shield over the area of the trapdoor, securing it prior to triggering the release.

Turning to them, "Ready?" Lexi asked with a smile. Both agreed affirmatively. Lexi opened the hatch while they observed. The water raced into the shield, expanding the waterproof fabric into a tunnel. Activating the flashlight on her wrist, the interior illuminated. "I'll go in first, then Gertie with Joseph coming in behind. Once we're inside, one of the pods shuts the hatch and extricates the water before we activate the gelatin and exit the waterproof barrier."

Lexi placed both hands on either side of the entryway and pushed herself in, moving around the corner and dropped all the way down the stairs. "Alright, Gertie, you're next."

Lexi felt the movement of the tunnel as Gertie entered. Within, Gertie's mumbling and exertions reached Lexi's ears, while her light helped to illuminate around them." Bumping against Lexi, Gertie said, "Alrighty, I'm behind you."

The tunnel squirmed as Joseph entered and squeezed around the tight corner. The hatch closed behind him and the pod extracted the water, collapsing the tunnel. They shook out the gelatin and jiggled around, mixing it up. After a couple minutes, the gel expanded. Lexi opened the hatch and walked out using her hands to propel her, with Gertie then Joseph following. "Scoop up the gelatin and toss it into the tunnel." Gertie and Joseph helped her, as best they could.

"Shall we continue?" Once Lexi received their affirmations, she led them to the next doorway. Showing them where the trigger lay, she opened the door leading to the hallway.

"The architecture of this structure is phenomenal! It is completely waterproof!" Joseph commented.

"And withstood the weight of the ocean!" Gertie ran her hands along the brick lain walls.

Lexi reached the final doorway leading to the secret chamber, guarded by the skeleton. "This trapdoor took us longer to find the mechanism. A fake trigger confabulated us for a day. Shamus discovered the real lever. Here it is."

The door slid open, revealing a dark room. As they entered and shown their lights around, both exclaimed in astonishment. Gertie ran to the bookshelf, shining her light on the array of titles. Exclamations but no actual words fell as she read through the names. Tears rolled down her cheeks as she looked from one book to the next, pointing and glancing to Lexi.

Joseph studied the objects. He started on the left side, working his way around and then in the center. Taking particular notice of the items worn by the skeleton sitting upon the throne, Joseph eyed them without touching.

Returning to the doorway, he shown his light on the guard. Speaking his first words, "You mentioned another skeleton exists?"

Lexi nodded. "It lies within the other hallway." She felt along the wall, hitting the trigger, activating the door. It slid open, revealing the remains. Shining her light on the pile of bones, she studied it closer. "What the hell?"

Joseph looked over her shoulder, "What's wrong?"

"It's wearing different attire!" Scrutinizing closer, "This skeleton differs substantially from the initial one. The hair appears longer." Lexi splayed her light along the tunnel, it turned left. "By Poseidon's trident, I discovered a new tunnel!" Lexi walked around the bend. She followed it a short way before reaching a dead end.

Feeling along the doorway, air flowed through along the top. Similar set up to the other two doors. She searched for the trigger.

"Lexi? Lexi?" Joseph's voice echoed along the corridor, anxiety colored his tone.

"I'm here." Lexi sighed, returning to the chamber. Now probably wasn't the best time to explore. "I reached another door. Air flows from the other side. No marks indicated the location on our map."

"How many doors lead off the chamber?"

"We thought only two. I accidentally triggered this one." Lexi walked into the room and surveyed it. With a wry look, "It's on this wall." Five feet on the other side of a bookcase against the wall stood the actual doorway. Finding the trigger, the door opened up, exposing the remains. "There he is. Right where we left him."

"I prefer skeletons to stay put," Joseph quipped.

"Me, too." Lexi stated. "Are you two alright? I want to return to the entrance and let Ricardo and Jareth know I discovered another tunnel. Ricardo brought the maps with him. Perhaps, he can ascertain where it travels to or starts."

"We're fine. There's plenty to keep us occupied," Joseph replied, smiling.

Gertie waved a hand, still unable to form words. She completed her initial perusal of one bookcase and began the next. With a pad, she recorded titles and authors, picking up where Jareth left off.

Lexi jogged down the corridor, jumping up the steps until she reached the entrance. "Jareth, Ricardo, can you hear me?" Lexi asked.

"I hear you. Is everything all right?" Ricardo responded, his voice scratched over the link.

"Yes. I stumbled on another doorway out of the chamber!"

"Really? Where is it?"

"Five feet from the small building entrance, to the right. Another skeleton lay outside the door. The corridor turned

140

immediately, then straightens. Around the door, air trickled." Lexi described. "See if any notation occurs on the maps correlating to this."

"I'll look. Professor learned to pilot the hydro-pod and extract sand from a building," Ricardo's voice smiled over the link. "Professor believes completely in the efficacy of the hydro- pods."

"Good to hear! I'll return to the new tunnel and locate the mechanism to open it."

"Do you intend to enter?"

Lexi hesitated. "I don't think so. My primary mission today requires me to guide Joseph and Gertie in and out of the chamber. We must plan for an exploration expedition."

"Okay, see you after a while."

Racing back to the chamber, Lexi found Gertie and Joseph pursuing the same tasks prior to her departure. "I want to locate the trigger to open the door to the new tunnel."

"We're fine here," Joseph replied, taking inventory of the objects. Gertie waved absently in Lexi's direction.

Back at the dead end, Lexi felt around, searching for the spot. After about half an hour, she still failed to locate the mechanism. Frustrated, she stepped back and leaned against the wall.

The wall moved. Not the door, the wall! She spun around flashing her light into the room. A deep, dry musty smell permeated the hall. Items glittered and glowed.

Awestruck, she entered slowly. Gold, ancient artifacts, objects from the Aztecs lay stacked and scattered around the room. The Spaniards failed to ransack this room when they conquered the Aztecs. Unbelieving, Lexi felt along the bricks of the wall, looking for the trigger device. She mirrored her stance against the wall. Her fingertips ran over the coarse stones fingers laid against it. Gently sliding up the bricks she discovered no cracks or protuberances.

She stepped back, shining her light, searching the area. What action activated the wall? She remembered the cold of the stones sunk into her right shoulder. Clicking her microscopic lens into place, she studied the location. The blocks surrounding it bore signs of it sliding back and forth. Placing her weight on it, she pressed hard, but it failed to budge. She

141

braced her left knee against the wall, balancing on her toes. Then she pressed her weight on her shoulder. The brick moved and the wallclosed. *So, that's how it works. Weight on the floor and against the wall at these spots triggers the opening!*

Lexi surveyed the spot on the floor for the second mechanism. The small stone fit evenly amongst the others, completely unnoticeable. Leaning against the wall with her foot on the brick, she engaged the door, parting them, revealing the gold once more. Against the doorway, Lexi gazed about, in awe. Realizing all this gold stockpiled down here, would that knowledge increase the likelihood of someone attempting to liberate one of the pods?

Lexi pondered the thought as she surveyed the contents. Greed brought out the worst in people. The only way to access the gold required the pod and a suit. She sighed heavily. Closing the room once more, Lexi surveyed the wall, searching for other triggers. Air trickled through the doorway which indicated it opened somehow.

Through her microscopic monocular, she peered at the wall, illuminating it with her light. After about half an hour, Lexi thought she found the mechanism. Between the bricks, she discovered a thin wire. It felt similar to the other triggers used to open doors. It only took a few moments of contemplation before Lexi tripped the mechanism and the door slid open, leading down another corridor.

The prevailing emotion at dinner could only be described as exuberant. The Historical Society team members detailed the wonderful sights witnessed at the underwater city. Excited beyond belief, they discussed plans for excavating Tenochtitlan, lost treasures found and postulated how the items came to be located at the bottom of the ocean.

"Is there any way to transport more people to the secret chamber? Can people exit the pods somehow and enter the tunnels?" Joseph savored the lemony dill sauce on the crab.

The brains of the expedition considered the proposition. "If we designed a waterproof tunnel from the pod hatch to the doorway of the corridor leading to the secret chamber," Tink thought out loud.

"Someone in a waterproof suit must assemble it from the oceanside," Shamus continued.

"We need to pump air into the tunnel, inflating it," Tink

stated.

"Swimmers move the tunnel from pod to pod without water entering it, preserving the pods and the corridors." Shamus mused.

"What about removing the underwater suits, placing them in the pocket of the pods and return to the surface for more to swim down," Lexi interjected. "I think we must continue to explore, searching for other tunnels, perhaps other treasure rooms."

"When we obtained supplies, I made sure to procure enough to construct more than plenty of underwater fabric." Tink said, "We continue to fabricate more suits."

"I propose building a multiple passenger hydro-pod!" Professor jumped into the conversation.

"I hate to be concerned about the money, but," Lexi interjected once again, "what specifically is in it for us? We provide the hydro-pods and pilots, maps leading to the city and the treasure room, actual location of the city, actual location of the chamber and how to access it and the tinkerers inventing the technology allowing access."

"We'll provide you with a Letter of Acquisition with a list of merchants. Almost any port you dock, a boat master will provide you with any and all services for your ship. How about a vast array of technology upgrades, like the visual communication system?" Professor stated. "You'll be paid with a trunk full of gold, which we deliver to you immediately. Basically, name your price."

Lexi felt at a loss. His offer seemed more than adequate. Glancing around the table, she saw no reason to disagree with his offer from her crew. "Tink, Shamus, can you start on a waterproof tunnel to run from the pod to the corridor as well as more underwater suits and a multi-passenger pod?"

"I brought a tinkerer and an apprentice aboard my ship. I know they'd jump at the chance to offer assistance on these projects." Captain Briscoe offered. "I also employ two deck hands with promising technological know-how."

Tink and Shamus looked at each other. With some unspoken communication, they reached an agreement and Tink responded, "We appreciate all the assistance possible."

Assignments concluded, the crews headed towards their assigned places. Lexi, Kabe and Brannon followed Professor to the *El Camino* with a propulsion pad to transport the trunk full of gold. Two crew members carried the heavy chest above deck and placed it on the pad. Professor handed her the key. Placing it in the lock, Lexi opened the lid. Various gold items gleamed in the sinking sun. The trunk overflowed with coins, jewelry, goblets and the like.

"Wow," Kabe breathed.

Lexi closed the cover. "Okay, looks good," she smiled. "These four will accompany you back to assist Shamus and Tink." Professor pointed to a young lady and three gentlemen as they approached. "The young lady is Ahnika. The gentlemen are Roger, Geoffrey and Karl." Introductions circled around the deck, then the party returned to the *Star Sapphire*. Lexi took them to Tink's workshop where Shamus and Tink already started working on the waterproof fabric. Kabe and Brannon stowed the chest.

Lexi returned above board. Once she secured the pods, she disabled them as well. Night fell over the ships while Lexi prepared for the morning excursion.

Ricardo brought the maps to the *Star Sapphire*. They searched for any notation marking the corridor Lexi found, to no avail.

"Do you think the Conquistadors missed that corridor?" Ricardo asked, carefully studying the map of the secret chamber.

Lexi shrugged. "Perhaps. It opened in the same manner as the other doors, from the secret chamber. The construction of the tunnel is similar but the trapdoor within the corridor doesn't appear to activate in the same manner as the other two."

"Which direction does it traverse?"

"It takes an immediate turn to the left and travels in this direction," Lexi demonstrated on the map.

"Hmmm. The entrance may originate from another room in the temple," Ricardo mentioned. "Unless the tunnel changes direction." Turning to Lexi with a smile, "It'll be fun to find out!"

Laughing, Lexi nodded. "Yes, it will. Hopefully, we can focus on it while the Historical Society works on the chamber."

144

Ricardo hesitated, "What do you think of the Historical Society?"

Lexi sighed, "I'm reserving judgement for a few days."

He nodded, in agreement. "Actions speak loudly."

"We'll figure out at breakfast who's doing what. With any kind of luck, Tink and Shamus will finish at least the wa- terproof hydro-pod tunnel. Then, we'll go in as well as the team." Lexi rolled the maps up. "Go ahead and take them, if you like."

"Alright, I want to continue to study them." He took the maps from Lexi. "See you at breakfast."

Lexi walked him out of the lookout. Ricardo kicked his new propulsion boots into gear and left the deck. Shamus found spare time to make him a pair after noticing how Ricardo envied the others. Wobbly at first, Ricardo found his balance and leveled off.

Entering the bridge, Lexi checked the radar. No ships showed up. Stars glittered brilliantly across the sky as the moon illuminated the night, both reflecting off the surface of the ocean. A slight breeze blew from the northeast. Everything looked good for the night.

Up one flight of stairs, Lexi entered the quarters she shared with Khara. She stood in front of a mirror brushing her waist length red hair. She wore an emerald green nightdress. The halter top accented her voluptuous bosom as the skirt flared over her thighs. Jareth lay in bed watching her.

His gaze turned to Lexi as she untied the drawstring of her trousers, allowing them to slide to the floor. Releasing the cinch around her waist, she pulled her billowy blouse over her head. She stood before them wearing blue bloomers covering her nether regions and a sky blue bustier.

"Get on the bed." Lexi spoke in a low voice to Khara. Khara flashed her a sultry grin and sashayed to the bed.

She crawled across to Jareth, her rear end exposed to Lexi. "Stop."

Freezing in her tracks, Khara stopped, glancing over her shoulder, smiling wickedly at Lexi. Lexi walked up behind her and nipped her on the cheek of her buttock. At Khara's gasp, she reached her tongue out and licked her clit from behind, slowly sliding her tongue between her labia, over her vagina and up her rear. Khara moaned low, soft and long. Lexi re-

145

peated her ministrations. Again, again, and again. Very slowly. Juices flowed from Khara as she whimpered. Lexi licked up her essence, sliding her tongue up and down her thighs and back to her clitoris.

Khara laid her head on the bed, turning her head to watch Lexi as Lexi slid her arms between her legs, lifting her leg up, spreading her wider, her tongue slowly licking.

Khara moaned, "Oh yes."

Pausing for a minute moment, Lexi met Jareth's gaze.

He laid back on the pillows, stroking his penis, watching the two of them. "I want you inside me."

He needed no further encouragement, jumping out of bed, he moved behind Lexi and slid straight into her center. Grabbing her hips, he pounded into her repeatedly as Lexi continued her gentle assault on Khara's sweet spot and labia, tickling them with her tongue. Khara cried out as her orgasm rushed over her, Lexi joining her as Jareth pounded repeatedly, abusing her vagina until he sank deep into her, moaning roughly as his cum flowed.

It took about twenty minutes before the three recovered. Lexi stood up first, stretching and moaning. "Mmm. Just what I needed." She pulled her trousers on and her blouse.

"Where are you going?" Khara asked tiredly, lying back on a pillow under the blankets.

"I'm sleeping between the pods."

Jareth laughed. "Seriously? Don't you think that's a bit over the top?"

Lexi looked him directly in the eyes and replied, "Nope." She walked over to the closet, pulled out a quilt, smiled at the two of them cuddled up. "Sleep well."

13

An unfamiliar sound of steam propulsion seeped into Lexi's consciousness. Instantly awake, she lay prone between the two pods, identifying the location. It came from over the ocean, above her. She grabbed her low light goggles, quickly pulled her boots on and belted her sword scabbard around her hips. Cautiously, bending low, she moved to the far side of the pod and surveyed the horizon. Three figures propelled towards the *Star Sapphire*.

Standing with the main mast blocking their view of her, Lexi silently climbed to the crow's nest. Two fishnets lay in the basket. She pulled them out as the figures landed on deck. She identified one as Matt and one as Terrence. The third she failed to recognize.

Matt and the other man landed beside one of the pods. Using low light goggles, they studied the connections securing the pod and pad to the deck. Lexi dropped one net on them, covering them both and dropped the second net, further entangling the thieves. Pulling her sword, she kicked her boots into propulsion and headed towards Terrence who stood guard, watching for movement from the pagoda. He wheeled about at the noises from the entwined men.

"Stand down! You trespassed and hold no right to board my ship!" Lexi ordered, hovering ten feet from Terrence, sword drawn.

He glanced at his comrades. They offered no help, from the tangled web. Indecision brushed across his face before he rushed Lexi. Lexi propelled out of the way, parrying his blow. "Jareth! We're under attack!" She yelled, spinning, window height to her quarters.

Terrence turned and lunged towards Lexi, sword raised.

Taller, heavier and stronger than her, Lexi knew her only

147

advantage lay in her agility and speed. He swung his sword in a wide arc, Lexi ducked, bumping his feet with her shoulder, knocking him off balance. As he struggled to right himself, Lexi hovered behind him and kicked him in the head. Swinging wildly, Terrence clipped her forearm, drawing blood. Lexi screamed in rage, flying back, as blood sprayed from the wound.

"Khara! Sound the alarm!" Lexi hollered, chasing after Terrence, avoiding his flailing blade as he struggled to regain his balance. His skill in propulsion boots appeared to be lacking. Dropping low, Lexi kicked his boot, disconnecting the system. Now, one boot flew forward while the other dropped. Unbalanced, his body fell towards the ground, one boot barely supported his weight, his head suspended above the deck. Barely. He swung his sword and Lexi parried the blow, then moved out of range.

Suddenly, the horn blared. "Finally!" Lexi stated. "Drop your sword, Terrence!" She hovered out of reach of his blade as Jareth joined her in the air, propelling to his other side, extending his weapon. Brannon and Kabe rushed on deck, brandishing long swords.

"Surround the two under the nets at the pods!" Lexi ordered as Captain Briscoe, Ricardo, Joseph and additional crewmen responded from the other ships.

"Stop moving!" Brannon ordered, brandishing his sword "If I cut these nets, you're really going to be sorry!"

Captain Briscoe landed on deck. He surveyed the scene: Terrence dangling by one boot while Matt and the other man lay trapped under the fishing nets between the pods. Lexi held her position, blood dripping down her arm. "Whatcha doin' Terrence?"

Terrence turned off the boot propulsion. His head hit the deck and he landed in a heap at Captain Briscoe's feet. He started to stand. "Stay put, Terrence. Drop the sword."

He hesitated. Captain Briscoe swung his sword, alleviating Terrence's sword and hand from his arm. Blood spurted across the deck. "I don't repeat myself. Professor and Jareth made the decision abandoning the plan to steal a hydro-pod from the *Star Sapphire*. It appears you disobeyed that order. Someone bandage his hand so he stops bleeding on their ship."

Khara moved towards him. Lexi grabbed her arm and

148

stopped her. "Don't go near that bastard."

Joseph knelt, removing his cravat and tied it tightly around the stump.

Lexi stood over the nets, sword in hand while Brannon and Kabe carefully removed one and then the other from the trapped men. As they reached their feet, Matt jumped and grabbed Lexi by the leg with one arm and sliced her calf, deeply with a knife in his hand. The other man barreled into Brannon and Kabe, knocking them down. Swinging her sword down, she sliced cleanly into Matt's forearm. He released her foot, but continued to stab at her with his dagger. Lexi parried his repeated stabbing blows until her blade found purchase in his wrist. Matt dropped his weapon as blood gushed forth.

Placing the tip of the sword at his adam's apple, "Put your hands up. Do not make a move or I will cut your throat." Lexi growled, hovering above him. Matt raised his hands, surrendering.

Kabe and Brannon wrestled with their attacker until they overpowered him, pinning him faced down on the deck with his hands bound behind his back and his feet tied up. In the process of subduing him, Brannon smacked his head into the deck several times. "Asshole! Come on to our ship and at- tempt to steal from us? Seriously?"

Captain Briscoe surveyed the captives. "Terrence, Matt, Ronald. We informed you the first priority for the Historical Society included excavating, obtaining and securing the objects stored within the Aztec city. We rescinded the order to steal the hydro-pod. You violated our decree. You trespassed aboard someone else's ship. You assaulted the captain. You attempted to steal an incredibly valuable piece of equipment, to the detriment of the Society's stated priorities."

"We followed the orders of our president!" Matt spat "Can I receive medical attention, please?" His attitude failed to take into consideration the gravity of the situation.

"Two high ranking members of the Society countermanded those orders, per Society bylaws. You stand in violation." Jareth stated angrily. "Jacob, George please retrieve Professor."

Two crew members nodded, and immediately propelled to the *Mountain Peak*. By this time, Noah, Shamus and Tink

149

crept above deck. Tink held a crossbow in her arms aimed at Matt. Noah leveled his and drew a bead on Terrence. Shamus raised his dart emitter targeting Ronald.

Terrence experienced an epiphany, suddenly realizing Captain Briscoe and Jareth's intentions. Taking a shaky breath, "We weren't trying to…"

"Steal *Star Sapphire's* hydro-pod?" Jareth responded. "Terrence, move over here by Matt and Ronald." Following Jareth's order, Terrence sidled slowly to the other captives. He kept his arms raised, blood flowing, falling to his knees.

"Get up! We attempted to perform our orders as per the president," Matt responded haughtily. "What can they do to us?"

"Execute us," Ronald responded in a gravelly voice. Matt whipped his head around gazing at Ronald, to Jareth, finally resting on Captain Briscoe. His severe miscalculation of the situation donned his features. As he studied the events in his mind, his mouth fell, stunned. He turned to Terrence, questioning.

Jareth landed next to Captain Briscoe. Noah moved beside them while Shamus and Tink propelled to Lexi. Khara sank behind her, with a medical bag. Gingerly, she placed a tourniquet on her arm and leg to slow the profuse bleeding.

The two crewmen propelled to the deck with Professor, depositing him between Jareth and Captain Briscoe. He surveyed the scene. "What happened?"

"Apparently, Matt, Ronald and Terrence attempted to steal one or both of the hydro-pods, unaware Lexi slept between the two. They attacked her," Jareth summed up.

A steely look entered the Professor's eyes. "Why did you attack after we countermanded the order?"

"The president offered us a substantial sum to obtain a hydro-pod for him," Matt stated, resignedly.

Leveling his gaze upon the trio, Professor stated dully, matter of fact, "You sold out the priorities of the Society for personal gain?"

The three men froze, offering no response. "I didn't ask a rhetorical question." The Professor continued in the same dull tone.

"We didn't look at it in that light," Matt responded, shakily. Lexi looked to Shamus. He shrugged his shoulders, bewildered

"We do," Professor commented. "The punishment is immediate execution. Agreed?"

"Agreed." Jareth and Captain Briscoe responded.

"Wait!" Lexi broke in. "Execution for attempted theft seems heavy handed. As the person affected by their crime, I disagree. Banishment, imprisonment, loss of a hand seem more appropriate!"

"Their crimes include selling out the stated priorities of the Society for personal gain which we punish with death," replied Professor.

Captain Briscoe drew his sword and beheaded Matt and Ronald.

"Wait! This is not appropriate!" Lexi attempted to come forward, but Khara held her arm, as she treated her injuries. "God damn it, let go of me, Khara! Stop!" Lexi screamed at Captain Briscoe.

But it was too late as Terrence's head disconnected from his body.

In stunned silence, the crew gaped at the carnage. Lexi recovered first. "Clean our deck and get the hell off our ship."

"Lexi, this is a clear violation of the Society's-," Jareth tried to explain.

Cutting him off, abruptly, "Remove these bodies from our deck and get off our ship. We will resume this discussion at a more appropriate time of day. I require medical treatment."

"We'll send our physician over to treat you," Professor offered. Shaking her head, "Don't bother. Just take the carnage and return to your ship." Hastily, the others picked up the body parts, departing for the other vessels. Jareth and Ricardo remained behind. "Go with them, Jareth. I need time to pro- cess this." Lexi stated coldly.

Surprise colored his features, but Jareth dropped his head, nodded, turned and propelled to the *Mountain Peak.*

After they left, Shamus turned to Lexi. "Please, let me stay. I am not a part of the Society and don't want to be, after that."

Lexi looked up at him and nodded. "I believe you." Tink exhaled heavily, relieved. Ricardo looked to Lexi. "I'll go where you order me to. But I want you to know, I am with you, with *Star Sapphire.*"

"Go below deck. You can sleep in the library for tonight." Lexi replied. Ricardo eagerly nodded and stood next to Noah. "What have we gotten ourselves into?" Noah asked, hesitantly.

"In the morning, I'll visit the *Mountain Peak* and discuss our continued involvement," Lexi stated.

"No. Let's do it here. On our turf," Kabe stated. "We defend ourselves here, protect ourselves."

"Let's not place Granny, Mom or Khara in danger." Lexi said.

"We take care of ourselves just fine. Hell, Granny probably single-handedly ended the civil war! You know how handsome Abe looked in a top hat!" Khara retorted. The rest of the crew burst out laughing at her comment. "Tink and I will rig up an offensive and defensive system while everyone travels to the city in the morning. We'll work with Kabe and Noah, keeping everyone else off the ship. Jareth, Professor and Captain Briscoe plan to accompany you, along with the other members of the team."

"I'll help, too." Khara stated. When surprised looks shot her way, "No one suspects a pregnant lady of anything except mood swings and weird food cravings. Hell, if I went to the *Mountain Peak* and asked for gunpowder and pears, they'd asked me, "How much?", give me what I wanted and escort me off ship as quickly as possible."

Another round of laughter came from the crew. "Our secret weapon, Khara, the pregnant lady," Kabe commented.

The next morning, *Star Sapphire* served breakfast above deck. The team, Jareth and Captain Briscoe arrived to eat. Khara and Caroline laid food out and everyone dished up their plates.

"The Historical Society invites you into the exclusive membership. You provide a variety of assets furthering our mission of preserving knowledge, art and technology for future generations. We provide knowledge, funding and assets furthering expeditions at other sites," Professor announced once they began eating.

"No, thanks." Lexi responded.

Silence fell over the table. "Lexi, this presents quite an opportunity for you and your family." Jareth replied. "We share the same goals."

"That may be true, but how we achieve the goals and our priorities obviously differ substantially. We refuse to steal from honest, hard- working people and our first priority lies with our family and the well-being of our family. So, no. We will not accept your invitation."

"Noah, Brannon, Kabe, Tink, Shamus, Ricardo, does Lexi speak for you?" Captain Briscoe asked.

Replies in the affirmation surrounded him from the table. "If you wish me to abandon my workshop aboard the *Mountain Peak,* I completely understand. I request allowances to retrieve my personal belongings." Shamus announced.

Not looking surprised, "You may, of course, gather your belongings. I certainly do not wish to end our working relationship, Shamus, or Lexi. I want to find a way to work together," Jareth responded. "We already proven we're a winning team."

"It's abundantly clear we refuse to be subjected to your rules, laws and punishments. We strongly disagree with the manner in which you handled the attempted robbery." Lexi stated forcibly. "My crew, my family abstain from accountability to your alleged authority. We reject it, we fail to condone it, we decline to be a party to it. Ricardo requested to be considered a member of the *Star Sapphire.* We accepted his request. He is now a member of our crew."

Jareth, Professor and Captain Briscoe paused. "Ricardo, is this true?" Jareth asked.

Without hesitation, Ricardo answered, nodding, "I am a member of *Star Sapphire.* I swear allegiance to them and recognize them as my employer, my captain, my family. Caroline is the closest thing to a mother I've ever known and by far and wide, Granny is the only grandmother I've ever had the privilege of being claimed by. The rest of the crew accepted me without qualms. Jareth, you brought me here, but they made me family."

Silence surrounded the table for several moments. With a sigh, Captain Briscoe responded, "We're sorry to hear this. In our defense, part of the initiation into the Society clearly indicates acceptance of the laws, priorities and punishments stated within the rules. Those men agreed to the terms. They knew the risks associated with the choices they made. I won't apologize for how we handled the situation."

"Duly noted." Lexi stated flatly. "My family, my crew, members of the *Star Sapphire* reject membership to the Historical Society. Any acts against our family, crew and/or members of the *Star Sapphire* will be considered acts of war. Is that clearly understood?"

The members of the Historical Society nodded.

"Now that we dealt with that sticky wicket, we finished the tunnel, allowing us to transfer five people to the corridors. We can transport personnel down in pods and enter the corridors through the tunnel," Shamus stated. "Today, we complete two more suits and start on a third pod. What size do you want the pod to be?"

"Since we finished the waterproof tunnel, we thought a passenger hydro-pod may prove most beneficial to the expedition. Our design carries five passengers and a pilot," Tink explained. She took out a roll of papers and handed them to Lexi.

Perusing the blueprints, Lexi nodded, then handed them to Jareth. "That sounds fantastic!" Jareth smiled, studying the scrolls. "Do you possess what you require to build," glancing at the title of the design, "a passenger hydro-pod?"

Tink and Shamus nodded. "I acquired enough supplies to build two pods, so I believe we already obtained the parts."

"What would it cost for you to build this pod for the Society? Perhaps with less controls allowing someone without genius level of intelligence to operate it?" Captain Briscoe asked. Tink and Shamus looked at each other and then turned to Lexi.

"Calculate the purchase price of supplies and the length of time required to construct it. Do you want your tinkering crew to assist in building it? While assisting, they begin to learn how to perform maintenance tasks and repairs," Lexi suggested.

Nodding, Captain Briscoe replied, "Yes. We appreciate that."

"I vote we commission a passenger hydro-pod from the *Star Sapphire*." Professor proposed while forking a bite of fruit frittata into his mouth.

"I second it and offer the suggestion we commission a waterproof tunnel to accompany the pod." Jareth replied.

"I agree on both suggestions. We reached a consensus and the motion passed. Provide us with the cost of the two items and payment will be arranged, in any form you request."

"Very good. Now, who wishes to swim and who prefers riding in a pod, utilizing the new tunnel?" Lexi asked.

Joseph raised a hand, "I'll swim."

"I request travel within a pod, please," Gertie stated.

Everyone turned to Professor. "As intrigued as I am regarding the chamber and its treasures, I want to explore the city more, from a pod, this morning. As an archeologist, my true love lies in unearthing structures buried by time. The hydro-pod allows a delightful opportunity to excavate all sorts of wonders!" Professor demonstrated remarkable skills at operating a pod the day before, putting around the city, clearing sand from buildings. Gertie chose to accompany him.

"Ricardo and I hope to explore the new corridor and determine its destination, if that's alright," Lexi commented.

"Very good. Yes, please continue your search, discovering where it leads to. There may be other rooms filled with treasure!" Professor declared exuberantly.

Captain Briscoe sighed heavily. "To be honest, I feel a little anxious at the thought of traveling underwater. But I must assess the scope of the project, estimate the cost and identify potential obstacles as we continue forth."

"Ride down with me. After you tour the corridors and chamber, we'll traverse the city," Jareth offered, grimacing. "The breadth of the overall exploration seems incredibly overwhelming."

Raising his eyebrows in surprise at Jareth's admission, Captain Briscoe replied, "Let me procure paper and a pencil to take notes."

Within half an hour the expedition sank into the ocean. The swimmers started earlier and the pods met them as they made their way.

Captain Briscoe quickly overcame his anxiety as he gazed at the schools of fish gliding around. "Incredible! I never dreamed of such a mode of travel!" The swimmers waved when the pods propelled passed. In the distance, structures of Tenochtitlan came into view. "Oh my."

Prior to entering the corridor, the pods waited for the swimmers to assist in setting up the new waterproof tunnel. Jareth made a small circle around some of the buildings. Captain Briscoe stared out in wonder, wordlessly assimilating the magnitude of the city. To date, perhaps a third of the buildings peered out from mounds of sand. To expose the entirety of Tenochtitlan, many more structures required excavation.

"Here come the swimmers. We found the tunnel at the guard station to be easier to access. The one in the temple travels around a tight corner and down stairs in a narrow hallway. For larger people, it proves quite ungainly," Jareth explained. Lexi and Ricardo swam to the pod and removed the shield from the pocket, affixing it across the hatch opening, then extended it through the doorway, over the trapdoor in the floor. Once secured on both ends, the hatch on the pod and the panel covering the entry way opened. Captain Briscoe climbed through as it flowed along with the currents of the ocean but remained in place. After he reached the corridor, Lexi removed the shield from the pod and attached it to the other pod, allowing Gertie to access the secret chamber.

"If we invert the tunnel, can we use it to enter? It's pretty much the same as the shield we used before." Lexi commented through the communication link in her helmet.

Tink responded, "Yes, we built it to work for both modes of transport. Hypothetically, the only thing accidentally entering the pods, would be gelatin."

The new tunnel worked sublimely, transferring everyone into the corridor. Gertie and Joseph continued inventorying items and placed several in bags to transport to the surface. With the waterproof tunnel, it appeared safe to remove objects from the secret chamber. Gertie chose several pieces of jewelry and a vase; pieces not susceptible to water damage, as opposed to books. They discussed which held more value to the Society and prioritized the non-waterproof objects initially.

Meanwhile, Lexi and Ricardo provided Captain Briscoe a tour of the secret chamber and the three corridors. He studied the books lining the shelves. "How in the world did these titles appear here?" Removing one, he opened it, reading the publishing information. "Published in 1860? How?"

Gertie shook her head. "At this point, we don't know. We continued the catalogue Jareth started. Nothing we found provided any clues as to the origins of this library. Based on publishing data, these books appear to be placed just prior to the flood. It seems someone intended to protect this knowledge."

Shaking his head, "Amazing, simply amazing."

Lexi led him through the corridor to the temple and explained the process to gain entry. They located Ricardo in the new hall. Lexi showed Captain Briscoe the triggers she found thus far. Except the gold room.

When they reached the closed door, Ricardo stretched his arm up and felt around the door. "Air seeps through along the top," he commented. "It should be safe, right?"

Shooting him a sheepish look, "I think so. I felt air, too, so I assume the other side appears dry." Lexi replied. She slid her hand along the bricks until she located the loop. "Shall we?"

Ricardo nodded.

"Seriously? You just open the door?" Captain Briscoe reached an arm out, barring further action.

"How else should we do it?" Lexi inquired, raising an eyebrow.

"If water flowed on the other side, air wouldn't blow through the top," Ricardo explained.

"When we initially entered the tunnel from the temple, that provoked fear. We held no knowledge of what lay on the other side," Lexi explained. "At this point, we're fairly confident of what to expect. If you want to wait in the chamber, feel free."

Heaving a deep breath, Captain Briscoe stepped back, then nodded. "Go ahead. This proves how important you are to this project."

The door slid to the left. Shining their lights down the corridor, it turned abruptly to the left. Sticking their heads through, they peered along the brick lined walls. The corridor smelled mustier, older than the others they discovered. Initially, the corridor appeared similar but on further examination, the bricks measured larger. The builders placed a different substance between the stones, fortifying the construction.

"Do you think this corridor was built at a different time by different builders?" Ricardo carefully studied the inlaid bricks.

"Yes, I think so." Lexi shone her light around as she cautiously walked down the corridor. It curved towards the right. That seemed odd. Why would it veer? Why not a straight line? "This construction seems very odd. Did they build the tunnel around something?" Ricardo remarked, as he surveyed the wall.

"I agree. I'm going to count my footsteps, see how this measures out," Lexi replied, retracing her steps back to the door. Once there, she counted off until she reached the ninety degree corner. She continued counting until she reached the next corner. "The two hallways are approximately equal."

"Do you believe a corridor winds around a room?"

"It provides the impression that something exists here," Lexi tapped her finger on her chin, contemplating where a door might be located. Ricardo began searching the bricks, looking for an opening. The entrance to the gold room used a mechanism triggered on two spots, the ground and the wall. It seemed plausible this room operated on a similar mechanism. For the first room, the latch lay near the sliding door. "I'm going to search near the entry way." Ricardo nodded.

Shoulder height, she shined her light and using her microscopic lens, she gazed at the bricks, not finding anything. Lexi studied the floor, searching for a small brick trigger.

She almost made it to the corner when Ricardo exclaimed, "I think I located it! This brick seems to move, but it isn't opening the..." He stopped mid-sentence as the wall separated.

Ricardo seemed to step on the foot trigger as he pushed on the brick, Lexi thought to herself, rushing to the opening. The room housed a musky, animal odor. Shining their lights into the room revealed... nothing. Lexi cautiously entered, il- luminating all around. In a corner to her left, a skeleton hung shackled to the wall, wrapped in chains. No clothes lay in sight. The shackles and chains gleamed silver in the light.

"Are the remains bound in silver?" Ricardo asked, astonished, as he carefully studied the bound figure.

Wrinkling her nose, Lexi responded, amazed, "It appears so." Long chestnut hair tangled around the bones and silver links. "Look at those teeth! The canines are quite pronounced!" This room seemed to be a dungeon. Finding nothing else of interest, they exited the room, closing it back up.

"That was disturbing," Ricardo observed, shakily.

Lexi nodded in agreement. "Shall we continue our search?"

"Yes, let's." Captain Briscoe followed behind, reluctantly. As they turned the next corner, the hallway went another twenty feet and dead ended in a rock wall. "Shall we search for another secret room?" Ricardo asked, gazing down the bleak corridor.

"While you two continue your investigations, I intend to rejoin Jareth in the hydro-pod and finish the survey of the city. Your abilities leave nothing to be desired. Good work!" With that, Captain Briscoe beat a hasty retreat back towards the chamber.

Ricardo and Lexi exchanged a look.

Lexi tried to hide a smile. "Shall we? Hopefully, we discover something better than a dungeon!"

They each took a side and began to look for a trigger. After about an hour of hunting, Ricardo cried out in triumph. "I found it!" Pressing on the wall and floor, he released the opening mechanism and the bricks parted, exposing another room. A pile of bones lay in front of the entry.

Oddly, the clothing encasing the remains reminded Lexi of early New England colonists. Two hundred years prior.

Completely confused, Lexi looked back at Ricardo.

"Is that," sounding bewildered, Ricardo asked, "a pilgrim hat?"

14

"I think so," she exclaimed, surprised. Lexi shined her light inside the completely bare room. Other than the pilgrim. "Another dungeon?"

Ricardo stated, "This corridor leads to the dungeons?"

"Seems like it." Lexi sighed. "My stomach tells me it's almost lunch time. Why don't we return to the chamber?"

He nodded, activated the door to close it and followed Lexi down the corridor. They passed the first dungeon and came to the door before the gold room. Lexi tripped the catch and walked through. Ricardo followed and closed it behind them. As she continued down the hall, Ricardo paused. Turning, she saw him hesitate where the opening lay leading to the gold room. He ran his hand along the wall, his left hand discovered the latch for the door, his right foot pushing the mechanism, activating it. The wall separated. Lexi walked back to him.

"You found the other room?" She asked, shocked. Silently, she wondered how he knew where to search.

Completely speechless, he looked at Lexi and around the room then back and forth. Wandering inside, gazing at items, he finally found his voice. "The bastard Spaniards missed this room!"

Lexi laughed. "My thoughts precisely."

"More gold exists in this room than most nations possess!" Ricardo commented, walking around. "Magic resides in this room."

"Good magic or bad magic?"

"Ancient magic. Sometimes, it's hard to tell which is which," Ricardo murmured, gazing at the treasures. "If I'm making an inappropriate suggestion, please correct me. I believe we need to keep this room to ourselves."

Lexi nodded. "My thoughts exactly. I, uh, discovered it yesterday." Hesitating, "I wish this tidbit to remain between us until we're a little more...," she paused, "certain of the Society's intentions."

"I agree."

"How did you know to search here for an entry?" Lexi asked.

He shrugged his shoulders. "I don't know. Something pointed me to this locale. I just knew where to press to gain entrance into the treasure depository. That's how I found all the triggers down this corridor. I just," he paused, slightly bewildered, "knew."

"Huh. Well, we better return to the chamber."

In the chamber, Joseph held several pieces of jewelry. "There you are. Did you discover anything interesting?"

"The dungeons. One set of remains shackled and wrapped in silver chains. In a separate room, a pilgrim skeleton lay in the doorway," Ricardo informed Joseph. "Kind of unnerving."

Lexi nodded, shuddering. "To say the least. The corridor seems of older construction than the other two."

Intrigued, Joseph responded, "I'd love to see them after lunch!"

Gertie walked into the chamber. "See what?" Ricardo described the dungeons and the skeletons. "Yes, we must conduct an examination upon our return! We focused primarily on transporting items into the pod. We want to ensure the safety of all the objects. Initially, we chose objects water won't damage before attempting to retrieve books."

"The new tunnel works well?" Lexi asked, surveying the work achieved in their absence. Bare spots appeared on the shelves and throughout the room where items had lain before. Smiling brilliantly, "Like a dream! I will however, exchange my dress for trousers at lunch. Climbing through the tunnel in a dress proves to be cumbersome." Gertie replied, grasping her skirt.

"Are you prepared to leave? After you exit, we'll close up the tunnel and shield, following behind," Lexi suggested.

Joseph nodded, "Over lunch, let's regroup and prioritize tasks. Your findings of the dungeons and specimens pique my curiosity. I know the Professor will wish to observe them as

161

well."

The two researchers carried packs into the corridor.

Gertie climbed through the tunnel, into the pod. Once inside, Lexi sealed it. The appendages unhooked the tunnel from one pod and attached it to the second pod. Then, Joseph entered with Ricardo closing the hatch behind him. After Joseph reached the pod, the appendages released it, pushing the tunnel into the corridor, effectively inverting it while Lexi and Ricardo donned underwater suits. The swimmers safely exited the corridor, with no water leaking within. Finally, Ricardo placed the shield in the pocket and the expedition ascended.

Everyone regrouped at the dining table. Ricardo and Lexi described the discoveries in the dungeons.

"Did you disturb the skeletons?" Professor asked.

Both shook their heads, "We left them untouched, knowing you'd desire to examine the specimens as discovered." Lexi replied.

"We need to send for a physician specializing in the study of remains. I want Dr. Barnes-Kilpatrick," Professor stated, as he forked a bite of broccoli into his mouth.

Joseph nodded in agreement. "I concur. With the age of the skeletons in the corridors and the secret chamber, we need to ascertain their identity. Based upon the dated items, the books don't seem to match the time frame of the ruler and his two subjects within the chamber. The remains appear to be someone of great importance. But the specimens in the dungeons sound as if they're much older and their situations show signs of being quite remarkable."

"After lunch, I want to view the dungeons," Professor remarked.

"As do I," Joseph agreed.

"If it's alright with everyone, I wish to stay aboard ship to study the drawings Lexi procured. I'll add the new corridor and dungeons to the map." Ricardo added, "I hope to find something, anything to indicate…" He sighed. "I don't know what I want to find. The maps denote many symbols. Perhaps, I can identify or link up, or…" He ran a shaky hand through his hair. "I'm not ready to return to the dungeons."

Lexi empathized. "That's fine. We appreciate your assistance in every matter. I'll guide them down." Lexi drank her tea. "Ricardo found the access points to the dungeons. Without his assistance, we may not have found the entrances. His work on the maps led us to the chamber to begin with."

After lunch, the team met in the chamber. Lexi demonstrated to Jareth and Professor the access to the dungeon corridor.

"I comprehend how you mistook the entrance to the corridor," laughing, Jareth stated. "It looks similar to the temple corridor. I wonder if any other tunnels lead from here?"

Lexi shrugged as the door slid open, revealing the skeleton guarding the entrance. She stepped back as Professor observed the body. "This one dates older than the ones in the chamber and the other tunnels." Using his cane, he cautiously moved the sparse clothing and inspected the bones through his microscopic lens. "I estimate these bones pre-date the objects within the chamber by approximately two hundred years!" He glanced back at Lexi. "Continue on! Careful stepping over the specimen! We need to leave it untouched until the doctor arrives."

Guiding them down the corridor, she surreptitiously blocked the entrance to the gold room while triggering the next door to slide open. "Notice the size of the bricks? Larger, rougher? The mechanisms work differently than the other passages. Ricardo and I believe construction on this one occurred at an earlier time." Lexi pointed out as the door slid, revealing the next hallway.

"You are correct in your assumption. Very interesting! The construction matches the style and age of the chamber but differs from the two access tunnels," Professor stated as he followed Lexi, peering at the walls.

They turned the corner and zigzagged back towards the direction they just traversed, "This seems odd. Why waste time and energy constructing squirrely tunnels?" Jareth asked. "We wondered as well and started searching for a hidden latch. Ricardo found it over here," Lexi replied as she accessed the clasp, separating the bricks to expose the room. Lexi entered, shining her light on the remains shackled and wrapped in silver chains.

"By the mermaid's tail!" Professor whispered, moving next to Lexi. The other members of the team entered the dungeon.

Luckily, Gertie changed from her flowing skirts to trousers. She fainted. Jareth caught her before she hit the rock floor. "I'll take her to the chamber." He swept out of the room, carrying her down the hall.

Joseph knelt down beside the remains. "More light please." Lexi stepped back, illuminating the skeleton with her wrist torch.

"Hand me your light and I'll hold it, too." Lexi offered. He nodded and gave her his torch. With her arms spread out and a light in each one, she brightened the prisoner. "Before you become too engrossed in this one, do you want to examine the pilgrim?"

The two scholars, looked to one another, torn between studying this specimen versus the other. Reluctantly, they nodded. Smiling, Lexi led the way back into the corridor just as Jareth came around the bend. "We're headed to the pilgrim's dungeon."

Jareth replied, "Alright. I laid Gertie on a pillow. She decided she wants to stay in the chamber for now." He flashed a wry smile.

At the next cell, Lexi triggered the wall, exposing the skeleton lying a little ways within the entryway of the room. She shined the lights on the remains. "A two hundred year old New England pilgrim incarcerated under the lost Aztec city of Tenochtitlan beneath the Gulf of Mexico." Jareth stated, matter of fact, shaking his head, bewildered.

Professor and Joseph stared at the remains, speechless.

Both glanced to Lexi, the remains and back to Lexi.

"I think you stumped them, Lexi." Jareth smirked.

She shook her head, "I just opened the door. Gentlemen?" Lexi prompted them. "What do you want to do now?"

Joseph leapt over the skeleton, flashing his light on it.

Leaning down, he closely peered at the remains. "The hat, apparel, boots. Everything appears period correct."

"Don't touch anything! We must await the arrival of Dr. Barnes-Kilpatrick!" Professor stated. "This may be the mystery of the century!"

"I agree. I'm curious if the specimen truly proves to be a pilgrim." Joseph explained. "Too bad the skeleton lays concealed by the clothing." Scratching his head, "I can't fathom a reason for a puritan to be imprisoned this far south of New

England!"

"Why don't we prepare for Dr. Barnes-Kilpatrick's arrival? He needs light in both dungeons." Professor stated. "The only way to obtain better illumination requires transport of candles and lanterns.

"Which ship is he arriving on? Should we set up a laboratory for him or will he have one?" Joseph asked.

"He travels on the *Washington,* with his own laboratory and team." Jareth replied. "He was excited about the chamber and the skeletons we found initially. With the discovery of the dungeons, he'll be ecstatic!"

"Another Society ship?" Anger edged into Lexi's voice. "When do you expect his arrival and how many "safety" personnel aboard?"

Professor and Joseph turned to Jareth, who sighed deeply. "The *Washington* serves merely as a science vessel. Dr. Barnes-Kilpatrick owns the ship. He uses it for his own, personal expeditions and studies. I assure you, he harbors no interest in the pods whatsoever. His area of expertise surrounds the study of corpses, bodies, skeletons, mummies, the like. I worked with him on other projects. After he tours the chamber, corridors, and dungeons, his team transports the remains to his ship where he conducts his studies of the bodies. Once transferred, he bares no interest in what transpires here. The question he wants answered, who's in the chamber?" Jareth smiled reassuringly at Lexi. "As soon as he hears about the dungeons, however, his focus will alter."

Shooting him a skeptical look, Lexi turned to Professor and Joseph. "I concur with Jareth's assessment. Dr. Barnes-Kilpatrick stays extremely focused on his study of bodies. Like you, he contracts specifically with the Society for individual projects, maintaining his autonomy. His crew serves him and him alone." Professor shook his head. "While intrigued with your technology, he possesses too many scruples to steal."

"What's his expected date of arrival?"

"Probably mid-day tomorrow. When I contacted him, his ship departed from Panama Port headed for Colorado." Jareth replied.

"We better set up more light sources for him," Lexi stated resignedly.

They returned to the chamber where Gertie stood in front of a shelf. "I apologize for my sensitive constitution! I failed to prepare for the actual body of a human who died chained in a dungeon." She fanned herself, as the thought caused her to experience the vapors, again.

"We understand. Rather a shocking spectacle! Not as gruesome a picture, the pilgrim still paints an overwhelming atrocity," Joseph commented, sympathetically.

"A thought occurred to me. If the chamber and the dungeon corridor were constructed prior to the other two passageways, where lies the original corridor leading to the chamber?" Jareth asked, spinning around in the center of the treasure room.

Lexi paused and looked around. "Another corridor exists."

"Are you certain the dungeon corridor doesn't contain another entry?" Professor asked Lexi.

She shrugged. "We searched for a couple hours and didn't find anything else. Ricardo planned to study the maps I obtained to see if he could discern any other passages. Let's see how things transpire once Dr. Barnes-Kilpatrick arrives, but perhaps, Ricardo and I can continue to search for corridors. We seem to be pretty effective at locating them. Whether intentionally or unintentionally," Lexi said with a wry smile.

"I will communicate with the pods and instruct them to ascend to the surface and return with lanterns and candles to illuminate the dungeons and the chamber pending the doctor's arrival," Joseph stated as he moved towards the corridor leading to the small building.

"As much as I desire to study the two prisoners, I better focus on the books," Professor announced.

Jareth and Lexi glanced at each other. "I'll utilize the time to search for another corridor," Lexi said.

"As will I." The two studied the room. "It appears to be octagonal in shape. The initial three corridors each originate at a side." Jareth observed. "Shall we start searching this wall?"

Nodding, Lexi replied, "Sounds good to me."

"How did you trigger the corridor before?" Jareth asked after several minutes.

"I tripped it like the other two. But I fail to see a similar mechanism on this wall," Lexi replied. They searched two more sides to no avail, before the first pod arrived with the load of lighting equipment.

Joseph crawled back and forth in the tunnel between the pod and corridor, transferring lights from the pods. Lexi and Jareth carried the items into the dungeons and the chamber.

"I wonder if enough oxygen exists to burn candles and lanterns, not to mention all the people breathing down here? This area represents a closed system without any way to generate oxygen." Lexi pointed out.

Everyone considered her query. "Let's assign this task to Tink and Shamus. Perhaps, they possess the knowledge to create a pump to increase the oxygen output." Jareth shrugged, "It seems simple considering their inventions utilize oxygen processing."

Lexi nodded, as she continued to distribute lighting equipment.

"May we load books to transport to the surface?" Gertie asked, a hopeful expression etched on her face.

Nobody disagreed. Lexi grabbed a stack of books, winking at Gertie and headed towards the pod. As lighting equipment left, books took their place, leaving barely enough room for passengers. Once they unloaded and reloaded, the team returned to the surface.

On deck of the *Star Sapphire*, Gertie took a commanding stance pertaining to the handling of the books. Discussion surrounded the shelter and storage of the multitude of titles.

Captain Briscoe and Gertie stood toe to toe vehemently discussing their safety.

Taking stock of the situation, Lexi broke in loudly. "What about the *Mountain Peak*? The ship is new, with a beautiful empty library allowing easy inventorying and monitoring, without co-mingling with personal collections."

Jareth hid a smile, "I agree. All my personal books still remain in my chests. My library shelves hold nothing but dust. It provides the perfect spot to maintain the treasures of the chamber."

Gertie nodded vigorously. "It's imperative to protect the entire collection and keep it together! Jareth's ship offers the perfect option!"

"I disagree. The Society owns the *El Camino*," Captain Briscoe butted in.

"Yes, but the Society doesn't control this venture. It's a joint project between the *Star Sapphire, Mountain Peak* and the Historical Society. My ship furnishes the perfect solution, as the Society owns a part of it, I own most of it and am a high ranking, voting member. Captain Canatolli agrees. Professor, Joseph? Your opinion?"

"Our quarters lie aboard the *Mountain Peak*. This provides us ample opportunity, access and control. As the team appointed by the Society, I believe the *Mountain Peak* yields the perfect receptacle," Professor acknowledged. "I agree," Joseph replied.

"You're outnumbered," Jareth pointed out to Captain Briscoe. "The overwhelming opinion dictates the treasures rest upon the *Mountain Peak*."

He huffed angrily, walking away.

The crew worked at loading the books onto a propulsion pad and delivered the cargo to the *Mountain Peak*. Meanwhile, Lexi descended below deck to discuss a machine to generate oxygen with Tink and Shamus. After conversing, they determined a generator could easily be rigged, providing all the oxygen necessary.

Two Society tinkerers gleefully took on the task while the rest worked diligently through the night and next morning fabricating and building the passenger pod. Lexi and Jareth volunteered to assist. Tink assigned tasks to them within the pod, bolting seats down and other chores within their abilities. Noah and Brannon worked on fabricating the outer hull while Shamus installed the communication system. Tink built the propulsion system and the Society tinkerers installed it as she designed and incorporated a simpler control panel. Other skilled crew members assisted with metallurgy, mechanics and propulsion.

Kabe and Ricardo camped between the pods, pouring over maps of the city. Crew members not otherwise assigned loaded illumination devices into the pods under the watchful eyes of the cartographers.

Granny and Khara delivered snacks and drinks to the tinkering workshop, the map designers and the library builders. Joseph checked on everyone and settled in to assist the cartographers with changes to the map and attempting to locate other unknown corridors, chambers and the like. Professor and Gertie spent the evening sorting and inventorying the treasures brought up from the ocean floor, assisted by others from the *El Camino*. A sense of urgency enveloped everyone with the impending arrival of Dr. Barnes-Kilpatrick.

The next morning, all the members of the expedition broke for a quick breakfast, after grabbing a nap. Finishing the passenger hydro-pod proved to be the highest priority, with the oxygen generator and illumination devices delivered to the chamber coming in a close second. Lexi understood how to operate the oxygen generator as it worked on similar principles to the pods and the *Star Sapphire's* oxygen distribution system. They unloaded the illumination devices in the chamber while Lexi set up and started the oxygen generator.

Everyone else continued work on the passenger hydro-pod. Radio contact with Dr. Barnes-Kilpatrick placed their estimated arrival just after lunch. His airship caught a favorable wind and sailed rapidly to the rendezvous point. After hearing about the mysterious dungeon corridor, Dr. Barnes-Kilpatrick ordered the experimental solar panels engaged, increasing their speed. He reached the other ships in time for lunch

At first light, Kabe and Ricardo relocated to the bridge. Once the doctor's ship appeared on radar, they announced his arrival. As the *Washington* pulled alongside and dropped anchor, the pods broke the surface as well as the swimmers in underwater suits. Dr. Barnes-Kilpatrick, along with his crew, stood along the deck, watching the pods dock and the suits propel to the top deck. Tink maneuvered the passenger hydro-pod out of the drop door on the side of the *Star Sapphire* and onto the top deck. She exited the pod in a flourish and using her propulsion boots, she flew to the *Washington*, inviting them to lunch. Needless to say, the *Star Sapphire* impressed the newcomers.

Dr. Barnes-Kilpatrick, his captain, Captain Daniels, and expedition leader, Rock Reynolds climbed aboard a propulsion pad and journeyed to the *Star Sapphire* where Khara served a lunch causing a king's mouth to water. He peppered questions regarding the chamber, dungeons and technological miracles they witnessed as they pulled alongside the airships. Once they finished lunch, Tink piloted the passenger hy-dro-pod with travelers Dr. Barnes-Kilpatrick, Captain Daniels,

Rock, Professor and Captain Briscoe. Lexi, Joseph and Jareth swam down in underwater suits with the two pods following. Ricardo and Shamus rode in one while Brannon and Gertie operated the other. Everyone met in the chamber.

Dr. Barnes-Kilpatrick and his people expressed amazement as they gazed at the chamber. Immediately, the doctor gravitated to the three skeletons in the chamber. Lexi opened the corridor leading to the dungeon. He performed preliminary inspections of each specimen, with Rock taking notes. Paying no attention to the other objects, he surveyed the remains guarding the other two entrances.

Indicating the skeleton at the beginning of the dungeon corridor, he noted, "This skeleton appears about two hundred years older than the other five. His mode of attire is reminiscent of the Aztec natives pre-dating us about two hundred years. Remarkable."

"If you think he appears remarkable, wait until you see the other two. In the dungeons," Lexi stated with a sly smile. She led the way down the corridor, showing him the levers to access the next entry. As they moved through the second doorway and turned the corner, Dr. Barnes-Kilpatrick stopped. "This makes no sense. Why does the hallway turn back towards the way we came?" He questioned. "It seems like a waste of resources."

Lexi continued to the trigger point. She accessed the mechanism and the bricks slid apart, exposing the first dungeon. Entering, Lexi illuminated the room with her torch and lit the candles and lanterns set up earlier. The doctor entered the room and gasped as he gazed upon the poor soul wrapped and entrapped within silver bonds.

"By Neptune's trident!" He placed his monocle to his eye and peered closely at the skeleton. He surveyed the manacles binding the wrists, the long chestnut hair reached below the shoulders, silver chains circled 'round and 'round the body. "The canine teeth protrude significantly! Move the lights closer!"

Lexi obeyed, placing the lights semi-circle around the remains, allowing for intense scrutiny. "The bones appear to be approximately two hundred years old. No clothing covers the body. The chains and shackles seem constructed of silver."

He glanced to Rock. "Make a note to determine the amount of silver whether it's one hundred percent or a mixture of other elements. Shorter than average phalanges bear nails longer than typical upon the fingers and toes. Your dagger, Rock."

Rock withdrew his dagger on his belt and handed it to the doctor, handle first. The doctor used the blade to move the hair back, displaying the skull. The head appeared elongated with the nose and mouth more animalistic than human. "Land be with us. I believe this may be a werewolf! Wrapped in silver, the snout, canine teeth, claws! The body unclothed. We need to compare body measurements and bone structure to humans and wolves. The skeleton appears female." Awe whispered into the doctor's monologue. "I believe this discovery proves to be the first documented werewolf skeleton ever!" Dr. Barnes-Kilpatrick low voice conveyed the importance of the prisoner. He didn't disturb the bones, only the hair. "We need to photograph the remains prior to performing any action or moving it. Allow no one in this room without my express permission! Has anyone touched the remains?"

Lexi shook her head. "No. We understand the importance of preserving specimens in the precise condition discovered." A wide smile crossed his face, "Perfect! Thank you. As much as I want to remain here," the doctor paused briefly, "let's investigate the other corpse you encountered."

She exterminated the lights after everyone vacated the room. Leading the way down the corridor, she lit the lights outside the opening into the second dungeon. Triggering the mechanism, the bricks spread, revealing another room. A pile of bones lay almost in the center of the room. Quizzically, Lexi studied it before gently leaping over the corpse, to light the room. The pilgrim hat lay in the center of the room, the clothing and boots all faced away from the door.

"Why is there a pilgrim here?" Dr. Barnes-Kilpatrick bellowed. "Is this a prank? I find no humor in the scenario!"

"Sir, it's no prank. We found the pilgrim here, trapped in this dungeon, below the city of Tenochtitlan." Jareth explained. "That's why we asked for you, specifically. We require your expertise to find answers to the mysterious inhabitants of the dungeons."

The doctor glared at Jareth and then whipped his head around to Lexi. Lexi knelt down, studying the skeleton. She looked up to Joseph and Professor. As everyone entered the room, taking care around the remains, they waited for Dr. Barnes-Kilpatrick to begin his preliminary assessment.

"Is this... This isn't..." Lexi hesitated.

Professor shook his head.

"Weren't the bones in middle of the entry way when we left yesterday?" Joseph asked, looking at Lexi.

"I thought so," She answered softly.

Dr. Barnes-Kilpatrick looked at Lexi and Joseph. "Did someone move these bones?" He demanded.

"The opportunity for someone to move the skeleton didn't exist," Lexi stated, bewildered.

Warily, he looked at Lexi and moved closer to the corpse. Placing his monocle to his eye, he studied the attire, bones and boots, intently. "The clothing appears time appropriate. The rate of decay for the apparel and skeleton indicates," he hesitated, "placement close to two hundred years ago." The clothing, hat and hair obscured much of the bones from view. He sighed deeply, "I refuse to move anything prior to photographing the scene. I'm unable to determine much at this point, and hesitate to speculate at all. Finding a pilgrim this far south seems," he paused, searching for the appropriate term, "highly unlikely. No explanation comes to mind. Rock, we need a camera, measuring stick and evidence containers when we return tomorrow."

Rock nodded, making notes. Dr. Barnes-Kilpatrick moved around, bending, stretching, twisting and turning, trying to observe as much as possible, without disturbing the remains. Sighing in frustration, "I can't glean any more knowledge unless we move the corpse. Let's return to the surface to prepare everything required for tomorrow, now that we understand what the situations entail."

172

15

The next morning, Dr. Barnes-Kilpatrick's party and the expedition team met at the pods and travelled to Tenochtitlan. The doctor decided to focus on the remains wrapped in silver, initially. His team spent the morning photographing the scene, ensuring complete documentation of the dungeon and its inhabitant. By lunch, Dr. Barnes- Kilpatrick deemed it permissible to transfer the skeleton in a pod.

Meanwhile, the team continued cataloging and moving books for transport to the staging area within the *Mountain Peak*. The pods ascended multiple times to unload the precious cargo. Thrilled by the magnitude of the written treasures, Gertie frequently squealed with delight, while Professor reminded himself to continue loading, instead of reading. Lexi, Jareth and Ricardo proceeded with attempting to locate other corridors off the chamber, to no avail.

After lunch, the photographer returned to the dungeon to photograph the pilgrim while the rest of Dr. Barnes-Kilpatrick's team remained aboard, beginning work on the silver encased skeleton. The afternoon and evening passed without incident or new discoveries.

Someone opened the door to Lexi's bed chamber, entering low to the floor. "Unless you wish to find a dart impaled within your body, identify yourself immediately!" Lexi growled lowly, trying not to disturb Khara.

"Lexi! Glad you're awake!" Shamus whispered. "You need to come to the dark room."

"Now? Seriously?" Lexi relaxed, a little.

"Yes, now. And bring Jareth. You must see this. Keep your lights off. Sneak down. Don't let anyone know you're awake," Shamus said softly. He opened the door and exited the room, creeping downstairs.

"What's that about?" Jareth whispered, rolling over, kissing Lexi.

"I don't know, but we better find out." Lexi slid off the bed, grabbing a negligee and a sword, she crawled to the door. She clicked her low light monocle in to aid her sight.

Groaning, Jareth followed her off the bed and slipped his trousers on. Pulling his sword from his scabbard, he crept after Lexi. "Is it okay to leave Khara?"

"I'm booby trapping the door. Don't enter without me," Lexi informed Jareth, as she fiddled around near the door.

"Alrighty, thanks for the warning."

The two made their way downstairs and to the small room on the lower deck housing the dark room.

"Sorry for the subterfuge. Dr. Barnes-Kilpatrick heard I can enlarge and prepare color photographs. He requested I develop pictures for him of the specimen wrapped in silver." Shamus sighed and handed them large, color prints of the remains.

"His ship contains a dark room. Why did he request you make copies?" Jareth asked as he took the pictures. Lexi stood beside him, studying the pictures after he did.

"I think he wanted confirmation."

"Confirmation? Confirmation of … Wait, let me see," Jareth glanced back to the pictures Lexi held. Lexi looked at the photograph in his handed and sorted through her pile until she found a similar one. They compared the two prints side by side.

"What in the fires of hell! Is there, there is…" Lexi stuttered. Comparing the pictures, minute differences became obvious. Shamus' enlargements accentuated the growth. Tissue formed on the bones. Tissue formed on dead bones. One picture showed clean white ribs. A later picture showed tissue stretching across and between the ribs.

"It appears the bones experienced cell growth." Shamus stated, softly. "You are my captains. I informed you of my discovery."

Lexi grabbed the pictures from Jareth's hands and turned angrily towards the door. "Lexi!"

She whirled around. "You should probably dress a little

more appropriately. The doctor may suffer a heart attack if he viewed you in your present attire." Jareth stated with a sexy smile.

Lexi glanced down, as did Shamus. A navy silk night dress fell to her thighs, accentuating her breasts. Shamus averted his eyes, his first acknowledgement of her apparel. Rolling her eyes, Lexi turned and exited, taking the stairs, two at a time, quietly. Once on deck, she continued to her quarters, not bothering to crawl. She disarmed the trap prior to opening the door. Quickly, she threw on a shirt and trousers, not bothering with a corset. She placed her belt and scabbard low on her hips and slid her sword in. Then, pulled on her propulsion boots.

Jareth dressed quickly beside her.

"What the hell are you two doing?" Khara asked, sleepily.

"Nothing major. The doctor asked us to come and discuss his findings. He's too eager to wait 'til morning. I'll trap the door behind us, honey," Lexi answered softly.

"Be quiet when you come in or sleep in the lookout," Khara replied, yawning as she rolled over, burrowing under the covers.

"Alright, baby." Lexi re-set the trap as she and Jareth left. They propelled to the *Washington*. Lights glowed from several different cabins on the ship.

Jareth pointed to a set of lights, Lexi followed, carrying the pictures. He rapped on the door. The doctor answered. When he saw them, he sighed, glancing to the ground. He stepped out and led them below deck. They walked through a maze of hallways until they reached a steel door with a lock. Dr. Barnes-Kilpatrick pulled a key from a vest pocket and unlocked it. He swung it open for them to enter.

The barren room held only a steel table. A variety of instruments hung along the wall. The opposite wall held a collage of pictures of the skeletal remains. The photos ranged from the dungeon wrapped in chains to the laboratory, to the bones minus the silver, to tissue growing.

Numerous light fixtures swung from the ceiling. He inhaled deeply, as he stared at the empty table.

Patience failed to be Lexi's best virtue. Many members

of her family, if not all, stated patience wasn't a virtue Lexi possessed, even at a minimum. "What the hell do these pictures indicate?" Her voice expressed anger tinged with fear.

Sighing, "I'm not sure. I never saw anything like this before. I've never seen..." His voice became shaky, then calmed after a couple breaths, "I never encountered a skeleton comprised solely of bones, regenerate tissue." He took a couple more breaths, then continued, "I don't know if it was, is alive." Lexi and Jareth gaped at him. "Where is the... specimen?" Lexi asked as she gazed around the room.

Dr. Barnes-Kilpatrick heaved a deep breath and slowly exhaled. "It disappeared about three hours ago."

"What do you mean, 'the bones disappeared'? Bones lack the ability to rise up and walk away independently!" Lexi yelled, completely shaken.

Hesitating, the doctor replied, "These bones may have."

Silence drowned the room.

Jareth recovered first. "Are you saying, these bones regenerated tissue, organs, muscle, a brain, stood up and walked out?!" He ended in a high shriek.

Speechless, Dr. Barnes-Kilpatrick, nodded resignedly.

As realization of the information and the situation dawned on Lexi, she spun around and kicking her boots into propulsion, literally flew through the maze of the *Washington,* and landed aboard the *Star Sapphire.* Brannon slept between the pods. Lexi kicked his boots to wake him up.

"Search the deck for anyone not of our crew! Now!" Not waiting for an answer, she then propelled to her quarters, disarmed the door, "Khara! Below deck, now!"

Khara sat up, completely disoriented. "What?!"

"Just throw on a robe and run below deck into the library, right now!" Lexi's tone left no room for argument or objection. Khara grabbed a robe and raced after Lexi. At the bottom of the stairs, Lexi placed Khara behind her as they descended to the lower levels.

"Everyone to the library, now!" Lexi pounded on her parents, Granny, Tink, Ricardo and Kabe's doors. She heard muffled responses. Entering Granny's room, she helped her into a robe, covering a negligee causing her to blush crimson. She pushed her into the library, next to Khara and returned to her

176

parents' room. They met her at the door, both in robes. "Library, now!" Not hesitating, she ran to Tink's room. Shamus received less than twenty minutes of sleep. Tink threw a robe over her jammies as she pulled him out of bed and dragged him to the door. "Library!" Lexi ordered as she closed the door, heading to Kabe's room. He met her in the hall. Ricardo stumbled into a chair.

Once everyone gathered, Lexi took a few moments to breathe. "Don't allow anyone we fail to recognize by name aboard ship. Period."

"What's happened?" Noah questioned, concerned.

Lexi sighed, shaking her head. "You won't believe me." "The bones wrapped in silver grew tissue and began to reform into a human, or being, or whatever," Shamus stated, shakily.

Bewilderment, disbelief, fear, astonishment flashed over the faces of the assembled crew. "It's true." Lexi replied. "Somehow, the bones began to regenerate. As of now, the whereabouts of the skeleton appears unknown. The mobility, ability, agility, motivation of the… thing is unknown. Khara, Granny, Mom, Dad stay here in the library. Lock the door behind us. Brannon started a search above deck. The rest of us will search below. Once we clear our ship, we'll go from there."

Noah stepped to the front and nodded, locking the door as they exited. The rest of the crew separated, Kabe and Ricardo searched the library level while Tink and Shamus headed below to her workshop. Lexi returned topside to assist Brannon. It took about thirty minutes to ensure no outsiders boarded the *Star Sapphire*. Jareth radioed he intended to stay aboard his ship to conduct a search. He declined any assistance. Brannon, Kabe and Lexi set up a watch for the remainder of the night.

The next morning, the ship captains, the team and Dr. Barnes-Kilpatrick met aboard the *El Camino*. After searching all the ships, no intruders, strangers or unidentified bones were discovered. No one reported any incidents or mishaps.

"Exactly, what do you know, at this point, Dr. Barnes-Kilpatrick, regarding the corpse?" Lexi asked.

Scratching his head, Dr. Barnes-Kilpatrick summarized

his findings, "We ascertained the skeleton belonged to a female. She appeared to be approximately twenty-five to twenty-eight years old, five feet two inches in height, dark brown hair. Bone structure revealed Anglo-Saxon descent."

"Did the bones truly display signs of regenerating tissue?" Captain Briscoe interjected hastily.

Dr. Barnes-Kilpatrick removed the photographs from his tweed carrying case. He handed over the enlarged color pictures Shamus developed the previous evening. "Thanks to the darkroom abilities of Shamus, we obtained these enlightening pictures." The team and the two captains studied them. Pronounced exclamations proved to be forthcoming in a matter of moments.

Professor studied the pictures using a magnifying glass while Joseph peered through a microscopic lens monocle. "It does appear tissue reformed along the bones," Professor acknowledged, awestruck.

"Based on lore, we believe these remains belonged to a werewolf," Dr. Barnes-Kilpatrick stated. "To my knowledge, this proves to be the most scientific study ever performed upon a werewolf skeleton."

"Could the werewolf," Gertie twittered, "be alive?"

Shrugging his shoulders, "The evidence indicates tissue began to regrow on the bones. If tissue reformed, then it indicates some type of existence surrounded the skeleton. I don't know if the being possesses the ability to regenerate muscle, organs, blood, arteries, veins," Dr. Barnes-Kilpatrick hesitated slightly, "consciousness."

"According to lore, silver paralyzes and harms a werewolf," Joseph informed the group. "As a means of self- preservation, perhaps the werewolf entered into a hibernation state. Once the silver chains were removed, the werewolf regained consciousness and her ability to regenerate, kicked in."

"What length of time is required to reform an entire body?" Captain Briscoe questioned as he compared photographs.

Shaking his head, "No idea. Completely new area of science. Without photos as proof, I would refuse to believe it possible."

For the first time, Rock spoke up. "Once our team removed all the silver from the remains, this picture documents

178

the unadorned skeleton." Pointing to the photo Joseph held, "The photographer snapped that picture about two hours later. Within two hours, her body showed that level of regeneration."

"Removing the silver bondage seemed to be the catalyst for the regeneration?" Lexi clarified.

Dr. Barnes-Kilpatrick and Rock nodded.

"Could someone steal the remains?" Professor asked. "The value of this discovery appears immeasurable."

Dr. Barnes-Kilpatrick and Captain Daniels exchanged a look. "It's possible, but I don't believe likely. No one other than our crew lives aboard the ship. We travelled together for years and I trust each and every one of them. We failed to secure the laboratory. We accounted for the whereabouts of our crew members during the time the bones disappeared."

"I vouch for my crew," Lexi stated unequivocally. "And Jareth."

"My crew joined her crew and are accounted for," Jareth replied, flippantly.

The group turned to Captain Briscoe. "I'm unable to account for all my crew members and won't vouch for them. We searched crow's nest to belly, bow to stern and discovered nothing. I'd suspect my crew of stealing the silver chains before stealing bones," Captain Briscoe remarked wryly.

"Joseph, as an occultist, what's your take on this?" Lexi inquired.

"I desire to perform research regarding werewolves. Aside from what I already mentioned, the knowledge I possess coincides with Dr. Barnes-Kilpatrick's evidence. If amenable to Captain Canatolli and Dr. Barnes-Kilpatrick, I request to peruse your libraries for documents and books containing more information regarding werewolves. I intend to pass on today's expedition to the secret chamber. I think this line of study requires a hasty response."

"Feel free to access our library," Lexi spoke without hesitation.

Dr. Barnes-Kilpatrick nodded in agreement. "We already pulled the books mentioning werewolves for further research. One of my research assistants worked through most of the night. Feel free to compare notes with Maria."

"Very good. I'll start with Lexi's library, to cover as much information as quickly as possible," Joseph replied.

"What plans do you hold for the expedition team and Dr. Barnes-Kilpatrick's team today?" Lexi asked.

"A werewolf running amok fails to deter us from exploring the most important discovery the History Society ever encountered," Professor remarked, then glanced to Dr. Barnes-Kilpatrick. "Doctor?"

"Agreed. Excitement overwhelmed my team to begin studying the pilgrim. We intend to enact far more extensive security protocols, especially aboard ship," he announced.

"Very well. With Joseph staying aboard, there's a spot for an extra person, Doctor, if you want to send another along," Lexi pointed out.

"Actually, we travel with a historian on board specializing in the pilgrims and the New England colonies. He may possess valuable knowledge, benefiting the study of the other dungeon inhabitant," Captain Briscoe offered.

"Mr. Henry Lancaster?" Jareth asked.

Nodding, "Yes, he joined us in Albuquerque."

"He specializes in that time period and civilization," Jareth reiterated, approvingly.

"Very good. I want an expert's opinion on the authenticity of the remains," Dr. Barnes-Kilpatrick replied.

"Identify the personnel traveling with us, grab your supplies and let's head out in thirty minutes. We intend to track visitors coming and going from our ship and continue to maintain a night watch," Lexi informed the group. Looks of surprise met her announcement. "My grandmother and a pregnant woman reside aboard my ship." The looks melted towards understanding.

Thirty minutes later, members of the expedition party met by the hydro-pods. Divided amongst the passenger hydro-pod, hydro-pods and the underwater suits, they descended to the chamber. Lexi led the way to the second dungeon which incarcerated the pilgrim. When the bricks slid apart, the re- mains lay against the opposite wall.

"That thing moved! When I first entered the dungeon it rested in a different position than now!" Lexi exclaimed. "Initially, it lay right in front of the entry way. I leapt over it the first time I entered. Now, it's situated against the wall!"

Mr. Lancaster shot an annoyed look at Lexi. "Now, really dear. You mustn't let this business of the werewolf affect your tender sensibilities. The pilgrims proved to be kind, god-fearing people. They worshipped a loving, gentle god, shying away from anything surrounding the occult or supernatural." He stated in a condescending tone.

"I wonder if all the people they accused of witchcraft share your opinion." Lexi decided she didn't like him, instantly. He walked in and knelt to study the skeleton. Dr. Barnes-Kilpatrick's team set about snapping photos while Lexi arranged the lights, then stepped back as they began their studies. Mr. Lancaster inspected the attire closely, noting the workmanship of the stitches through a magnifying glass from his hat to his leather shoes. He took notes with a lead pencil. Even the buckles fell to his scrutiny. "May I move him?" He directed his question towards Dr. Barnes-Kilpatrick.

"Yes, we thoroughly documented the position of the specimen," the doctor nodded.

Mr. Lancaster removed the top hat, exposing the skull.

Moving the light, he inspected the inside closely while the doctor peered intently at the skull through goggles. He adjusted the lenses several times, before satisfied.

"Anglo-Saxon descendent, appears thirty to thirty-five years of age. Black curly hair, teeth in excellent shape." Dr. Barnes-Kilpatrick mumbled while one of his assistants wrote down his observations.

"Inside the hat, a label indicates the maker. Baker & Sons, London, 1615. Remarkably well preserved," Mr. Lancaster noted. "May I remove the cloak?"

Nodding, "By all means." The doctor stepped back relinquishing space to Mr. Lancaster.

Kneeling down, he worked at the ties around the neck bones, finally releasing the garment. The remains lay partially on top of the cloak. A white billowy shirt encased the torso and arms, while black breeches reaching below the knees, obscuring most of the skeleton from view. Mr. Lancaster studied the clothing, intently, peering at the stitching and ties, survey- ing the ruffles at the throat and hands.

"Remarkably, everything appears authentic. With no moisture, insects or sun, the fabric preserved incredibly well. I hypothesize a pilgrim landed in Mexico aboard a ship blown significantly off course. May I study the articles of clothing and any personal effects further?" Mr. Lancaster remarked, rising.

"Of course. Once we undress the remains, we'll send the clothing and accoutrements to you. Our only interest lies in the bones," Dr. Barnes-Kilpatrick replied. "What say we transport this fine gentleman to my laboratory and study him further."

"Agreed."

The doctor's assistants carefully placed the body in one of the waterproof bags, carrying it to the passenger pod.

After Mr. Lancaster, Dr. Barnes-Kilpatrick and his group ascended, Gertie and Professor started on the books, again. Meanwhile, Lexi and Jareth tried to locate another passage way, to no avail.

Lexi began to wonder about the gold room. Could the original tunnel to the secret chamber originate from somewhere within? The construction of the corridor indicated its creation occurred prior to the other hallways. The openings triggered differently. The manner of construction suggested the dungeons were additions, not part of the original structure. Nearing lunchtime, Lexi decided to speak with Ricardo and determine if he discovered anything on the maps.

By transporting books and objects from the room to the pods, Lexi and Jareth assisted Gertie and Professor. Once on board the *Star Sapphire*, Jareth propelled over to check on Dr. Barnes-Kilpatrick while Lexi located Ricardo in the lookout with Kabe.

"Any luck?"

They shook their heads, grimly.

"We searched throughout the chamber to no avail. I think I know where it might lay." Lexi shot a knowing glance to Ricardo. He nodded in agreement.

"We went over the maps extensively. You and Jareth physically searched. Where else could it be?" Kabe questioned, dejectedly.

Hesitating, for a few moments, "We kinda found another room we failed to mention to anyone."

Kabe shot a look at Ricardo. "You and Jareth?"

Shaking her head, "No, Ricardo and I. We discovered a room the Spanish Conquistadors overlooked during their invasion. It overflows with gold objects."

Staring at her open mouthed, "Overflows?"

"It proves difficult to walk through."

"We decided to wait, pending our developing relationship with the Historical Society," Lexi replied.

Kabe looked back and forth between them. "Who all knows?"

"Just us three."

"What is the oldest building within the city?" Ricardo asked.

Lexi thought a moment. "I have no idea. Perhaps Professor might be able to identify which one. Why?"

"We could try searching the building for a trigger. It's only a hunch but the original tunnel seems far older than the rest of the corridors. It stands to reason it originated in an older building," Ricardo replied. "Did anyone search the dungeons for hidden corridors?"

Lexi shook her head. "No, Dr. Barnes-Kilpatrick, his team and Mr. Lancaster's sole focus resides on the prisoners. Let's check the dungeons. Are you coming down? You developed quite a skill locating hidden corridors, trigger mechanisms and dungeons." Lexi flashed him a winning smile.

Ricardo hesitated, then nodded. "The dungeons freak me out. But I don't believe the conquistadors discovered them, the gold room or the original corridor. The maps led us to this point. Now we need to locate the rest of the Aztec hidden sites."

"Good luck with that. I'll stay here, guarding the ship and family," Kabe grinned. "Swimming to a city under the ocean and scouting for hidden tunnels beneath the city, fails to fill my cup of tea!"

Jareth landed on deck, propelling over from the *Washington*. Lexi yelled down to him and he climbed the stairs to meet them. "How are things in the laboratory?"

"Mr. Lancaster continues to study every stitch of clothing while Dr. Barnes-Kilpatrick and his team photograph and measure every nuance of the skeleton. Crew from the *El Camino* built security measures into the laboratory and they setup a guard schedule." Jareth, hesitated and sighed, then glanced at Lexi. "Are you certain the remains moved from a different location?"

"Ricardo, when we initially opened the dungeon, where

183

did the pilgrim lay?"

"Directly in front of the entrance. We both leapt across the skeleton to access the room," Ricardo replied. "Why?"

"Today, the bones rested against the far wall. The entry way opened unobstructed."

"Yes, I am definitely not traveling down there! Have any of the other remains relocated themselves?" Kabe shivered.

Lexi shook her head, "Not that I noticed. Did Dr. Barnes-Kilpatrick and his crew think the bones changed placement?"

"Half do, half don't. He changed their protocol. Now, pictures will be snapped immediately upon finding a specimen. A camera became standard gear for his expedition, as of this morning," Jareth explained. "I reinforced your observations. In fact, I'll apprise them of Ricardo's recollection, as well."

"What about the pictures taken yesterday?" Lexi questioned.

With a wry look, "The photographer apparently messed up. None of the pictures developed appropriately." Jareth explained. "Are you two returning to continue the hunt for the original corridor?"

Ricardo nodded. "We just discussed where to focus our search."

"We decided to start in the dungeons. We don't believe the corridor is there, but we looked everywhere else."

"Alright. I might check the dungeon corridor again, see if you missed something." Jareth paused, then asked, "Ricardo, at some point, could you examine the secret chamber again? You demonstrated quite a talent for finding hidden rooms."

He nodded as Jareth kicked his propulsion boots, returning to the *Washington*. Ricardo glanced at Lexi. "Let's wait and see if he finds it," Lexi replied with a wry look. They climbed down the stairs.

Professor and Gertie waited at the pods with Brannon. "May we utilize the passenger hydro-pod? We can transport more items in the larger pod since less passengers accompany us," Professor inquired.

Lexi replied in the affirmative. "In fact, Let's remove the unnecessary seats, providing more space." Lexi suggested.

184

Gertie clapped her hands with glee. "Wonderful!"

Climbing in, Brannon unhooked three seats and handed them out the hatch to Kabe. Kabe placed them on the deck out of the way. Lexi, Ricardo and Jareth suited up and dove into the ocean while modifications occurred aboard the passenger pod.

They reached the underwater city as the pod entered the water. When Gertie and Professor arrived, the search for the original corridor already commenced.

Jareth scoured the brick walls while Lexi and Ricardo started in the dungeon holding the werewolf. The lights remained after the crew transferred the skeletons to the laboratory. They carefully studied the bricks and floor, looking for the variety of trigger types discovered in other parts of the underground structures.

"Here's something," Ricardo indicated on the wall. Pushing a brick, resulted in a section of the wall rolling out, like a drawer.

"That's different," Lexi commented, standing up and walking over to the section of the wall. A number of items lay concealed in the hidden compartment. A thick gold chain with a canine tooth set as a pendant, a gold band held a large ruby, a leather bound small book laid on top of a folded dress and a pair of leather boots. The style of dress hailed to early colonial period.

"Jareth, come look at this!" Ricardo called out.

Searching the first section of the corridor, he responded quickly. "Ricardo located a drawer of sorts, storing clothing and belongings of the werewolf!" Lexi stated, excitedly.

Jareth raised his eyebrows in surprise. "Really?" Shining his light into the drawer he gazed at the contents. "Huh. Interesting. I'll take the trinkets up. Mr. Lancaster will be unable to contain his excitement," flashing a smile.

Lexi rolled her eyes. "Let's continue our search of each dungeon." They picked up where they left off, discovering several small cubby holes with assorted items, probably from other past prisoners. Moving into the pilgrim's dungeon, their search revealed nothing.

"I assume they wouldn't leave him unbound if any hidden holes existed in his cell." Ricardo reasoned. Lexi nodded in agreement. Exiting the dungeon, they encountered Jareth in the second corridor.

"Any luck?" Lexi asked. He shook his head. "We're returning to the chamber to look for triggers similar to what we discovered in the dungeon."

"Okay. I'll be here."

The rest of the day revealed no new discoveries. Dinner and the evening passed uneventfully. In middle of the night, Kabe's voice sounded quietly across the communication system. "Lexi? Jareth?" Jareth groaned, and Lexi responded with a mumble. "Um, two people just left the *Washington* in a row boat."

Lexi groaned and Jareth mumbled, "Contact the *Washington* and ascertain their knowledge of the departure."

"Alright." The link fell quiet for several moments. "The bridge reports awareness of the departure. They appear to be on a date."

Laughing, Lexi responded. "Thanks for your diligence, Kabe."

"Sorry to bother you."

"I'd rather be safe than sorry," Jareth murmured. "Since we're awake," he nuzzled her neck. Lexi rolled on top of him, spearing his penis into her vagina and rocking slowly, back and forth. He moaned softly as she slowly rubbed her clit along his pubic bone, his cock sliding in and out. Juices flowed from her, dripping down his testicles. Unable to stand it any longer, he grabbed her by the hips, holding her still and pounded repeatedly into her. She tried to suppress her moans, not wanting to wake Khara while Jareth rammed into her. The best way to quell her cries, she decided included engaging her mouth in some kind of activity. Sucking Jareth's nipple and encircling her tongue around it, his skin muffled any sound. He held her hard against him, burying his face within her hair as their orgasms flowed together.

Sated, entangled in each other, they drifted back to sleep. The early morning watch belonged to Lexi. She quietly rose, showered and dressed. Kissing Khara and Jareth, she exited their chambers and climbed down to the bridge. "Mornin', Kabe. Did the love birds make it back yet?"

Shaking his head, he laughed. "No, not yet. I apologize

for waking you." He handed her a hot cup of tea.

"Mmm. Thank you. I'm glad you did. With all the insanity occurring, we can't be too careful." She sipped her tea, "Anything else unusual happen?"

He shook his head. "I wore my night goggles all night. The two lovebirds were the only thing I saw. Interestingly, one of the people in the row boat? Their body temperature registered significantly cooler than the other."

Laughing, "A scantily clad woman?" Lexi hypothesized.

"I feel like a cad, busting them!"

"Get some rest. Who knows what adventures today may hold."

Kabe left the bridge, heading below deck to his quarters. Gazing at the radar, Lexi scanned for ships, but none other than the four registered. She wondered if the row boat should show up, but wasn't sure if the radar acknowledged objects, magnetic interference or some other scientific thing a majig beyond Lexi's understanding.

Placing her goggles on, one low light lens and one heat seeking lens, she kicked her boots into propulsion, and conducted a circuit around the ship. Nothing untoward showed up. Where did the row boat row off to? Lexi considered performing a perimeter check around all the ships, but worried about tripping their individual watches.

Considering her options, Lexi paused and then propelled to the bridge. Activating the local communication system, she announced to the ships, "*Star Sapphire* intends to perform surveillance around the circumference of the ships. Does anyone object?"

The *El Camino* and *Washington* responded in acquiescence of the patrol. No response emanated from the *Mountain Peak,* as Jareth slept aboard the *Star Sapphire.* Lexi immediately rose above the airships and propelled at least one hundred feet away. Flying by the *Washington,* she observed one row boat missing. She checked around the other ships and peered into the early dawn as far as possible. No row boat in sight.

Landing on deck of the *Washington,* she approached the bridge.

"Good morning. I'm Captain Canatolli of the *Star Sapphire.* Who took your row boat?" Lexi questioned the mate commanding the bridge.

He looked at her, confused. "What do you mean? Our row boats are accounted for."

"Look through low light goggles. Your row boat left between one a.m. and four a.m. Two crew members on a date? Our watch observed and called your bridge?"

He laughed, "No... I think you suffer from confusion."

- "No. You appear uninformed. My watch observed the boat leaving. It's gone now. Call Captain Daniels and Dr. Barnes- Kilpatrick, immediately."

He hesitated.

"Immediately!" Lexi demanded.

The mate activated the intraship communication, contacting the captain and the doctor. Within less than two minutes both reached the bridge. "My watch observed your row boat leave your ship between one a.m. and four a.m. this morning. Kabe contacted your bridge and verified the departure. Just now, I performed a perimeter search and see no sign of the boat. Is everything all right?"

"I authorized no one leave of the ship," Captain Daniels responded, worry creeping across his features.

"Let's check the laboratory!" Dr. Barnes-Kilpatrick announced, rushing downstairs. Lexi followed, drawing her sword. Below deck, she grasped the shoulder of the doctor, moving passed him, cautiously but quickly jogging to the laboratory. Outside the door, a crew member slumped againstthe wall, a pool of blood puddling under the body.

Checking his pulse, Lexi turned to the doctor, shaking her head. Motioning to Dr. Barnes-Kilpatrick to stay back, Lexi leaned against the wall, grabbed the door knob and flung the door open. She whirled around and entered the room. The doctor flipped a switch, illuminating the room. Blood splattered against the walls and floor. The remains of what could barely be classified as human lay upon the floor with body parts strung throughout. The stench of blood and excrement permeated the air. As Lexi surveyed the scene, she realized more than one body fell to the brutalization. Nothing living remained in the laboratory. Dr. Barnes-Kilpatrick activated a lever on the wall, sending a loud alarm, ship wide.

"How many staff worked in this room? Who is unaccounted for? What happened?" Lexi shrieked, fear overcoming her. She rushed out of the room and through the maze of corridors until reaching the deck then propelled to her ship, activating their alert signal. Rushing to her quarters, Khara and Jareth lay snuggled together.

"Khara, below deck, now! Find Dad! Jareth, get dressed!" Activating the ship communication system, "Brannon, Kabe, Ricardo, Tink, Shamus to the bridge! With arms! Everyone else to the library!"

Groaning, Khara rose. "I really hate my slumber disturbed. Two mornings in a row? Really?" Lexi threw a robe around her and led her below deck while Jareth dressed and grabbed his sword.

"What happened?" Noah herded Caroline and Granny to the library.

"Something terrible aboard the *Washington*. I'm not sure yet. Keep them safe until we determine what occurred. Only us onboard our ship!" Lexi replied as she slammed the door. "Lock it!"

Shamus, Tink, Ricardo, Brannon and a very sleepy Kabe met Lexi at the stairs leading to the top deck. "The *Washington* suffered a catastrophe. The row boat failed to be an innocent date."

Kabe moaned softly, "No."

"We don't know what happened, but at least three died. The boat seems to be missing. I assume they're identifying bodies and unaccounted for crew." Lexi filled them in as they reached the deck.

"Perform a perimeter check. Stand guard at each point until we receive more orders. I'll head to the *Washington*."

Jareth met them on deck. "Will you and Brannon come with me to search my ship?" Jareth asked, looking at Lexi. They nodded and followed behind him. "I want to begin at the bottom deck." He hesitated. "Lexi middle deck, Brannon top deck, if you please."

They both nodded in agreement and went to their assigned places. Within minutes they met above deck, clearing his ship. Lexi whistled to Tink. Tink and Shamus propelled to the *Mountain Peak*, taking a stance at bow and stern, with Brannon at the bridge. Lexi and Jareth propelled to the *Washington*.

The captain and doctor met them on deck. "A guard stood outside the laboratory. My third team worked on the pilgrim remains. Two of the four man team make up the massacred bodies within the room. Two are missing. The unaccounted crew members appear to be Katerina de Marco and Karl Chekov. Third mate David McCormack manned the bridge when your watch contacted us regarding the row boat. His mental status," Dr. Barnes-Kilpatrick paused, "appears to be," pausing again, "afflicted."

"Afflicted?" Lexi asked. "What the hell do you mean, 'afflicted'?"

"He seems to be experiencing severe disorientation," Captain Daniels, replied.

"The pilgrim remains?" Lexi questioned, hesitantly.

"Also unaccounted for."

16

The four captains devised a perimeter and set up a series of overlapping watches between the ships until the sun rose. The *Washington* was the only ship to suffer losses of life. As the sun illuminated the oceanscape, the four captains, first mates, Dr. Barnes-Kilpatrick and Professor met aboard the *Star Sapphire.*

With a heavy sigh, Dr. Barnes-Kilpatrick noted, "Obviously, our security precautions proved ineffective. The *Star Sapphire* observed the perpetrator leaving the ship. Unfortunately, we underestimated the abilities of the specimen. We allowed our desire for knowledge to supersede common sense. Five crew members paid the ultimate price."

"Should we look for the row boat?" Jareth asked.

"I don't truly understand how our radar works, but I searched for the row boat when I came on watch duty at four a.m. It failed to show up on the display. I didn't see it when I performed the perimeter check around all the ships within a few minutes, using low light and heat seeking goggles." Lexi informed everyone.

"Which direction did your watch observe it sailing in?" Captain Briscoe questioned.

"I'll trade places with Kabe. He can answer your questions," Brannon stated, propelling to the ship. Within moments, Kabe landed at the captains meeting.

"The row boat set out in a northern direction, about 2:30 am. I only saw two people aboard." Kabe paused. "A third may have lain prone in the boat. The person opposite the rower, displayed a significantly cooler heat signature than the rower."

"Probably due to activity level," Captain Daniels pointed out.

Lexi asked, "What did you discover about the pilgrim?"

Captain Daniels looked at Dr. Barnes-Kilpatrick, who tried to disappear. Once all eyes turned on him, he responded. "Based upon the carnage in the laboratory, the pilgrim appears to be a vampire."

Loud exclamations of fear, disbelief and anger overwhelmed him. Raising his hands in the air, "When Jareth returned and stated a second crew member believed the remains changed position and moved, we instituted extra precautions. But apparently, not enough."

"In our research, we discovered vampires enter a state of hibernation if they fail to partake in blood for an extended amount of time. My hypothesis surrounds the belief once the skeleton came into close proximity with living beings, filled with blood, the hibernation period…" he paused, "ended. The beast slaughtered at least three of our crew. The lore states vampires possess the ability to compel victims to perform actions against their nature. I believe the vampire compelled our mate to cover the escape with the two crew members as hostages or unwilling accomplices. As of now, the mate still exhibits significant confusion and disorientation."

Silence surrounded the meeting. Lexi finally spoke. "We need to set up a watch on each ship and a perimeter around all ships. Myself and my crew volunteer to serve. This situation demonstrates we need to proactively protect each and every ship and the entire expedition. Obviously, these creatures exceed our understanding and capabilities."

"I concur," Jareth replied.

"As do I," Captain Briscoe acknowledged.

Professor nodded, "Agreed."

Peering at Dr. Barnes-Kilpatrick, Captain Daniels stated, "For the sake of my crew, I support your suggestion."

"Of course, whatever we need to do to ensure the safety of everyone. I appoint Captain Daniels as my proxy to work with the rest of you setting up arrangements." Dr. Barnes-Kilpatrick agreed. The rest of the captains appointed proxies to work setting up arrangements.

"I intend to return to Albuquerque to pick up crew mebers and supplies in a day. Provide me with a list of needs or if you require crew to be dropped off or picked up," Jareth announced.

Lexi hid her surprise. This was the first she heard of Jareth leaving the expedition. "I'll inform Tink and Shamus. One or both of them may wish to accompany you or at least, provide you with a list of items to obtain. Let's divide into two groups, if possible. One group devise a watch protocol and the other group decide upon an expedition plan."

"Do we need an expedition plan?" Captain Briscoe asked. Lexi retorted, "Dr. Barnes-Kilpatrick, what do you intend to do? Bring up another skeleton for study? The other examinations transpired very encouragingly," she responded sarcastically. "To date, we let loose a werewolf and a vampire into the modern world."

Her response effectively quieted Captain Briscoe. Dr. Barnes-Kilpatrick hesitated and replied, "I want to continue my studies, yes. I agree we need to take better precautions. We obviously mishandled the last two specimens."

"Why don't those of us involved in the expedition head up to the lookout to discuss priorities and the next course of action," Lexi suggested. "The rest, develop a watch detail for the ships."

Nodding, everyone made their way to the appropriate place. Kabe notified Joseph and Gertie while Brannon dealt with setting up guards for night watch.

Once the expedition members reached the lookout, Professor declared, "We need to enact a greater stance upon safety. The beings we discovered, pose a substantial risk to the party, crew and expedition. We lost two of the specimens and five crew members. Are there any," he paused, searching for the correct word, "abnormalities anyone noticed with the other skeletons?"

No one replied. Lexi shook her head. "The remaining corpses seem to be," trying to find the correct terminology, "not dead as long? Not trapped down there for such an extended period of time?" Looking to the doctor for assistance, "Suffer from the non-living state for a shorter time frame?"

"We understand your point. Have you or your crew noticed them changing positions or moving?" Dr. Barnes-Kilpatrick asked.

"No, the remaining specimens behave appropriately for skeletons," Jareth remarked, looking towards Lexi.

193

She agreed. "They maintained their positions and provided us no reason for concern." Lexi replied. "But, I suggest performing a more thorough study prior to moving them to the surface. I realize my suggestion flies in the face of your empirical analysis in a controlled setting, but for safety sake…," Lexi allowed her comment to trail off.

"I performed a preliminary check of the objects, searching for cursed or magical items. Nothing indicated any concern, but I'll return and re-examine everything," Joseph volunteered.

"Did you study the items we found in the werewolf dungeon?" Lexi asked.

Surprised. "No, I didn't realize you discovered anything!"

Jareth broke in quickly, "I'll bring the items by. We failed to find another corridor to the secret chamber. But we decided to continue searching based on the triggers discovered in the dungeon. We found no hidden compartments in the pilgrim's dungeon. I imagine the focus remains on the chamber."

"We want to continue to remove the books and objects. Already, we relocated most of the inventory to the *Mountain Peak*. Since Jareth intends to return to civilization, perhaps we need to speed up the transferring process. I intend to travel with him, studying the books while he garnishes supplies," Gertie offered.

"I prefer to stay. If it's alright with Lexi, I intend to work in a hydro-pod continuing to excavate the city. The hydro-pod provides a fascinating mode of uncovering the sunken city," Professor stated.

Lexi felt torn between Jareth and Gertie leaving with the objects and books. With everyone occupied elsewhere, Lexi and Ricardo gained the opportunity to explore the gold room without interruption. However, Jareth possessed the objects and books. Of course, she held the secret of the gold room.

Smiling, Lexi replied, "Sounds like a plan to me. Ricardo and I offer our assistance in moving items from the chamber to the pods."

"How much study do you recommend we perform in the chamber prior to moving the specimens?" Dr. Barnes-Kilpatrick asked Lexi.

Hesitating, "From someone with no knowledge of the occult or the study of human remains, I suggest stripping off the clothing and observe the bones for several hours at a minimum, before transferring to the laboratory. Both situations may have been averted if longer periods of observation occurred prior to transferring them."

Shaking his head, "To record empirical data, the study needs to occur within our laboratory, where we control as many variables as possible," Dr. Barnes-Kilpatrick disagreed.

"And how much empirical data did you collect in your laboratory prior to the remains disappearing and killing your team?" Professor asked the doctor. "I concur with Lexi. At a minimum, the skeletons need to be undressed and scrutinized for a significant length of time to preserve life and learn the appropriate manner in which to maintain possession of the bones."

Dr. Barnes-Kilpatrick sighed, dropping his gaze to the floor.

The rest of the team voiced agreement, including Captain Daniels.

"Take whatever tools, instruments, cameras and personnel you need to preserve the integrity of your findings," Lexi stated. "The pods leave in thirty minutes."

The members returned to their ships in preparation for departure. Lexi informed Ricardo about the new approach the expedition party intended to use towards the secret chamber. With their help, hopefully the books and objects would be cleared out by the time Jareth planned to pull up anchor.

They reached the chamber prior to the pods, as the rest of the team loaded gear for Dr. Barnes-Kilpatrick. Jumping into their tasks, Lexi and Ricardo carried pre-packed items to the entrance, awaiting the arrival of the pods.

Once the hydro-pods materialized, the doctor's gear and team unloaded, then books and objects transferred on. Gertie and Professor packed items while Joseph performed aura analyses prior to loading.

195

Dr. Barnes-Kilpatrick chose to hold off studying the remains wearing the jewelry and crown, seated upon the throne. Instead, he focused on one of the guards. After snapping a number of photographs, an assistant removed the adornments and scant clothing. A table had been brought down. Laying out the bones, the team began their preliminary study. Two crew members, one at the skull, the other at the feet began a thorough evaluation using microscopic goggles. Lights illuminated the skeleton. A third crew member jotted notes observed by the other two. Dr. Barnes-Kilpatrick monitored their actions and kept a close watch, ensuring the bones failed to move, regenerate tissue or perform any action atypical of a skeleton. After lunch, Dr. Barnes-Kilpatrick and his team deemed the bones safe to transfer.

The team transported most of the contents of the chamber to the *Mountain Peak*. Professor, Gertie and Joseph decided to move everything, then Gertie intended to inventory and catalogue the items while the ship sailed to port. The team estimated the rest of the items could be transported by tomorrow. That evening, the crews determined who travelled with Jareth and provided him a list of supplies to obtain. Shamus and Tink devised a list based upon the orders placed by the Historical Society and Dr. Barnes- Kilpatrick. Of course, the doctor desired a passenger pod along with a number of underwater suits. The waterproof tunnel attached to a pod allowing access to the corridors, instantly became popular to the individuals uncomfortable with the underwater suits.

Khara and Caroline decided to accompany him as well. Kara wanted to find a physician to examine her and the baby. Granny chose to stay. She found Dr. Barnes- Kilpatrick incredibly handsome but rather standoffish. Meanwhile, Professor seemed to be more adventurous and entertaining. This proved a rare opportunity for Granny as two eligible bachelors travelled in her vicinity!

By lunch the next day, the team moved all the objects to the *Mountain Peak* and Dr. Barnes-Kilpatrick cleared two more sets of remains to transfer to the laboratory. With the shelves cleared, Ricardo and Lexi focused their search for another corridor along the areas previously concealed. Since a number of the doctor's crew remained behind, ensuring the non-movement of the specimens, Lexi and Ricardo waited to explore the gold room.

Jareth settled his passengers and readied the airship to leave by the next morning. He borrowed members from the *El Camino* to assist in the operation of his ship until he recruited more sailors.

A couple hours prior to quitting time, Ricardo located a hidden latch, previously concealed behind books on the shelves. Once he triggered it, a portion of the wall slid away, revealing a room. Shining lights inside displayed walls covered in artwork, piles of rolled up canvas and sculptures exhibited on ledges and tables.

"Look at this!" Ricardo exclaimed, slowly entering the room.

Lexi jumped up from her place on the floor and gazed in for herself. "Oh my. Impressive!"

The members studying a skeleton rushed over to view the discovery. "Wow! That is some find!"

Curious, one of the team walked in and shown a light on a specific painting, studying it closely. "Do you know what this is?" Pablo questioned, shock flowing through his voice.

Lexi and Ricardo looked at him, shaking their heads. "This is *The Scream*, thought to be destroyed in the flood!" Glancing around the room, Pablo moved towards another canvas. "This is a Picasso, that, a Rembrandt! What are these paintings doing," waving his arms, "here?"

"Don't ask us. We have no idea. We merely locate the secret rooms," Lexi replied, peering at the works of art displayed.

"Is there an art historian onboard one of the ships? These need to be handled with specific care!" Pablo inquired, carefully studying a Picasso through a microscopic monocular.

Shrugging her shoulders, "Not that I'm aware of. I'll let Jareth know to bring someone back with him."

"Let me see the camera. I'll snap pictures," Pablo gushed. "Remarkable, simply remarkable!" Another person handed him the camera and he took photos of the room, including as many pieces as possible in each photograph. Once he finished, his mates deemed one set of bones safe to transfer to a pod and they returned to the surface, while part of the team remained behind, supervising the last skeleton.

Lexi and Ricardo decided to enter the gold room. They removed lights from the dungeons and set them up to provide illumination. The glittering gold almost blinded them.

As they inspected different objects, Ricardo voiced his observations. "These items appear to be constructed by native people. The detail and workmanship indicate designs reminiscent of the Aztecs, or even earlier, the Toltecs."

Lexi gazed at him several moments. "You're not a port urchin."

He smiled at her. "I am, and more." Ricardo continued to study the multitude of items, almost as if he looked for something specific.

Meanwhile, Lexi examined the construct of the room, searching for the corridor. She ruled out the wall the entrance lay on and to the right and left as those ran into the other tunnel or the chamber, leaving the wall straight across from the entrance. While the other two rooms showed some sense of organization, this appeared like the items were placed haphazardly. The wall in question lay concealed amongst treasure. To trigger an opening probably included a foot be placed and a brick move shoulder height as the other openings along the dungeon corridor. Treasure concealed the floor while the area of the wall, shoulder height, lay exposed. Lexi decided to search for the wall trigger first. If found, then she'd know where to focus the search on the floor.

Glancing at Ricardo, he remained immersed in the items. Lexi realized he kept picking up carafes or pitchers, studying each one, intently. Saying nothing, she began her perusal of the wall. After about twenty minutes she experienced more luck than Ricardo, locating the release about a third of the distance along the wall.

Over her shoulder, "I found the shoulder trigger. I need to move items in this area here," indicating the spot, circling her hand above.

He nodded, briefly looking at Lexi, as he studied a carafe made of gold, adorned with pieces of red, blue and green stones. Sighing he returned it and continued his search. Lexi carefully picked items up and moved them back from the area she centered on.

An assortment of gold and silver items, adorned with

gems, lay piled along the wall. Items ranged from cups to daggers, from jewelry to short swords. She spent little time studying the objects as she cleared them out of her way.

"That's it!" Ricardo cried out in glee, hurdling over a stack to reach Lexi's side. He gazed at an item she grasped in her hand.

Lexi studied it. It appeared to be a wine decanter constructed of solid gold with embedded sapphires. The inside was stained a crimson color. "This?" She asked questioningly. "Seriously? This is what you're looking for?" She laughed and handed it to him.

Grasping it in both hands, he gazed at it in wonder, sinking to the floor. Reverently, he ran a finger around the mouth of the pitcher. "Yes, my family searched for generations, seeking this carafe."

"Hmm." Lexi responded before she returned to her task. After several more minutes, she cleared the area and began her examination for the next mechanism. Knowing what to look for, it took a short amount of time to locate the spot. By placing her toes on the brick and pushing with her right hand, she activated the opening. The bricks slid apart, revealing a corridor.

"Ha ha! I found it!" She exclaimed excitedly. "Are you finished playing with your wine decanter? Want to come explore the corridor with me?" Lexi asked Ricardo. He still occupied his spot on the floor, communing with the carafe.

Almost as if she woke him from a trance, he jerked his head up, shaking it to clear away cobwebs. "Of course! Good work!" He jumped to his feet, carefully placing the vessel on a rock shelf along the wall.

Lexi activated the light on her wristband, illuminating the hall. It led straight about five feet and rounded a bend. They walked along rough, uneven stone. The construction of the stone walls demonstrated crude workmanship. Along the corridor lay gold items of treasure.

Larger items rested in wider alcoves, like a suit of armor, an elaborate head dress, a vase filled with gold nuggets.

The corridor opened into a cavern. Shining their lights around revealed baskets filled with dry grains, seeds, plants, vegetables and fruits. The leaves and pulp decayed, leaving only dried pits or seeds. Lexi recognized many of the seeds, but a few escaped her knowledge.

"This appears to be a root cellar of sorts," Ricardo observed. "Do you think these seeds retain their vitality?"

Lexi shrugged, "That's a Khara, Mom and Granny question."

On the far side of the cavern, loomed a dark corridor. They cautiously shown their lights, peering down. The corridor traversed ten feet before reaching a dead end. The construction differed in the dungeon corridors than from the tunnels they initially found. Lexi and Ricardo searched the sides until Ricardo located the trigger imbedded in the brick, then searched the floor, locating the other.

"I found both mechanisms." Ricardo asked.

"Do you feel air leaking through?"

He shook his head. "I feel nothing."

"We never climbed in elevation. I think we remain below the water level."

"Unless water leaked in," Ricardo pointed out.

Lexi shot him a wry look. They both peered at the wall. Running their hands along the surface, neither detected any flow of air seeping through. "Let's talk with Shamus and Tink. Maybe they can design a tool to aid us."

Ricardo nodded in agreement. They returned down the tunnel and into the gold room. Picking up the wine decanter once again, Ricardo studied it, then whispered some words. Lexi barely discerned his utterances. It sounded unlike any language she heard before. Replacing the carafe, he turned to Lexi. "I'm ready."

They exited the gold room and returned to the secret chamber where the doctor's team finished loading the last of the remains into a waterproof bag. "Any luck?" Pablo, the aspiring art historian asked.

"We ran into a brick wall, literally," Lexi smirked. "Not sure what flows on the other side. Water, air or what? We'll check with Tink and Shamus regarding some sort of tool for us to use to peek through." She shrugged her shoulders. "How about you? Did your bones stay put?"

Rolling his eyes, "Yes, the remains behaved as remains should."

Chuckling, everyone returned to the entrance. "If you can't develop the photographs, let me know and our crew will work on it."

Pablo shook his head, "I'll make sure we print the photos before bed. I'm excited about the paintings and intend to research specific pieces."

"You seem to know a lot about art," Lexi observed.

"My mother taught art history. I learned by osmosis," Pablo smiled.

As the sun set, Pablo landed onboard the *Star Sapphire* carrying the pictures. He found everyone in the library. "Here's the photographs of the art room."

Granny looked over Lexi's shoulder perusing the pictures. "Once upon a time, I gained employment as an art thief. Several of these paintings hung on the walls of the Louvre in Paris. How in the world did the *Mona Lisa* end up here? The Egyptian antiquities came from the Louvre." Studying the photographs intently, "The Prado in Madrid displayed these paintings by Goya, Raphael, El Greco, and Velazquez." Gasping, "The Tiber statue? It can't be! Paris to here?" Granny exclaimed, tears filled her eyes. "I'm going down! I must see these!"

Staring at Granny intently, "Someone hired you as an art thief?" Pablo asked hesitantly.

Tink shook her head, "She spent a lot of time on the Sea Nile."

Shamus choked back a laugh. Lexi rolled her eyes and turned to Granny. "You recognize some of these works?"

Tears rolled down her cheeks and she nodded, "I assumed they were destroyed in the flood. Or looted. Of course, this is only a small percentage of the great works of art housed in the two museums. But these paintings resided in Europe prior to the flood."

Pablo nodded. "She's correct. These masterpieces belonged to the Prado and the Louvre. It's astounding to see them in Mexico!"

"I'll speak with Dr. Barnes-Kilpatrick and see if we can borrow you tomorrow. If you and Granny start cataloguing the artwork you recognize, it would prove most helpful," Lexi remarked.

"I already asked Dr. Barnes-Kilpatrick. He gave his permission for me to assist." He smiled and looked at Granny. "It is my honor to work with such an esteemed scholar as yourself." He reached for Granny's hand and kissed it.

Giggling, "I, too, look forward to our collaboration," Granny responded.

Noah rolled his eyes, sighing, "Land sakes!"

Word spread across the three ships regarding the room filled with the world's most recognized masterpieces. Several crew members from the *El Camino* and the *Washington* showed up along with their captains in hopes of viewing the treasures.

"I offer to forgo our study of the remaining skeletons, allowing others the opportunity to examine the art room. Provided, I am one of them. From my ship, myself, Pablo, Juliette and Henry," Dr. Barnes-Kilpatrick announced.

"I request myself, Daniel, Sophia and Jacob accompany the team to Tenochtitlan," Captain Briscoe asked.

Lexi nodded. "Who wants to swim?"

Granny, Professor and Pablo volunteered. Lexi, Ricardo and Brannon piloted ships to the city. The swimmers donned suits and dove in, while everyone else settled into pods. The newcomers asked for a tutorial on the operation and demonstration of the pods and appendages, and use of the propulsion system to clear sand from structures. Once the swimmers arrived, the tunnel latched to the pods and the corridor, providing a waterproof entry.

Inside, they marveled at the chamber. Dr. Barnes-Kilpatrick's crew members studied the remaining bodies until everyone met in the room. Lexi opened the access, revealing the art room. Ricardo and Pablo carried lights into the room, illuminating the masterpieces. Oohs and ahhs accompanied the sight of the newfound treasures.

The art aficionados raced inside, in different directions, gazing at the pieces thought to be lost to the flood waters. Each performed a quick perusal of the displays, then more slowly, began to study them. Lexi listened to the party identify different works. More than one person pulled out a monocle to study minute details. Around the room, the assembled group reached the conclusion the artwork proved authentic. A few tears rolled down the cheeks of the gathered personnel.

Dr. Barnes-Kilpatrick successfully studied and contained the skeletons of the guards and the servants. He remained confident the final corpse, the ruler, appeared safe to bring aboard. His team stripped the clothing and adornments from the bones and laid it out on a table. They proceeded to document and photograph the condition while ensuring nothing changed or moved.

Lexi traversed back and forth between the art room and the chamber. Granny worked with Pablo and Captain Briscoe identifying the pieces of art. Surprisingly, Granny recognized more of the masterpieces than any of the others. Lexi ensured Granny truly understood the tenets she discussed. She smiled as Granny provided a lesson in art history to the other two gentlemen.

After lunch, placing the bones in a waterproof bag, Dr. Barnes-Kilpatrick proclaimed the bones safe to transfer. He left the chamber, entering the art room, checking on the progress of identifying the items. Granny greeted him warmly, showing him several pieces of rolled canvas. They discovered numerous famous paintings when they glanced through the scrolls.

Ricardo carried the bag containing items worn by the skeleton to the pod. They decided too many people hung around for them to work in the gold room or the newest corridor.

Removing the last of the skeletons worked to reduce the number of people within the chamber. The expedition chose to wait until Jareth returned to transfer the artwork. An art curator joined Jareth and intended to oversee the project.

Ricardo picked up the carafe from the bag. Pulling a matching dagger from a sheath at his hip, he sliced open his wrist, placing it over the carafe, catching his blood. Milking the cut, he encouraged it to flow freely until filled a quarter of the way. The skeletal remains lay out on a table. He removed the clothing and adornments from the bag and re-dressed it. The final adornment, the crown, he placed upon the skull, with tremendous reverence. Then, he held the decanter to the mouth and poured the blood, whispering words not spoken for centuries.

As he finished, nothing happened. And then, a hurricane hit.

17

Behind the rib bones, a tiny silvery flash of lightning struck. It spun, gathering velocity and volume, quickly filling the chest cavity and forming muscles, tissue, veins, arteries, organs and skin. Ricardo stepped back from the table. Dark skin of the Natives enveloped the skeleton as long black hair grew from the skull. The eyelids opened, revealing deep brown eyes. The lips parted into a smile as he levitated to his feet.

Dropping to his knees, Ricardo whispered, "Oh, mighty Tlaloc! Rise again!"

Tlaloc looked down upon him. "You seem familiar."

"My family carried your ceremonial dagger, ensuring it's safe return to you," Ricardo replied, holding the dagger out to him.

Tlaloc gazed around the room, recognizing several skeletons laying out on tables. He touched them and they began to regenerate, life springing into the bones. "What is this, a cavern?"

Shaking his head, "No, it is an airship, a boat." Ricardo replied. Pointing to the door, "Here is the exit."

"Where are the rest of my servants, my guards?"

"I'm not sure, but I can find them!"

Nodding, Tlaloc ordered, "Do so, now."

Ricardo jumped to his feet and opened several drawers built into the wall of the ship. The remains lay on trays. Pulling out the metal sheets, he displayed them for Tlaloc.

"Very good." He touched each one in turn and life flowed through.

Out of nowhere, a gust of wind blew, along with thick gray clouds. A crack of thunder boomed as lightning split the sky. Immediately, Lexi jumped out of bed and ran for the bridge. The storm surrounded the ships. Lexi fired up the steam and wind engines. She flipped on the deck lights. Flicking a switch, she released the moorings. The *Star Sapphire* swerved, unbalanced as the ship blew away from the others. Lexi tried to place as much distance between them and the rest of the ships, to avoid damage.

Brannon burst through the door as a torrential downpour slammed onto the deck. "Love the new captain's uniform!" He grabbed the controls for the equalizers and thrusters to even out the airship's path.

Lexi smiled, rolling her eyes. "I didn't take time to dress. As soon as I felt the wind, I ran to the bridge. Where did this storm come from?" She glanced down at her apparel. A green silk night gown hung to her knees, accentuating her breasts.

Shaking his head, "The horizon appeared bright and clear when I retired to bed," Brannon responded.

Kabe burst through the door, head soaking wet, drops of rain rolling down his face. "Well, at least you come by your fashion sense honestly. I just bumped into Granny and the Professor. All I can say is I wish I was blind."

Brannon and Lexi chuckled. Kabe increased propulsion and changed the angle of the wind turbines, propelling them away from the others and straightening their course. The other ships released their moorings and sailed away, placing a safe distance between them all, to ride the storm out.

From the deck of the *Washington* a mini hurricane twisted into the sky. "What the hell?!" Brannon exclaimed as Lexi and Kabe stared open mouthed as the twister rose up into the clouds.

"Are those," Kabe hesitated, "people inside the hurricane?"

"They look like Indians?" Lexi observed, questioning. Groaning loudly, "By the whiskers of Poseidon's beard! I bet it's the Aztecs from the secret chamber!"

"I shouldn't laugh, but I swear we're cursed with these remains. What did we let loose this time? Storm denizens?" Brannon asked.

"No, actually it's Tlaloc, the Aztec god of rain, earthly fertility and water. He's ascending back into the heavens, taking his rightful place, commanding and protecting his followers," Ricardo replied, entering the bridge, shaking the rain off his head.

Lexi, Brannon and Kabe looked at each other, quizzically. "How do you know that?" Lexi asked softly.

"My family held the honor of protecting the ceremonial dagger for Tlaloc. After I found the carafe he drank blood sacrifices from, I realized I must assist him to return to our world," Ricardo explained.

"You resurrected an Aztec god?" Brannon questioned hesitantly.

"Reincarnated, actually." Ricardo corrected.

Silence drowned everything else out on the bridge as they watched the hurricane whip the balloons around. The crews valiantly attempted to keep the ships airborne but away from each other, navigating the tumultuous air currents. Like clock- work, Lexi, Kabe and Brannon worked together, manning the controls, maintaining altitude and ensuring the ship remained on an even keel.

"I feel the need to put clothes on. Ricardo, take my place," Lexi ordered, "I'll be right back."

Ricardo slid over, taking the controls from Lexi. She jogged upstairs to her quarters and quickly pulled on trousers, a blouse, a waist cincher and propulsion boots.

Over the communication link, Noah asked, "Everything all right?"

"Everything's fine. Ricardo resurrected the Aztec god of hurricanes and we're trying to keep the ship airborne without smacking into any of the other ships," Brannon answered.

"Reincarnated the god of rain and water," Ricardo corrected.

Noah didn't respond. Within moments he entered the bridge with Tink on his heels. "Wow. We're watching a hurricane." He observed out the windows as the other ships bounced around the skies, buffeted by the winds generated by the god of hurricanes.

Suddenly, the *Star Sapphire* lurched precariously towards the ocean waves. "One of the ropes broke!" Tink shouted, bolting out the door with Lexi behind her. Both kicked their boots into high propulsion, to fight against the turbulent winds. Tink grabbed a bag from a storage box as Lexi shot into the air, trying to catch the flaying rope.

The wind battered the cord about before Lexi finally grasped it. Using her boots to counteract the gusts, she gained control, just barely. Stretched tight, it no longer reached the bracket welded to the deck. "Damn! Take another rope out of the pack!" Tink hollered over the wind, turning her back to Lexi. Lexi pulled out the coiled roll.

Threading the end through the hole, Tink clipped a cinch onto the end, forming a loop around the bracket. Using a pincher from her arm bracer, she squeezed the cinch tight around the rope. Lexi flew towards the balloon to anchor it around the harness. But the blimp smacked into her, sending her spinning into the wind. Brannon appeared behind her, throwing an arm around her waist and grabbing on to the ropes.

"Good catch!" Lexi said with a smile. The two of them propelled back to the balloon, looping the cord through the harness and back down. Tink met them in the middle with another clip. Between the three, they fastened it, pinching it tight, securing the balloon to the airship once more.

"The *Washington*!" Tink exclaimed. "She broke a rope, too!" The three propelled through the swirling winds over to the ship. Two of the crew struggled to affix the rope back to the harness. Lexi and Brannon assisted by grasping the trappings and stretching it away from the air filled fabric, allowing the others to thread it through. Tink placed another clip on the end and pinched it together, securing it. But the balloon sagged heavily.

"It lost too much hot air!" Tink diagnosed, "We need to fly into the balloon. The steam from our propulsion boots will help to inflate it!"

"Won't we get boiled alive?" Lexi hollered over the howling wind.

"Once we feel the heat increase, we exit!" Tink sank down and then rose inside the balloon. Lexi hesitated momentarily before following her. The others flew behind them. Inside, the moist air felt cool and clammy. Tink hung upside down at the top of the arc, her propulsion boots spewing steam. Lexi copied her head under heels stance off to the side with Brannon assuming a similar posture opposite her. The other two circled below them, adding to the heat. The balloon started to inflate, regaining shape, as the temperature rose.

"Alright, let's take a look from outside." Tink authorized the exit from the interior.

The five propelled out and surveyed the result of their ministrations. Substantially fuller than before, the balloon still lacked the ability to completely maintain flight of the boat.

"Take the repair pack. I'm going to the engine room. It seems like the propulsion unit isn't firing correctly." Tink announced as she dropped towards the deck.

Lexi swooped to the bridge of the *El Camino*. "Do you require assistance with anything else, Captain?"

"Something's wrong with our engines," He reported, struggling with the wheel of his mighty ship, trying to keep it upright.

"Tink went below to offer her assistance," Lexi informed him.

Captain Briscoe heaved a sigh of relief. "Where the hell did this storm come from?"

"We'll discuss that once we survive it. I'll refill the pack and my boots. Holler if you require our assistance," Lexi remarked.

"If you need our men to aid with retying ropes, I'll keep them available," Captain Briscoe offered.

Nodding, "Thanks. In this wind, five work perfect. I'll tag Shamus in while Tink works with your crew," Lexi exited the bridge and propelled back to her ship where she re-stocked the pack with rope and clips. As she flew by the bridge, she noticed Shamus watched out the windows, observing the storm and the other ships. Once finished, she returned to the bridge to warm up.

She stood in front of the pipe circulating hot water up the pagoda to heat all the rooms. "Brrr. Tink's helping the *Washington* with their engine. Shamus, do you mind assisting with harness repairs, as needed?"

"No problem. Within my arm brace, I built a similar tool to Tink's," glancing out the window, "It looks like it could be a long night." No sooner than he spoke, the *El Camino* lost a rope.

Lexi, Shamus and Brannon flew towards the ship. Brannon yanked a coil of rope from her pack and cinched it around the bracket as Shamus clipped it on. Lexi sprung towards the balloon. Two of their deckhands met her. One pulled the harness out from the balloon. An unexpected gust of wind whipped the blimp into one of the men, sending him careening through the air. Lexi reached out to grasp him as he flew by, but missed. He plummeted towards the ocean. Entering into a dive, Lexi tried to catch up to him, to no avail. She pulled up abruptly about twenty feet before the waves. The crew member crashed into the scalding water.

Brannon screamed for Lexi over the howling wind. He and the other crew member held on to the rope but it flung them around like toys. Kicking into high propulsion, she raced towards them, catching hold. Adding her power to theirs, they guided the cord to the harness and quickly threaded it through, then Shamus secured it with a clip.

As soon as they finished, Lexi caught sight of one of the small balloons which supported a pod, break free of the rope. The propulsion team returned to the *Star Sapphire* to secure the line. Even though a shorter length, little room remained to maneuver around. But they fixed it, just as the rope on the other pod snapped, releasing the balloon.

Rushing over to it, Brannon grasped a rope still tied to the blimp. Lexi grabbed ahold, too, trying to keep it from blowing to Africa. Shamus propelled to the top, pushing down, attempting to help return it to the deck. Two deckhands from the *Washington* and two from the *El Camino* surrounded the balloon and assisted in easing it back down. Kabe and Ricardo met the balloon and grabbed the rope while Lexi affixed another rope to the harness, dropping it to the deck as she sat on the balloon, holding it down. Shamus clipped the first rope down and then secured the second rope. All the deckhands, Lexi and Brannon laid down on the balloon briefly, to rest. But only for a moment.

Lexi refilled the pack with clips and rope, then she met up with the others as they replenished the steam in their propulsion boots. Scanning the eastern sky, she searched in vain for the light of the morning sun, as the storm screamed around them. "Head up to our bridge to warm up and dry off a little 'til the next catastrophe," Lexi offered.

The last one to the deck, Lexi looked to the hand from the *El Camino*. "I'm sorry about your shipmate. I tried to catch him, but," she trailed off. "What was his name? I need to radio your captain."

Nodding his head, "Thank you, sir. I already notified my captain. His name was Geoff." They rested for about fifteen minutes before an alarm sounded, signifying the engine required ocean water.

Groaning, Lexi headed towards the door. "I'll extend the tube down. If the wind blows too hard, someone might need to guide it."

"Affix an anchor to the end of the hose. That will send it straight down," Shamus suggested. "An anchor rests beside the kiln. Just tie it to the handle of the tube with a piece of rope. Once it reaches the water, we don't necessarily need the anchor again. Might as well leave the hose in the water. Who knows how long this storm intends to last?"

"Thanks, Shamus." Lexi exited the room, with a death grip on the railing, she made her way downstairs, to the deck, then below to the engine room. Following Shamus' directions, Lexi opened the trapdoor, dropping the hose with the anchor attached. She watched it plummet to the ocean and sink into the roiling waves. Throwing the lever, activating the pump, water flowed up into the holding tank, silencing the alarm.

On her way to the bridge, she popped into the library where Granny and Professor waited out the storm. Lexi provided them a brief update while Granny prepared hot tea for her to take to the bridge. "Keep the tea coming. Just let us know when it's ready. We'll send someone down. The wind is extremely treacherous."

With a tight hold on the tea pot, Lexi made her way to the bridge where enthusiastic greetings surrounded her. Everyone cuddled their hot tea for a few minutes before a line broke on the *El Camino*. The team raced to the line, quickly replacing and securing it. They crowded on to the bridge to see how the ship fared through the ceaseless winds.

"We're doing fairly well, considering. Right now, we're replenishing our water supply. The storm taxed our reservoir," the captain responded.

"I filled ours as well. Hopefully, enough rope remains to maintain the balloons through this storm!" Lexi remarked.

"Martin, grab several coils of rope and clips. Take some of ours. I appreciate you assisting with these repairs. This hurricane popped out of nowhere! We failed to prepare adequate-

210

ly."

Lexi sighed. "None of us made proper preparations. We'll discuss that once the storm passes."

Within minutes, Martin reappeared on the bridge carrying the supplies. "Thanks!" Lexi handed them to Brannon who placed them in her pack.

They received about a fifteen minute break before a line broke upon the *Washington*. Bidding Captain Briscoe adieu, the team vacated the bridge, propelling to the broken line.

The torque on the balloon snapped another line. The wind whipped it out, slapping Lexi across the chest, knocking the air out of her lungs, sending her tumbling through the sky. Using her boots, Lexi counter balanced against the wind, catching herself. She raced back to the balloon, lying on top of it, catching her breath while trying to hold it from escaping. Three deckhands joined her as Brannon grabbed one line. Tink appeared with a rope, looping it through the harness and clicking it on.

"You, okay?" Tink asked as she joined Lexi while Shamus and Brannon secured the other line.

Lexi nodded. "Wind knocked out of me," she gasped.

Tink knelt behind Lexi, sat her up and rubbed her back as the rain pelted them. "I repaired their engine. A fish clogged the filtration unit which shut down the entire system. After I cleaned the fish out, I put a screen over their uptake hose. We probably need more water for our engine by now."

"Already took care of it," Lexi stated, slowly catching her breath.

"What's up with this storm? How did none of us see it coming?" Tink asked, ringing water out of Lexi's hair, still rubbing her back.

"Apparently, Ricardo resurrected the Aztec god of hurricanes," Brannon answered.

"Reincarnated the Aztec God of rain and water," Shamus corrected. "He filled me in. So, our little port urchin serves as the keeper of the ceremonial dagger and holds the responsibility to reincarnate the god once he obtains the sacrificial carafe."

"Surely, you jest!" One of the deckhands from the *Washington* commented.

"Unfortunately, we don't. I intend to discuss it with the

other captains and expedition leaders once we make it through the hurricane." Lexi said.

"After all the craziness I experienced on this expedition, I believe damn near anything at this point!" Another deckhand commented, shaking his head.

A roundhouse of chuckles answered in agreement. "Shall we head to the bridge to await the next line break?" Tink suggested.

Grunts acknowledged her suggestion and everyone rose to their feet, flying to the bridge where the welcoming smell of coffee invaded their nostrils. Crowding around the steam pipe, the crew warmed up and dried off as much as possible. The next several hours they spent propelling from one ship to the next, securing lines. Once the sun peeked over the eastern horizon, the hurricane disappeared as quickly as it appeared.

The captains agreed to meet in an hour's time. All needed time to assess damages and determine what supplies may be required. Lexi and the rest of the crew handling broken lines, wanted a hot shower and dry clothes. She announced the crew from the *Star Sapphire* demanded the day to recuperate from the activities throughout the night. The pods wouldn't be running to Tenochtitlan today.

18

After warming up in a hot shower and changing clothes, Lexi felt ready to conquer the world. Noah provided her with a list of damages and required supplies. For the most part, the *Star Sapphire* weathered the storm well. Their inventory of rope and clips diminished significantly, however. Later in the day, Lexi and Tink planned to inspect the balloons and the seams to ensure no tears or leakage resulted from the storm. The rest of the crew caught some sleep while Lexi met with the captains and expedition leaders. Anticipating questioning directed at Ricardo's actions, he accompanied her.

Tea, coffee pots and a bowl of fruit sat at the table, on the *El Camino*. Caffeine proved to be in high demand this morning as no one received much sleep through the night. Lexi poured herself a cup of tea and sat down. Professor and Captain Briscoe already found seats and sipped coffee, looking at the world through bleary eyes. The group awaited the arrival of Captain Daniels and Dr. Barnes-Kilpatrick.

"We appreciated you and your crew's assistance. Without your help, our ship would have been lost," Captain Briscoe stated.

"Without all three ships and their crews, none of us would have survived," Lexi replied. "It took easily a five man team to secure lines. The pods required more. Without assistance from your crew and the *Washington*, we may have lost one balloon and perhaps sustained severe damage to our ship, not to mention the pods."

Dr. Barnes-Kilpatrick and Captain Daniels walked in at that moment. "It required all three crews to survive through the hurricane, but we appreciate your assistance tremendously." Captain Daniels stated as he plopped into a seat, pulling the coffee pot to him. Dr. Barnes-Kilpatrick nodded in agreement.

Everyone seemed a little surprised to see Ricardo sitting at the table. "We'll cover his presence in a moment. Can we discuss supplies and any damages first? I hope Captain Briscoe will contact Jareth to pick up more rope and clips before he leaves port. We used up a substantial amount of our rope inventory last night. Tink could fabricate more clips, but we'd prefer to use her expertise on pod production."

Nodding, "I already contacted Jareth and asked him to postpone his departure. We need rope and clips as well as balloon fabric. This morning, we discovered an area of our main balloon showing signs of shearing if not repaired imminently." Captain Briscoe informed the table.

"Tink provided substantial assistance in repairing our engine last night. She suggested modifications to improve efficiency and less problems with maintenance. Here's a list of what we need to implement her suggestions," Captain Daniels handed a list to Captain Briscoe. "The crew members working with you last night securing lines commented your propulsion boots seemed to last longer and provided more power than theirs. Your pack and Tink and Shamus' arm bracers reportedly sped up response time and proved to be a stronger alternative than our customary practice. Can we order these items through you? And receive training?"

"Our crew members noted the same advantages to your set up as opposed to ours. We, too, request to order these items." Captain Briscoe remarked, "Your people appeared more agile in the air with your propulsion boots."

"I'll talk with Tink and Shamus. I don't think a problem exists in providing the technology. Once you receive it, Kabe or Brannon can instruct you in the use of the items." Lexi responded, smiling, "As for our agility, we played tag and other games with propulsion boots since Tink designed them over fifteen years ago. It's merely a matter of practice."

Chuckles broke out around the table. "Is this a complete list, then?" Captain Briscoe questioned. Everyone nodded. He stood up, opened the door and hollered for a deck hand, who carried the list to the bridge, patching through to Jareth.

Sighing, Lexi said, "About the storm. Ricardo, explain." He nodded and described his actions of the previous night.

"If you decide to leave Captain Canatolli's employ, I offer

you employment, immediately," Dr. Barnes-Kilpatrick stated.

"Based on what?" Captain Daniels asked, completely surprised.

"He resurrected a god. I can't resurrect a squirrel, let alone a god!" the doctor exclaimed.

"Reincarnated," Ricardo and Lexi corrected.

"Which resulted in a hurricane that almost destroyed all our ships and our personnel!" Captain Briscoe pointed out.

"And I let loose a werewolf and a vampire, which culminated in the death of five of my own crew. Who am I to pass judgement?" Dr. Barnes-Kilpatrick stated.

"I'd be willing to hire you as well. Your skills piloting a pod, swimming in an underwater suit, knack for finding secret entrances and your diligence in studying the maps led you to the chamber," Professor offered.

Laughing, "Before you two enter into a bidding war regarding my crew member, he is still a member of our crew and our family," Lexi pointed out.

"And I'm not searching for a job, even though I'm quite flattered by your esteem of my abilities," Ricardo stated.

The crews spent the next few days putting ships back to rights, inspecting sails, ropes and masts. They repaired everything possible, trading supplies and personnel between ships. For items requiring replacement, they utilized available inventory and prepared to change out once Jareth arrived. Tink reinforced the rigging supporting the hydro-pods. The first mates devised a watch program encompassing crew from each ship around the perimeter and on deck with radio contact maintained throughout the night, utilizing radars and lowlight goggles.

Dr. Barnes-Kilpatrick and Professor spent time discussing the reincarnation principles with Ricardo. They tried to ascertain some way to protect the expedition from further attacks by Tlaloc. To no avail.

"My training centered around protecting the dagger, finding the carafe, then reincarnating Tlaloc once I found the proper body," Ricardo explained.

"How did you recognize the vessel?" Professor asked.

"Once I located the carafe I knew the vessel lay close. A god chooses the strongest, most powerful body. Obviously, the remains wearing the crown, sitting on a throne, portrayed the god," Ricardo shrugged.

"You'd think, being the person to reincarnate Tlaloc, that earned you some credit, your life holds value for him," Dr. Barnes-Kilpatrick.

Again, Ricardo shrugged, "Who am I to guess the thoughts of a god?"

The *Mountain Peak* rendezvoused with the other ships late afternoon on the third day after the storm, pulling up in close proximity to the *Star Sapphire*. Lexi propelled over, meeting Khara on deck. She kissed her, rubbing the baby bump. Khara melted into her embrace.

"My word! Have you no shame?"

Lexi slowly ended the kiss and peeked over Khara's shoulder at the irritating voice. A rotund man with heavy gray mutton chops stood ondeck in a leisure suit, wearing a top hat. He leaned heavily on a cane.

"I beg your pardon?" Lexi asked, slowly strutting over to him.

"Decent folk are present! Public displays of affection appear most improper! You need to be placed in the stockades for your behavior, young lady!" Mutton chops announced vehemently.

"Who is this?" Lexi demanded, using her thumb to point at him.

"Has the flood waters receded? I thought that voice belonged to you! Leonardo Diconi! What in Poseidon's underwear brings you to Mexico?" Granny exclaimed as she propelled to the *Mountain Peak*.

"Lady Eloise Von Barton!" Mr. Diconi looked flabbergasted. "I'm protecting assets from these Historical Society yahoos! We placed books and works of art in the underground chambers of the temple at Tenochtitlan. Apparently, some young female captain," rolling his eyes, "found our cache and started looting it!"

Granny walked over and kicked him in the leg. Hard. "That young female captain just so happens to be my granddaughter! Captain Alexandrea Canatolli, allow me to introduce this unfortunate sod, Leonardo Diconi, Master of Arms for the Societá per L'illuminazione Intellettuale."

216

Mentally translating, "Are you kidding me? There must be some sort of limit as to the number of secret societies involved in one expedition! I thought one seemed like too many. Then, there were two, which resulted in a god's temper tantrum! Three?" Lexi shook her head, "Nope, not doing three!"

"God's temper tantrum?" Khara questioned, glancing askance at Lexi. Jareth hid a smile.

"Of course, she's your granddaughter! If there's trouble to be found, you, Eloise, are always close behind!" Throwing his hands in the air, he shook his head disgustedly.

Lexi moved in front of Granny, pulling her sword, as Kabe, Brannon, Ricardo and Noah propelled over, landing behind her. Tink and Shamus flew to the crow's nest, drawing cross bows, nocking arrows.

A wide smile crossed Granny's face. "Leonardo, meet the rest of my grandkids and my son, Noah." Granny performed introductions.

"Granny, how do you know this," Lexi paused, "gentleman from the dark ages?"

"Back in my spying days, I contracted work with the Societá per L'illuminazione Intellettuale. He served as my handler," Granny explained, placing a hand on Lexi's sword. "Put that away, dear. He's harmless, just a blowhard."

"Eloise! Do not speak of our past involvement! That remains confidential!" He blustered.

She scoffed, "It's fine! They think I'm delusional." Captain Briscoe and Captain Daniels landed on deck.

Jareth introduced the captains to the newcomer. "We need to sit with Professor and Dr. Barnes-Kilpatrick to discuss the continuing expedition and ownership of the items within the chamber," Jareth announced.

"The Society sanctioned and paid for this expedition. We contracted with the *Star Sapphire* and Dr. Barnes-Kilpatrick for the technology, guides to the city and the study of the remains. Any and all items found within the chamber belong to the Historical Society." Captain Briscoe stated.

"Except we acquired and placed everything there for the sole purpose of preserving the knowledge," Leonardo argued. "The chamber belongs to us."

"Fine. We'll return everything to the chamber and you

can remove it," Lexi smiled sweetly.

"Let's wait for Professor and Dr. Barnes-Kilpatrick," Jareth responded. "I hope we can reach an agreement amongst all parties."

"When do you want to meet?" Lexi asked.

"As soon as possible. I know Professor wishes to explore more of the city and there's still another corridor to find," Jareth stated. "Let's call them over now. How about if we eat dinner while we discuss it?"

Within fifteen minutes, the captains, Professor, Dr. Barnes-Kilpatrick and Granny met in Jareth's dining room, with the newcomer. Everyone introduced themselves and their affiliation. Immediately, the two societies began arguing over ownership of the chamber.

"Leonardo, explain how the items came to be placed in the chamber." Lexi interrupted. "I refuse to take his word at face value. He needs to describe how they know about the chamber. How to access it. What's stored inside? How they obtained the items. Granny stated many of the paintings were displayed at the Louvre and the Prado."

The rest of the members of the expedition nodded. Leonardo replied, "Alright. Our scientists predicted the volcanic eruptions six months prior to the announcement. We gathered the important texts of many societies. The Spanish and French monarchs asked us to protect the masterpieces of their collections. Several members of our society participated in the," Leonardo hesitated, "exploration of the new world. We knew of the chamber beneath Tenochtitlan.

"The Societá per L'illuminazione Intellettuale decided to place as many books, paintings, sculptures, etc within the chamber. We brought four ships loaded with the treasures as well as armaments to protect the shipment. Our guide led us to the chamber via the temple. A trip wire lays embedded in the wall which opens up into a narrow corridor leading around a corner and down a set of stairs. At the end, rests another trap door. The lever appears wired near the top of the wall. It leads down another hall where a decoy catch and another trigger open into the chamber, an octagonal shaped room. Outside, the remains of a skeleton guard the entrance. Inside, another corpse sat on a throne with two servants in attendance. We built shelves to hold the books.

"Behind one of the bookcases lies a trip wire leading to another room where we placed the artwork. We developed a catalogue of all the items we situated inside the chamber." From an interior pocket, he pulled out numerous pages of a handwritten list. "Here's our inventory." He handed it to Professor.

"What about the other corridors?" Lexi asked.

He looked surprised. "We're only aware of the tunnel off the temple. Others exist?"

"Yes, at least three more. We found two. One originating from a building on the outskirts of the city and another tunnel off the secret chamber leading to two dungeons. You weren't aware of those?" Lexi questioned casually.

He shook his head. "No, we used the temple corridor. You mentioned three tunnels. Where is the third?" Leonardo questioned.

"Our attempts to discover the other tunnel remains fruitless, to this point. The dungeons and corridor leading to them differ significantly in construction. Older than the temple and the outbuilding. Reason leads us to believe one more tunnel of older construction exists, which, so far, we failed to locate," Lexi explained.

Shaking his head again, "We hold no interest in the actual city or any other rooms, tunnels or treasures. Our only interest lies within the items we placed for safe keeping," Leonardo stated. Lexi sat back in her chair, with a self-satisfied look. "Did you find anything of interest?"

Lexi turned towards Professor and Dr. Barnes- Kilpatrick. Professor looked towards the doctor. "Uh, yes. We found a werewolf, a vampire and the resurrected Aztec god of hurricanes, Tlaloc."

"Reincarnated, god of water and rain," corrected numerous entities around the table.

Leonardo looked at them, dumbfounded, turning to Granny for confirmation. "You missed the hurricane that buggar dropped down on us! Worst I ever encountered!" Granny fanned herself, "I lacked the good fortune to meet the werewolf or the vampire. The pictures of the werewolf provide me with nightmares every time I fall asleep."

"You possess photographs of a werewolf?"

"Just the bones regenerating tissue once we removed the

silver chains," Dr. Barnes-Kilpatrick reported. "It liberated itself at some point while unattended."

"And the vampire?"

Rocking his head back and forth, the doctor explained, "Well, the vampire killed three of my team, kidnapped two, stole a row boat and disappeared into the night."

"The Aztec god of hurricanes?"

"Rain and water. I'll take responsibility for that one. One of my crew members reincarnated Tlaloc and let him loose." Lexi acknowledged.

"So, your expedition lost a werewolf, vampire and the Aztec god of rain and water?"

"If you want to be completely accurate, Tlaloc took two servants and three guards with him, as well." Dr. Barnes-Kilpatrick added. "Do you think you would have experienced more success?"

"Wouldn't even want to try!" Leonardo contemplated the situation, shuddering. "I perused the books. Where's the artwork?"

"I began cataloguing it, but it still occupies the art room," Granny replied. "Jareth's ship provides the available space for storage. We awaited his return. The expedition party discovered the artwork after his departure."

Dejectedly, Leonardo asked, "The art remains in the chamber?"

"It does," Granny smiled like the dolphin who ate the tuna. "My grandkids appear to be the only ones who possess the knowledge and technology to transport the items to the surface." Everyone else hid their smiles. "Shall we start negotiations?"

"Let's take a few minutes break, Granny. I know I could use the water closet and a glass of wine," Lexi suggested.

"I agree. I want a break." Others around the table concurred. Lexi took Granny's arm and propelled her to the *Star Sapphire*. Jareth accompanied them. They returned to the ship ten minutes later, carrying a decanter of wine and each held a full glass. The smile Granny wore, looked like the giant white shark that ate the dolphin. Leonardo appeared worried.

"Where do you plan on preserving the books and artwork?" Granny asked, sipping her wine.

Leonardo hesitated. "At this point, we lack appropriate facilities to protect the artwork and the library of books."

Jareth spoke up. "The Historical Society owns several buildings safe from water where the items can be preserved and available to scrutiny by appropriate persons. We are more than willing to enter into an agreement with the Societá per L'illuminazione Intellettuale to preserve and maintain these valuable artifacts for future generations. Between your organization and ours, we can ensure the safety of these cultural icons for generations to come."

"No offense, Jareth, but do you possess the authority to make a deal like this?" Leonardo questioned.

"Between Jareth, Captain Briscoe and myself, we hold authority to enter into binding agreements on behalf of the Historical Society. In that same vein, do you have the authority to agree to a binding agreement on behalf of the Societá per L'illuminazione Intellettuale?" Professor turned the tables.

Leonardo paused, hesitated, froze, and paused again. Granny's smile looked like the giant squid that ate the great white shark. Sighing heavily, "Eloise and I, together, hold the authority to enter into a binding agreement for the Societá per L'illuminazione Intellettuale."

Lexi turned and shot her grandmother a look of pure awe. Granny winked at her. "I'm in complete favor of allowing the Historical Society to work in conjunction with the Societá per L'illuminazione Intellettuale to preserve the artistic masterpieces and written narratives for future generations of humans."

Leonardo nodded his head in agreement.

Jareth, Dr. Barnes-Kilpatrick and Professor, on behalf of the Society, agreed as well to work with the Societá per L'illuminazione Intellettuale in the preservation and protection of the priceless artifacts.

Professor questioned, "As an archeologist, the excavation of Tenochtitlan appeals to me tremendously. I refuse to acquiesce you hold any claim to the city. Do you entertain any issues with us further exploring this ancient city?"

Leonardo and Granny shook their heads. "No, the excavation lays beyond our means. At this point, our primary objective remains in procuring and protecting our caches of historically relevant works." Caches? Plural? Lexi filed this tidbit in the back of her mind.

"Along that same vein, if we find another corridor and/or secret room, any and all items stored within belong to whom?" Lexi questioned.

"We only claim ownership to the items we placed within the chamber for safe keeping. We lack awareness of any other corridors or chambers, therefore, we stake no claim on any other objects, especially if the pieces appear Aztec in nature. In our opinion, ownership belongs to the Aztecs," Leonardo articulated clearly.

Lexi swallowed her smile. Looking towards Professor, Captain Briscoe and Jareth, Lexi asked, "And the Historical Society? What is your stance regarding any other corridors and/or secret rooms?"

"Our priorities focus on working alongside the Societá per L'illuminazione Intellettuale regarding the objects they placed within the secret chamber and the art room. We take responsibility for the beings within the dungeons, per our contract with Dr. Barnes-Kilpatrick. We hope to continue excavating the city." Professor paused for a moment, "Given the issues arising with further exploration of the secret chamber, we hold no desire to continue, stake no claims or accept responsibility for any further findings or faults. We refuse liability for the Aztec god."

Nodding, "Is this the opinion of the Historical Society?" Lexi asked, face devoid of emotion. Captain Briscoe nodded in the affirmative. Jareth eyed Lexi speculatively, then agreed as well.

"The *Star Sapphire* intends to continue exploration of the corridors. We promise to provide assistance to both the Historical Society and the Societá per L'illuminazione Intellettuale in transporting the artwork to the surface and any other tasks. We finished transferring all the books from the chamber. Technological assistance will be provided as needed. Relinquishing, developing or teaching technology will be proffered on a contracted basis. We send two hydro-pods, the passenger pod and three underwater suits down twice per day, at a minimum. Our tinkerers work to develop more pods and suits, per your instructions. Let us know how many people and which mode of transport you intend to use. Ideally, inform us one shift ahead of time, but we tend to be quite flexible. We offer to furnish pilots for pods as needed."

"I desire to view the city and understand the process you use to gain access to the secret chamber. May I go tomorrow morning?" Leonardo asked.

"Of course. Do you want to transport by hydro-pod or swim in a waterproof underwater suit?" Lexi questioned.

He looked at her blankly.

"We will ride in the passenger pod. I'll show him how to enter the secret chamber and present him a tour of the art room and the dungeons," Granny offered. Lexi knew better than to argue.

"Gertie and Joseph desire to tour the art room. The three of us intend to descend in the morning. Gertie asked for a seat in a pod. Joseph and I can take a suit or pod. Whatever works. I don't mind swimming," Professor shot a triumphant look towards Leonardo.

Oh, gawd, the elderly gentlemen will be engaging in fist-icuffs over Granny, Lexi thought to herself.

The doctor shrugged, "My team holds no desire or need to venture down. If Pablo's knowledge of artwork is required he may accompany you. We're out of skeletons. I intend to set sail, tomorrow."

"Actually, I want to access your knowledge on a couple matters." Lexi stated.

Surprise flashed across Dr. Barnes-Kilpatrick's face. "Of course, at your service. What do you need?"

"Probably you, and a couple of your bone analyzers."

"Did you find another corridor?" Jareth questioned.

"Yes, but we can't tell if water or air exists on the other side of the wall. A skeleton guards the corridor. Hopefully, the remains are normal. Or at least, as normal as possible in that place," Lexi replied, rolling her eyes. "One more spot exists for a passenger."

The meeting resolved to the satisfaction of all the parties. Later that night, Jareth and Khara laid in bed, waiting for Lexi to join them. Once she checked the watch, the long range and short range radar, she strolled into their quarters.

Smiling, she untied her trousers, letting them sink to the floor. Her waist cincher followed. Slowly, she unbuttoned her blouse and slid it off her shoulders, standing in only a corset top and bloomers. Unlacing the corset, her breasts eased out.

Lexi slid her bloomers low on her hips, providing a peek of the thatch of hair protecting her clit. Crawling on the bed, Lexi stopped between Jareth and Khara, resting on her knees. She unwound the ribbon constricting her breasts, a little more. Rotating her hips, she stuck her thumb in her waistband, easing them down, sliding to her knees, exposing her treasure trove. Pulling on the ribbon of her corset, her breasts burst out, freed, her nipples thrusting up.

Jareth grabbed her hips and pulled her to him, until her nipple entered his mouth, nipping with his teeth. Khara rose to her knees, taking the other nipple, sucking softly. While Jareth bit, Khara suckled. He dragged it in his mouth, sucking it pert. Khara caressed the other nipple with her tongue, gently, lathing, sweeping her tongue around.

Lexi spread her knees wider apart, moving in to them. Jareth rubbed her clit with his thumb, while his pointer finger entered her vagina and middle finger slid deep into her anus. Lexi arched back. Jareth stroked her, each finger a different rhythm. Moaning deeply, Lexi thrust her tit deeper into Kha- ra's mouth, moving her hips against Jareth's fingers, rocking back and forth, with more force.

Lexi pushed Khara away from her nipple and sank down onto her sweet spot, her tongue flicking ferociously. Moaning, whimpering, begging Khara laid back as she quickly approached orgasm. Jareth moved behind Lexi, sinking his penis deep inside her. Lexi moaned in ecstasy as his testicles bumped against her nub. Thrusting harshly, he sank his cock in and out of her while she flicked her tongue against Khara's clit, two fingers inserted in her vagina. Khara cried out her orgasm and Lexi followed with Jareth right behind her. The three rode the waves until they sank, collapsing, spent.

Laying between Khara and Jareth, Lexi stretched and rolled to her back. Jareth whispered in her ear. "Let's adjourn to the lookout." Khara slept soundly. Jareth and Lexi rolled out of bed and snuck upstairs.

In the lookout, Jareth led Lexi to a corner. Kneeling down, he placed her arms on each side, grasping the window sill, knees wide apart. Grasping her clit between his thumb and forefinger, he stretched it down, tight. She moaned.

"What did you find under Tenochtitlan?" He stroked and stretched her tender button.

Moving her hips against his ministrations, "What do you mean?"

Pulling harder, he used his fingers to spread her vaginal juices around, up to her anus. "What have you found?"

She laughed and moaned. He tugged strenuously and she moaned harder. Jareth moved behind her, rubbing his manhood along her vagina, tickling her clit and just touching her anus. She moaned and pushed against him. He pulled back, the head just resting at her sphincter. Teasing.

"What did you find?" Jareth whispered in her ear. His cock poked at the entrance to her ass as he mercilessly flicked her aching nub.

Lexi ground her buttocks against him, trying to force him inside. He laughed and pulled back. She pressed her clitoris against his fingers, moving back and forth vigorously. His fingers slapped her clit then moved to her hip. She moaned in consternation.

"What did you find?" His hips encompassed hers, his hand cupped her breasts, pulling her up against him, grinding his hips against hers, allowing his shaft to rub between her legs. His fingers worried her nipples, almost painfully. Almost. She moaned, hungrily.

Tightly gripping her tits, he held her against him, rotating his hips against her ass, his cock hung between her legs, providing her no satisfaction. She reached down, grasping him in her hands, but he pulled away. Letting go of her breast he slapped her tender nub.

Whispering in her ear, Jareth ground his hips into hers, "What did you find?"

Lexi laughed, throwing her head back, she turned, her lips meeting his in a fierce kiss. Her tongue slid into his mouth, dueling, massaging his gums, along his teeth. She ground her hips into his, trying to slide his cock into her.

Jareth chuckled, sliding back and forth, slowly along her thighs, his pre-ejaculate leaving a trail. "What did you find?"

Pouting, she tried to lock her lips onto his. He slapped her ass, stood up and returned momentarily. He wrapped both her wrists in rope and tied them above her head, latching the loop on a hook. Lexi turned slowly, inserting a nipple into his mouth. He bit it. Hard, then sucked it tenderly while slowly sliding his cock between her thighs. One hand sank to her

225

throbbing nub, teasing it, mercilessly while the other encircled her breast, rubbing the nipple into a tight bud. She whimpered. "What did you find?"

"Screw me and I'll tell you."

His manhood continued to glide between her thighs, barely scraping her clit, nipping at her anus. She moaned. She groaned. She begged. "What did you find?"

Rotating her hips against his, she tried to insert his rock hard rod into her anus or vagina but he continued to tease her, she whimpered. He tugged on her clit. She began to orgasm. He stopped.

"Please!" She begged, grinding her hips against his. "What did you find?" His cock poked at her ass while his fingers tickled her labia tugging on her pubic hair.

"A room filled with Aztec gold! The conquistadors missed it in their invasion!" She burst out. He thrust into her ass as his fingers stroked her clit. She ground her hips against his, rocking back and forth as he pounded inside her while he tweaked her nipple and worried her tortured button. Quickly, she orgasmed. But he didn't stop. He continued to thrust into her as she reached another orgasm. He slapped her clit and juices flowed down his scrotum, causing him to orgasm. Jareth buried himself deep within her, one hand grasping her tit and nipple tightly while the other hand pinched her love button, throwing her over the cliff as he shot his cum deep inside. They moved together as waves of ecstasy washed over them, again, and again, and again.

When Lexi regained her senses, she hung by her wrists, with Jareth holding her tight against him as they finally stopped moving. He reached up and untied her wrists. She sank into his arms. Lying back against the bench seats, he held her. "You found a room of Aztec gold?"

"For the record, sexual torture is completely unfair and paybacks are a bitch."

He chuckled. "The room with Aztec gold?"

Sighing, "Off the dungeon corridor, I found a room filled with gold items. Obviously, the conquistadors didn't locate it. Ricardo located his carafe in there. Beyond the room, we discovered another corridor but we can't determine if water or air exists on the other side." Snuggling tiredly into his embrace, she continued, "There's an alcove with a variety of dried seeds, most I recognized, some I didn't. A couple of skeletal remains lay in the corridor."

"And at what point were you intending to share this information?" Jareth asked, as they lay entangled.

"Either this evening or tomorrow. I waited to see what side you landed on and what your next move entailed. After our meeting tonight, I decided to show you in the morning."

He pulled back, gazing at her in the moonlight. Lexi met his eyes, unabashedly.

19

The next morning, the expedition team gathered in the
chamber. Granny played tour guide to Leonardo, who continually expressed awe and wonder at the sights below the ocean
as they made their way to Tenochtitlan. Completely overcome
by the experience of traveling underwater, he gazed in wonder
at the structures visible beneath the sand dunes. Shaming him,
Granny finally convinced him to crawl through the waterproof
tunnel into the corridor leading to thechamber.

Once inside, standing on the rocky floor, breathing air,
"By Poseidon's trident! I must say, your grandchildren inherited your courage and ingenuity genes!" Leonardo bent over,
gasping.

Chuckling, "Yes, they're pretty terrific. Come along, old
man. Wait until you see the secret chamber and art room!"
Granny led the way down the corridor.

In the chamber, the door leading to the room storing the
masterpieces, stood open. Leonardo entered, speechless as he
gazed around at the collected treasures. While they conducted their inspection, Lexi led Jareth into the dungeon corridor
and triggered the opening into the gold room. She pushed him
inside the room, closing the entrance behind them. Using her
wrist torch, she found the other lanterns and lit them, illuminating the room.

"I inadvertently tripped the opening. Ricardo discovered
it independently," Lexi said. "Do you want to see the other
corridor?"

His gaze swung around the room, assessing the enormity
of the treasure trove. Wordlessly, he assented, carefully stepping over and around pieces of gold as Lexi triggered the hidden opening on the far wall, exposing a skeleton guarding the
corridor.

The sight of the remains caused Jareth to laugh. "Dr.

Barnes-Kilpatrick just might leave this place with an Aztec corpse yet!"

"I'll believe it when I see it. The hallway extends quite a ways," Lexi commented drily. She pointed out objects lying along the corridor. They reached the storage alcove holding the seeds. Surveying the assortment, Jareth displayed more excitement than in the gold room. "Some of these varieties, I don't even recognize! I can't wait to plant them to see what grows!"

"Do you think the seeds will produce?"

"I think so. The seeds appear dried and preserved." He knelt, studying the individual pods closely. "These may be worth more than the items in the gold room! There may be species thought lost!"

Lexi smiled. "The end of the line lies around the corner. We can't tell if water or air exists on the other side. Typically, air flows through, but here," she pointed down the corridor, "nothing."

Hesitating, he rose to his feet, following her. When they reached the dead end, Jareth inspected the area, noting the trigger. But ascertained nothing. "Air probably lays on the other side. Our elevation never increased." He noted.

"I agree, but if we're wrong..."

Jareth nodded. "Set up a waterproof shield, just in case?" "That's what I'm thinking. It's about lunch time. Let's return to the surface and grab all the necessary equipment," Lexi suggested.

"Agreed."

Retracing their steps, they entered the chamber where the rest of the party carried paintings out to the pods for transport. Ricardo glanced at Jareth and raised his eyebrows in question. Jareth smiled and nodded. Picking up a couple pieces, Lexi walked down the corridor and handed them to Joseph, waiting in the tunnel between the corridor and the pod. After loading the pod, the crew ascended to the ships.

Khara served lunch above deck on the *Star Sapphire*, to accommodate the growing numbers of the expedition party. With assistance from Caroline and Miranda, a young woman Jareth hired while at port, dishes of fruits, a salad and seared tuna lined the table laid out for the hungry crew. Several loaves of steaming bread provided a tantalizing aroma to the meal.

"Hot bread! How long has it been since we ate hot bread!" Tink gushed as she plopped into a chair, grabbing the knife and cutting a chunk off. Popping it into her mouth, she rolled her eyes and moaned. "It tastes wonderful."

"Miranda spent the morning grinding sunflowers into flour for bread. It's quite a labor intensive process but she ground enough for a few loaves. When time allows, she intends to prepare more to keep on hand," Khara explained, setting glasses on the table. "Jareth hired her to maintain his garden and kitchen."

The rest of the party found chairs and began dishing up. A young woman, in her twenties came up on deck from the kitchen, carrying two pitchers. Her chestnut hair fell almost to her waist in a braid. She wore a light weight simple dark brown cotton dress with a navy cincher, sleeves rolled up to her forearms. Thick, bushy eyebrows protected her chocolate eyes. A pendant hung around her neck, but Lexi couldn't make out the design.

"Everyone, this is Miranda. She's responsible for the fresh baked bread!" Khara announced as she approached the table.

A round of cheers met the introduction. Miranda smiled brightly and approached each person offering tea or lemonade. When she reached Lexi, "Thanks for the bread. It's abso- lutely delicious." Lexi met her eyes, then dropped her gaze, noticing the canine tooth pendant necklace. Glancing to her hand, she saw a ruby ring. Absolute shock moved through her brain as she recognized the jewelry found in the dungeon of the werewolf.

Miranda thanked her and moved to the next person while Lexi wordlessly watched her. Ricardo noticed Lexi's odd behavior, but remained unaware of the cause. As Miranda reached him, he expressed his gratitude and took his glass from her hand. He caught sight of the ring and raised his gaze to her neck, noting the tooth pendant. Ricardo and Lexi stared at each other with the hidden knowledge that Miranda was the werewolf.